EOGHAN

Book Cover by Y'all. That Graphic

Edited by Victoria Ellis, Cruel Ink Editing and Design

Proofread by Rose Sharon, Fairy Proofmother Proofreading, LLC

CHECK YOUR TRIGGERS

Your mental health and emotional well-being matters to me. You can find a list of possible triggers on the book's page on my website katerandallauthor.com or by scanning the QR code below.
Xoxo

For Matt. For always.

CONTENTS

CHAPTER ONE

EOGHAN

MY BROTHER IS A **twat**. And a cockblocker.

Three weeks ago, Finn made me look like an ass in front of one of the most stunning blondes I'd ever laid eyes on. The woman is his new wife's best friend, and he thought it would be funny to fuck with me. Not even married for four hours, and he was already acting like the stick-in-the-mud I constantly ragged on him for being. Shouldn't have surprised me, but Jesus, he could have backed off and let me talk to the girl. It wasn't like I was going to take Alessia's best friend, Gemma, home with me. *Maybe.*

Who am I kidding? I was ready and willing if she was. But then, Finn had to pull that ridiculous little stunt. Right before I struck up a conversation with Gemma, Finn paid one of Alessia's cousins to pretend that I'd made plans to take her to my hotel room. I didn't even have a room at the hotel, for Chrissake. Gemma took off before my brother could wipe that smug-as-hell smile from his damn face. Did I try to talk to her again that night? Of course. Did she avoid me like the plague? One hundred percent. When I eventually lost sight of her in the giant ballroom, I asked our security guard if he saw her leave. He confirmed the valet brought her car around, and she'd left not long after my brother and his new wife.

However, never let it be said I'm not a persistent man. Or a mild stalker. Whatever people want to call it. It's not as though I have nefarious intentions, but her ice-blue eyes have done...something to the part of my brain that usually tells me to forget about a girl who plays hard to get—not that many, or any, do. The way she looked at me, like she could see right through me, was oddly refreshing. I could get any woman in Boston with a smirk and a beckoning of my finger. Could be the Monaghan charm that my mother says I'm cursed with, or it could be the fact that I'm part of the most powerful crime family in Boston. Women love a little walk on the wild side. But the way Gemma looked at me told me she knew exactly what my game was, and she wasn't fucking having it.

And I liked it.

I need to see her again. See if my first reaction was due to the whiskey or from something else—which brings me to the little neighborhood kickboxing gym she's a member of. I may have had one of Cillian's tech wizards do some digging after making it clear that he'd better not get any ideas about running to my brother's lieutenant about our little fact-finding mission, of course. Nothing intrusive, just a general background search that included bank transactions for monthly subscriptions. I found two things of interest. One, she has a monthly subscription to an online lingerie shop—handy information—and two, I found where she has a gym membership. Now, I'm not sure if she's here today; like I said, I'm not an *actual* stalker. But I know she frequents the place, so I'm giving it a shot. Plus, I'm always on the lookout for new fighters. I organize fight nights in the basement of a couple of my family's bars. The fights rotate on a biweekly basis, and the cut the bar takes from the bookies on our payroll brings in a pretty little penny for my family business.

I step inside the warehouse-style gym and look around. The layout is impressive. It's a hell of a lot bigger than most others I've been to, with three rings spaced throughout and several sets of weights and hanging bags. The high ceilings have exposed ductwork, giving it an industrial, open feeling. The fast-paced rock music blasting from the speakers, paired with the determined looks in the patrons' eyes, makes one thing clear—these people are ready to throw punches. It's not particularly busy for a Tuesday evening, but the weather outside is shit, which is typical for springtime in Boston. Rainy as hell one minute, then warm and sunny the next. Never know what you're going to get this time of year.

Looking around the gym, I don't spot her at any of the bags or weight machines. My guy says she usually comes in after work a couple days a week, but maybe today isn't one of those days. Since I'm here, I may as well check out a few of the fighters. I step toward the ring in the right corner of the gym. The two guys inside are working hard at some mixed martial arts. It's my job to watch fighters and recruit the ones I think would bring energy and competition to my more seasoned guys. I find the hungry ones, the ones who want to get out and make some real money. That's what I provide and why we usually have a wait list for guys who want a shot. They make a hell of a lot more at one of my nights than any of the other small-time operations around Boston.

One guy in the ring is giving it his all. There's a look of determination on the kid's face that far outweighs the tired look in his opponent's eyes. Kid is doing it right, running circles around the other man. He's quick, I'll give him that, but he needs more training. That's okay. I can work with that. I have trainers to work with the guys who have the most potential. After the kid lands a complex series of punches and kicks, the tired-looking lumberjack of a man falls to the mat and taps out as blood pours from his lip.

"Sorry about that," the younger fighter tells him and reaches out a hand to help his opponent off the mat. When the bigger fighter swats his hand away, the kid shrugs and walks to his corner, grabbing his water and taking a long pull from the bottle. The other fighter stomps off to where I'm assuming the locker room is. Some guys get pissed when their blood gets spilled. Though he was a big guy and would probably make some money for my bookies, he's not right for what I do.

This kid, though...

At first glance, he looks to be in his twenties, but as I get closer and see him wiping the sweat from his face, I'd peg him to be eighteen, if that.

"Hey," I call out as he throws the towel over his shoulder and grabs his shirt from the rope.

"'Sup," he replies with a head nod, but he doesn't seem particularly interested in talking to some random stranger.

"Good fight," I say, and he simply nods again. *Okay.* I'm getting major screw-off vibes from this kid, and he clearly has no idea who I am. "Got a name?"

"Yeah."

Seriously?

He pulls the ropes apart and jumps out of the ring in front of me. The kid is probably about six feet tall, and he has a medium build but is absolutely covered in defined muscle as if he works his ass off to stay in tip-top shape. The black curls on his head make him look even younger, and those dark-brown eyes are looking at me like I'm a complete nuisance standing in his way.

I'm not going to lie. It's refreshing having someone who runs in these circles not know who I am. Most of the time, when I go to a gym like this, I have multiple guys trying to show off so they can be invited to fight in one of my bars.

"I'm Eoghan." I hold out my hand, but instead of

shaking it, the little punk looks at it then back at me. "Eoghan Monaghan," I say.

That gets his attention. Not that I need validation or anything, but Jesus. Okay, maybe I do need a little validation. Finn walks around this city, and everyone practically drops to their knees. I can barely get some kid who's still cutting his teeth in the ring to give me the time of day.

"Javier Rivera," he finally introduces and takes my hand in a firm shake.

"You know who I am?"

"I do, sir. The guys in here are always talking about wanting to get on your roster."

That's more like it.

"Sorry, just the way you were eyeing me when I was in the ring made me think you were trying to talk to me for other reasons."

The look on his face when he lets that little tidbit slip is hysterical. I've never seen a man look like he wants to physically take back the words that came out of his mouth and choke on them quite like Javier does right now. The laugh that explodes from me instantly relaxes him, and he chuckles a little at his minor faux pas.

"Nope, just checking out your form." I wince and smile in his direction. "Saying that now sounds a little weird." We both have a laugh, and I reach into my pocket, pulling out my wallet to retrieve one of my black business cards, which has just my name and phone number on it. These are the cards I reserve for the guys who I meet at places like this. The ones I think have a shot at making me and my family—and themselves, of course—some money.

"Give me a call. You need some more training, but the raw talent I saw up there"—I nod to the ring—"has my interest...piqued, shall we say."

Javier takes the card from my fingers and nods enthusiastically. "Thank you, Mr. Monaghan."

"Mr. Monaghan is my dad, kid. Call me Eoghan." I've never liked standing on ceremony the way my dad and brother always have.

"Okay. Thank you so much."

The excited enthusiasm rolling off this kid has me wondering about one very important detail.

"How old are you, by the way?"

"Nineteen, sir. I mean Eoghan."

"You live around here?"

"No, but I work here, cleaning up at night and doing a little maintenance here and there. Freddy lets me work out and train for free, so I don't mind the train ride. Beats any place around my neighborhood."

Just like I thought. *Hungry.*

Freddy is the owner. I've met him a few times since we're both in the fight scene. He opened this place up a couple months ago and has been asking for me to come check it out. It was a happy coincidence that this is the place Gemma makes monthly payments to from her checking account. *Okay, fuck, that does sound a little stalkerish.*

Deciding I might as well get a workout in while I'm here, I turn to where I saw the beaten fighter scurry off to.

"Can I get changed in there?" I ask, pointing to the small hallway.

"Yeah, man. I'll show you around when you're done."

"Sounds good, kid."

I head into the locker room and appreciate the simplicity. There are no fancy wooden lockers with an attendant ready to take your towel from you after you finish your shower. In fact, the showers themselves are sectioned off with those aluminum panels you would find in any run-of-the-mill high school locker room. Instead of oak or cedar lockers, these are metal. They're newer than the ones in the makeshift locker rooms we have. I like it. No fuss, no muss. This is where you go to train and work out, not bullshit in some fancy room with your buddies after doing an hour on a rowing machine like you find in a lot of gyms in the ritzy neighborhoods.

When I walk out in my workout shorts and a sleeveless shirt, Javier is grabbing a bag of towels. Damn, this kid goes right from training to working. "I'll be right back, just have to throw these in the laundry room."

I nod in his direction and look around at the other people. It's getting a little more crowded in here but not so much that there isn't plenty of space to do some weights. Maybe I can get in the ring with Javier and get a better feel for what he needs to work on, too.

As the kid walks up to show me around, I notice a woman with bright-blonde hair pulled back in a high ponytail. Her long legs are encased in a pair of tight black leggings, and her red tank top hugs her delicious form. Damn. I'm a sucker for a ponytail I can grab on to while I—

"Don't even go there, man. Many have tried. All have failed. Miserably," Javier says when he sees me eyeing the woman I came here to find.

"You know her?" Maybe I can glean some information from him. You know, more than I've already dug up.

"She's wicked good in the ring, but she doesn't really talk to any of the fighters. Some guy she met here took her out once, but now they avoid each other like the plague."

If it's the guy I remember her being at the fights with about a week ago, then good riddance. I saw him buying some coke at the fight night last week, then I saw him talking to her before my brother knocked out a big Russian guy to get to his wife. I was outside dealing with the asshole who dared grab what wasn't his, so I didn't catch Alessia breaking a girl's nose for fawning all over her husband. My bartender told me it was pretty fucking epic, though. When I learned my sister-in-law could fight, the idea of having a female fight night sprang to mind. Now, knowing Gemma not only likes to watch fights but trains at a gym, the idea is really starting to take root.

"Have you seen her spar?" I ask Javier as I watch Gemma tape up her hands and test it in her fist.

"A couple times. She's good. Kinda ruthless." Javier shrugs and walks me over to the weight set. I'm no stranger to a gym, and this one doesn't have any bells and whistles. There's really no reason for him to show me anything, but I can tell he's trying to impress me a bit, so I let him do his thing.

I load some weights onto a bar and lie down on the bench. "Give me a spot, yeah?"

Javier nods, and I do a few reps with him standing over me. When I sit up, I see Gemma from the corner of my eye. She's in the ring with a guy who looks twice her size. She's going through a routine of different kickboxing moves, and the guy is giving her a few pointers as she kicks the mitts he's wearing. I wipe my face, wander over to a bag closer to Gemma, and start throwing a series of punches. They're half-hearted at best, but that's not really the point. I'm trying to get the damn woman to notice me, but she's wrapped up in her own workout. Typically, female attention isn't lacking when I step into a gym, but this girl isn't paying anyone any mind. I respect it, even if it's irritating me.

Walking over to the ring she's at, I loop my arms over the ropes. "Fancy seeing you here, Gem," I say with my usual smirk playing on my lips.

"First off," she starts while she continues to throw her kicks. "It's Gemm-*aaa*. With an A. Secondly, I'm surprised you didn't recognize me, given how you kept staring over here. But then again, I suppose I am just another faceless woman you tried to hit on one night." She stops and stands in the middle of the mat with her fists resting on her hips. "Tell me, Eoghan, do we all just blur together in that brain of yours?" Even though she's slightly winded from her workout, she has no problem giving me the dressing down she thinks I deserve. Goddamn, I must be some sort of masochist because I fucking love it.

The man, who I'm assuming is her trainer, releases a snort of laughter at my expense. Asshole.

"You want me to take care of this guy, Gemma?" he asks. Like he's going to actually do anything. His eye catches someone behind me, and I turn my head to find Javier a few feet behind me, shaking his head at Gemma's trainer.

"Nah. I can handle him. Thanks, though."

She thinks she can handle me? Interesting.

"I haven't seen you since the night of the fights. How've you been?" *Smooth, Eoghan.*

"Busy not wasting my time stalking women at their neighborhood gyms." She's fucking sassy. And I'm so fucking busted.

I cock my head and watch her stalk toward where I'm standing. She bends over, grabs her water bottle, and takes a long drink. I've never been one to wax poetic about the way a woman's throat moves while she swallows mouthful after mouthful of anything, but seeing her head tilted back and exposing her long neck with sweat dripping down it gives me the sudden urge to jump into the ring and trace the beads of sweat with my tongue. What is it about this woman that has me so damn... what's the word? Struck stupid. Yeah, that's a fair description.

She sets the bottle back down and picks up a towel, wiping at her face and neck. "What are you doing here, Eoghan? This isn't your regular place."

"I know Freddy. He's been wanting me to come check it out. Said there's some talent around here."

Gemma quirks her brow as her lip tips up with a disbelieving smirk. "Really?"

It's not a complete lie. "Yes. Really. How could I have known you worked out here?"

Her blue eyes narrow into slits. "Considering your brother runs the Irish mob in Boston, I have no doubt you have the means to find out."

"You think awfully high of yourself, Miss Dalton. Don't you think we have better things to spend our time and resources on?" We absolutely do. I may have overstepped when I used Cillian's guy to help me out, but it's not like anyone is going to tell me no.

"So this is pure coincidence?" Gemma asks, still giving me a narrowed gaze. God, I fucking love seeing that look on her face.

"Why do you hate me so much?"

Gemma blows out a long breath and shakes her head, her blonde ponytail swinging from side to side with the movement. "I don't hate you, Eoghan. I've just known a hundred guys like you. Hell, I've dated half of them. You all want what's in front of you until the next pretty little thing walks by. Take the wedding, for example. You were chatting me up but already had a girl lined up to meet you in your room. It's the same old song and dance with guys like you—have a sure thing on the hook and a girl waiting in the wings for when you get bored. I'm not into guys with revolving doors in their bedroom."

"That whole thing at the wedding was my brother's doing. I was 'chatting you up' because I wanted to get to know you, not have you as some sort of backup plan. I'd never seen that girl before in my life. I think it was one of Alessia's cousins. Finn told me to stay away from you before the wedding, so when he thought I was getting too friendly, he cockblocked me. No offense."

Gemma's eyes widen in surprise for a split second when I tell her the truth about Finn's involvement. She lets out a little laugh and rolls her eyes toward the ceiling. "He didn't have to bother." She spears me with her gaze, the same piercing look that captivated me from the start, and looks down at me from the ring with her hands spread across the ropes like a queen addressing her subjects. She's ethereal. "Look, even if I wasn't well aware of the reputation you have in this town, you're my best friend's brother-in-law. That's a little too close to home for me." She kneels down until she's at eye level with me. "Your brother did us both a favor. No harm, no foul."

Gemma jumps out of the ring and stands in front

of me, raising her brows—probably wondering why I haven't walked away with my fucking tail between my legs.

"I want to take you out. Dinner or drinks, whatever you want. Let me prove the rumors about me aren't true." Granted, her impression of me is probably spot on, but I've been obsessing over this woman since I first laid eyes on her. I'm sure as hell not going to throw in the towel now.

"Does that usually work?"

"What?" I smile at her. A lesser man would probably run in the other direction, but her fire doesn't scare me in the least. Just the opposite, in fact.

"The whole *I'm so handsome and charming and I'm going to show you a good time* act you have going on." Gemma waves her hand up and down between us.

"You think I'm handsome *and* charming?" My mouth tilts in a way that most women find irresistible.

"No. I find you annoying and in my way," she says, taking a wide step around me to head to the locker room.

"I can work with that," I call out as she pushes through the door.

The small smile on her full lips doesn't escape my attention before the door closes behind her.

After watching Gemma walk out the door with a little flick of her hand to at least say goodbye to me, well, kind of, I head to Clovers—one of our four bars. There isn't a fight tonight, so the place isn't packed brick wall to brick wall, but we have a pretty decent after-work crowd. The bar is nestled in a blue-collar neighborhood, and unless it's a fight night, the customers are your usual salt-of-the-earth kind of people. My kind of people. There's no bullshit, well, aside from the occasional bar fight, but that's pretty typical in any bar across the US. But no one is here putting on airs.

This is where I have my main office. Though I keep one at every bar we own, those are mostly a catchall for the staff. This place is where I keep the books—legal and otherwise. No one comes into this office but me. There's one across the hall for my bar manager, but otherwise, this particular room is locked up like Fort Knox.

I have a seat at my desk to go over some invoices for the other three bars we own, but my concentration is shit. My eyes wander to the framed photo on my desk. It's the same one Finn has in his office—a childhood photo of the two of us with my grandfather. That man taught us the importance of brotherhood and family. I love my brother, don't get me wrong, but Finn really screwed me over with Gemma. We've always been competitive, but that's how brothers are. I'd lay down my life for him, just as I know he'd do the same for me. But I swear to God, I'd like to punch him in the face for his little stunt.

When Gemma and I were talking at the wedding, there was a connection. She can't deny that. Maybe it's the challenge, maybe it's my brother telling me not to go there, and I don't take kindly to being told what to do. Still, I think it's something more. There's something in those piercing eyes of hers that possess a fire I've never seen. Fire and ice, that's the sum of what I know of Gemma Dalton, but I plan on learning a whole hell of a lot more.

CHAPTER TWO
GEMMA

I T's BEEN A WEEK since I gave Eoghan the brush-off at the gym. It's adorable how he thought I didn't see him there or feel him staring at me while I was working out with my trainer. Eoghan is many things, but incognito isn't one of them. I don't think the man could be even if he wanted to. Which he doesn't. I've always had a knack for attracting good-looking guys, the ones that turned heads every time we went out. Guys who were charismatic and fun. All the things that Eoghan Monaghan is. That's why I need to stay far, far away from him. He's a perfectly nice guy to look at, and he even makes me laugh. And I can't forget charming. He's all of the things. And it's all bad for me.

After my last "date" at one of the fight nights held by the Monaghans, I've decided I can do without the charmers and the fighters. Sorry, but I have better things to do with my time than watch a group of guys snort a bunch of lines and ogle every woman in a skirt who walks by.

I've had it up to my eyeballs with the dating pool in Boston. If this is what's out there, I'd rather stay single with a menagerie of cats. I miss having a kitty since Alessia took Lucian home with her. After we graduated from college and she decided to attend Wharton for her MBA, I moved into an apartment building that doesn't allow animals. But I miss that little fucker, even if he did tear apart the old couch we had in our small two-bedroom apartment. He's an asshole cat, but at least he's consistent—more so than any man I've dated in the last five years after I split with my ex. They're all nice one minute and then chasing tail the next.

Actually, not so different from a cat, then.

When I graduated from college, moving to Boston seemed like a more logical choice than going back home to my mom. I worked my ass off at Yale for my fancy marketing degree and was determined to work in the fashion industry. There weren't exactly many opportunities back in Virginia where me and my mom had lived since I was born. There were many late nights I'd be awake—since I never had a set bedtime—that would be spent flipping through the magazines my mom left lying around. I loved looking at the pictures of beautiful women in exotic locations wearing fancy clothes and imagining myself in them. As I got older, I recognized the ads as some damn good marketing. Those people looked like they were having the time of their lives, and I wanted to be a part of it. I never considered myself a particularly creative person. I wasn't one to sketch elaborate dresses, and I didn't have an eye for photography, but I had an innate sense of what it took to sell a feeling. Even those damn car commercials with a dad sending his daughter off to college in the same type of car he took her to her first day of school in would get me every time. But the fashion world was my first love, and that's where I wanted to work.

When I landed an internship at a premier fashion house right out of Yale and eventually got hired on full time, I was shocked. My boss, Natalie, saw the fierce determination in me when I started, and she wanted someone she could mold into a version of herself. I was willing to be just about anything she needed in order to work for her, so that's what I did. I dressed the part, showed up earlier than everyone, and was usually the last one to leave. And it paid off. Now, I'm one of the youngest marketing executives in the industry. It's a far cry from the depressing childhood I fled when I left Virginia Beach at eighteen.

"Knock, knock." Sami, one of the models who regularly works on campaigns with our company, pops her head in my office. "It's been a minute, lady."

I wave her in and stand from my desk. "Sami, how are you?" I walk around to meet her in the middle of my office and wrap her in a tight hug.

The plus side of working at Aubine is I've gotten to know some of the sweetest girls. Many people think models are vapid women who don't care about anything other than being photographed at the most exclusive parties or clubs, but the girls Aubine hires are the exact opposite—at least most of them, Sami included.

"I was in the building for some fittings and wanted to come say hi."

"I'm glad you did," I tell her, releasing her from my arms and waving to a white leather chair before I step back behind my glass desk and have a seat. "You have a shoot coming up with us next week, right?"

We're launching a new campaign that's geared toward the new ready-to-wear line. Aubine Couture made its mark in fashion years ago and was the one-stop shop for the rich and beautiful to get the latest in all things high fashion. I remember being in high school and looking at the magazine spreads when Jean first made his splash into the fashion world. He came from nothing, just like me, and reinvented himself, just like I wanted to. I knew right then and there that if Jean Aubine could do it, so could I. Now, he wants to offer the feeling I had when I was a kid looking at all the gorgeous people in beautiful clothes to those who can't necessarily afford an Aubine exclusive. And that's where I come in. It's my job to sell the dream, and fortunately for everyone in the company, I'm damn good at it.

"Yup. I just got in last night for my fitting, and I have a whole two days here before I take off for a shoot in the Caribbean, then to Belize for Aubine's shoot."

"What are you going to do with all that free time?" I ask with a tilt to my lips. Sami is one of the most in-demand models in the industry. Free time is a long-forgotten notion for her.

"It's not what *I'm* doing. You should be asking what *we're* doing." Her grin matches mine, and I shake my head.

"Girl, I am so damn busy with this new campaign, and I just took a bunch of time off for my best friend's wedding and—"

"And, and, and," she says, waving her hand in front of her. "We both know what your idea of taking time off is. Instead of working a twelve-hour day, you work ten. We're actually in the same place at the same time, and we're going out tonight."

Sami has always been the kind of person where, whenever I see her, it's as though no time has passed. The company started booking her when she was fresh off the bus from Nowhere, Indiana. This gorgeous woman with long black hair and eyes so green it looks like she's wearing colored contacts has never lost the carefree and kind spirit I've come to love. She's one of the few who understands this is just a job, and it's fleeting. There is a limited lifespan to a model's career, and it's not particularly long, which is why she makes the most of her time and the opportunities her beauty has afforded her. She doesn't take it too seriously, unlike some of the other models I've had the displeasure of working with.

"I mean, I suppose it is part of my job to make sure the models are happy working with Aubine..." I shoot her a smile and hers widens, knowing I can't resist a night out with one of my favorite people. "Just tell me Camille isn't coming."

Sami winces at the mention of her name. Camille is one of the models working on this campaign, and I know she's here for a fitting today as well.

"She was in the room when Brit and I were talking about going out tonight. I couldn't very well *not* invite her."

That's the thing about Sami. She's too damn sweet for her own good. Camille is nothing but a whiny headache who uses her beauty and status to make other girls feel inferior. I really wish Natalie would stop hiring her, but her pretty face sells clothes, even if her stunning outside doesn't match her rotten inside.

I let out a groan, but the thing with being friends with someone who is just as busy as you is sometimes you have to concede. I guess spending an evening with Camille will be my concession this time.

"Okay. I can put on my big-girl panties and deal with her for the night." I wouldn't normally subject myself to Camille's company, especially since I know how sore my tongue will be with all the biting I'll have to do. But Jean loves having her in his clothes, which means I'll have to play nice for the evening. "I hope you know how much I love you."

Sami smiles wide in my direction and stands. "Meet me at the hotel. Your boss hooked me up with a suite as a thank-you for fitting Aubine into my schedule this week."

"My boss will also be hooking us up with bottle

service since I have to deal with Camille tonight." The smile I give Sami matches hers as she laughs on her way out the door.

"See you tonight," she calls, then blows me a kiss before shutting the door behind her.

When I get home it's already after seven, and I need to shower this day off. It was meeting after meeting after Sami came and insisted on going out. Honestly, if I had known my day would turn into what it did, I would have opted out of anything other than a bath, a glass of wine, and a steamy romance novel to get my mind off the day.

The photographer for the shoot next week is having some sort of existential crisis about something or other. From what I gathered during the twenty-minute conversation Natalie and I had with him on the phone, he wants to leave a mark on the world. He's frustrated that all anyone seems to want are staged pictures of beautiful people and how he's contributing to the ideals of a materialistic society. He swore he was quitting the fashion business and going to live in a hut somewhere he could meditate and become one with the earth or some shit. That was until Natalie offered him thirty percent more money than his usual rate and promised Aubine would make a donation to the charity of his choice in his name. When the phone call ended, she said she was glad to pay it since finding a new photographer on such short notice would have cost a lot more than a few thousand dollars.

Then, two members of my team got into a very heated debate over typography. Yes, it was a real thing, and at one point, I thought it was going to come to blows. I get it—I do. We work our asses off for the company, and sometimes that stress can manifest in...*unusual* ways, shall we say. But it was like separating kindergartners who would not stop poking each other.

I close the door to my modest two-bedroom apartment and flip on the light. After slipping out of my heels, my feet meet the plush cream carpet, and I let out a long exhale. Tossing my bag onto the cream leather chair, I head into my kitchen. I pull open my freezer, grab a bottle of vodka and some ice, and splash a healthy amount into a glass. I've always had a taste for good vodka, and the familiar burn hits just right as I take a sip. If I sit down now, I know it's going to take a monumental effort to get back up, but my light-gray chenille couch is calling my name. Giving in to temptation, I trudge into my living room and sink into the soft cushion. I love this couch. Hell, I love everything about my apartment. It's light and comfortable. I don't have to worry about beer stains on the rugs or cigarette burns marring the expensive fabric of my furniture. So unlike the apartments I grew up in.

When I was hired full-time, I moved into a nicer place, but not so upscale that if I lost my job tomorrow, I'd be on the street within the month. I think I'll always carry around that fear of financial insecurity that had been ingrained in me from childhood. My mom and I moved into a nice apartment once when I was little. I had my own room and everything. She'd met a guy and swore it was love.

It wasn't.

Turns out, he was married, and his wife didn't appreciate him keeping an apartment for his mistress and her bastard daughter—her words, not mine—with her money. The guy was filthy rich as long as he was married. She held the purse strings, and he thought he could get away with renting an apartment for us. I don't know if my mom knew the whole story or if it would have even mattered to her. Probably not. The only thing she ever cared about was having her bills paid by someone other than her. It was a real treat being home and getting to witness that train wreck when the guy's wife showed up. We were packed up, tossed out, and back to her sister's before she found us another run-down one-bedroom like she always did.

Now I keep my space tidy and clean. I have light-colored furniture because I'll be damned if I ever look at another brown-plaid couch that's been kept around long past its prime just so it'll hide the dirt. And there isn't a cigarette burn or a stain of questionable origin in sight.

Taking another sip of the vodka in my nearly empty glass, I haul myself off my couch and head into my bedroom. The lamp next to my bed is on, as it always is, even when I'm sleeping; it's just another habit left over from a fucked-up childhood. Bad things happen in the dark when you think you're alone. Obviously, I don't have to worry about strange men wandering in here looking for my mother, but I also can't sleep in a pitch-black room.

Setting my drink on the nightstand—under a coaster, thank you very much—I open my closet and pull out a dress I bought last week. I shrug out of my work clothes and put them in my dry-cleaning bag. When I lay the dress on the bed, my mind flits to Eoghan. The way the look in his eyes made me feel like I was the sexiest woman in my workout gear. He had a gleam of appreciation in his gaze when he came over to the ring I was working out in. What would he think if he saw me dressed to kill in the little sequined black number on my bed? *Whoa, where the hell did that thought come from?* It doesn't matter what he thinks. I have never been, nor will I ever be, a woman who dresses to impress a man. And I certainly have no intention of trying to impress my best friend's playboy brother-in-law. I shake my head as I style my long blonde hair into a topknot and head to my bathroom to wash the day—and all thoughts of Eoghan Monaghan—down the drain.

The line to get into the new club Sami insisted we go to is a hell of a lot longer than I would have expected, even for a Friday night. When one of the security guards walked the line, he spotted the four of us and either recognized the three models I was with, or he saw four beautiful women and decided to bring us to the front. Most likely the latter since the beefy man doesn't look the type to pour over fashion magazines in his off-hours, but hey, I could be wrong. Either way, we were brought to the front, and the velvet rope was opened for us immediately, much to the disappointment of the others waiting in line if the grumbles and groans we heard were anything to go by.

Now we're in the VIP level of the club, looking over the balcony at everyone dancing on the lower level and enjoying bottle after bottle of champagne. Blue laser lights flash throughout the dark space as music pumps through the speakers. Our section is lit with thin blue rope lights running along the railings, and the glass tables scattered throughout the floor have large smoked-glass bases with blue lights inside; it makes them look iridescent and dreamy. The name of the club, Blue Oasis, is definitely on brand.

Some people may think I'd feel inadequate or somehow dimmed by the stunning women I'm surrounded with, but they would be dead wrong. I don't suffer from low self-esteem or subscribe to the beauty standards that I can admit the people in my industry are responsible for creating. You don't have to be nearing six feet tall and weigh barely a hundred pounds to be beautiful. I'm not, and I feel damn good about myself. Being five-eight, I'm relatively tall for a woman, and I've always been on the thinner side—that tends to happen when you grow up without enough to eat on a regular basis—but I work hard to stay in shape. Not for anyone other than myself, though. The tight black dress I donned for the evening, along with the sky-high heels, accentuate my long muscular legs that I spend a lot of time working to keep toned and strong.

Years ago, when my best friend was assaulted by her boyfriend, she and I started training in a few different martial arts practices. I found my stride in kickboxing, while Alessia found her passion in boxing. Doesn't hurt that her husband trains with her now. He's quite the fighter himself, though I've only seen him in the ring once, and that was just for a minute before he knocked out his opponent to get to his wife. That was certainly a night for the books. As much as I've come to appreciate the relationship my best friend has with her new husband, and I love that she's finally found not only her match but someone who deserves her, I have to say, I'm not sure how I'd handle someone being so...possessive. Not that I've ever dated a man who would care enough, but I wasn't raised in the same life as Alessia. To her, it's normal, but it sounds stifling to me. At the same time, I've never been married to a hot-as-sin Irish mob boss, so there's that.

"I love that necklace," Sami says, plopping down on the couch next to me while she takes a sip of champagne. The other girls are dancing with a few guys who are in the VIP area with us, enjoying the attention.

"Thank you," I reply, my hand touching the aquamarine necklace I bought myself after my last raise.

Growing up, my mom never had money to spend on expensive jewelry, and while I'm hardly making millions, it's more than I could have thought possible sitting in the run-down one-bedroom apartment my mom and I shared while she was at work. My mom had other priorities for the money she earned while dancing in bikini bars, and it certainly didn't include anything for her daughter.

"Are you having a good time?" Sami asks, turning her big doe eyes on me.

"Of course," I reply, though it's a bit of an exaggeration. Am I having a bad time? No, but I'm not quite comfortable. Maybe it's the dress—though I do look fabulous—or maybe it's the heels, though again, they're amazing. There's just something I can't shake.

Two of the guys the other girls were dancing with come over to us with broad smiles on their faces as they look from us to the dance floor below.

"What are you ladies doing sitting all by yourselves

over here?" the one on the right asks in a flirtatious way that gives me the impression he doesn't really care about the answer. He just wanted an excuse to come talk to us.

"Well, you were over there"—Sami points to his other two friends, still occupied with Camille and Brittany—"and you weren't paying us any attention." Sami gives him a playful pout, and his grin gets impossibly wider, showing off teeth so bright they must be veneers.

"I'm sorry, sweetheart. I won't make that mistake again." The man holds out his hand to her. "Let's dance."

Sami pretends to consider his offer, but it's a coquettish act. When she slides her hand into his palm, the guy looks like he won the lottery. They head over to the other dancing couples and begin swaying to the beat of the heavy bass.

His friend has a seat next to me, and I eye him from behind the rim of my champagne flute. He's not bad looking by any stretch, but he looks like every other man I've met in places like this. His dark hair is slicked back, and the gleam in his brown eyes tells me he's not necessarily here for anything more than a good time. And honestly, good for him.

"What about you?" he asks. He's not giving off creep vibes; he seems like a guy looking for a fun time and hoping I'm it.

"What about me?"

"Would you like to dance?"

I look to the dance floor on the lower level and nod. There's no reason for this black cloud hanging over my head. So what if the guy is the same as any other man in this club or any other man I've met in the last ten years? We're here to have fun, and I need to shake myself out of this funk I've been carrying around with me all night.

I set my glass on the table and return his smile. "I'd love to. But let's go down there," I say, pointing to the floor packed with writhing bodies and people enjoying themselves. That's what I need. To be surrounded by people living it up. Hopefully some of that energy will rub off on me. This morose feeling that settled into me when I got home from work needs to fucking evaporate ASAP.

He holds out his hand, and I slide my palm into his. "Ronny." He flashes me another smile.

"Gemma," I reply.

Ronny leans in close and whispers, "You are absolutely gorgeous, by the way." His breath tickles my ear, and I feel...absolutely nothing but the desire to swipe the feeling away.

I give him a bland smile and lead him out of the VIP area to the dance floor. What the hell is wrong with me? It's just some dancing with a perfectly attractive man. Granted, his eyes don't carry the same sparkle of mischief as the ones I was thinking of earlier, but he also isn't part of a powerful criminal organization in Boston with women falling all over him, if the rumors are true. Yes, I did a little digging into Eoghan since the wedding. No, I am not proud of myself. What I found out about him from various sources is that he likes to party. He likes to be seen at the clubs around town, and he definitely likes having a beautiful woman or two on his arm. He's the Irish mob party boy, and that's the last thing I'm looking for.

When Ronny and I get to the lower level, he immediately starts grinding all over me like every other musclehead in the place. I take a step back and think he finally gets the hint that there should be at least a couple inches of space between us. *Thank God.* It doesn't take long for the beat of the music to envelop me and a smile to overtake my face as I dance to the ramped-up pop remixes playing through the speakers. This is what I need. A night of dancing and letting loose. After a couple more songs, I'm absolutely parched, and Ronny is decidedly less interested in being down here with me. I can't exactly blame him. He's realized that I'm here for fun, but not the kind he probably had in mind.

"Let's go back!" I yell over the loud music and point my finger to the VIP area.

Ronny nods and we make our way out of the crowd of bodies and back up the stairs. It's when we get there that I realize something is drastically different from when we left. The girls are still dancing, but it's not with Ronny's friends. I don't recognize these guys, but his friends have retreated back to the other side of the roped-off area and are chatting up a group of completely different women.

Then my gaze turns to the blue velvet couch I'd been sitting on just a few minutes ago.

"Hey there, blondie. Fancy meeting you here."

CHAPTER THREE
EOGHAN

I F IT WERE ACTUALLY possible to shoot daggers from your eyes, I would be a fileted piece of meat bleeding all over this gaudy electric-blue sofa. Gemma looks about one point three seconds away from reaching over the low glass table between us and strangling me with her bare hands when she spots me sitting and drinking her champagne. Well, it's not exactly *hers*. I've informed the staff to transfer her bill to my card, and this is a fresh bottle, but still.

After our run-in last week, I've been keeping tabs on her. A little *light stalking*, if you will. Not anything scary or weird, just keeping track of where her credit card is used. Good thing for her, too. When I saw that her card was swiped at this club, I called a couple of my guys, and we decided it was a good night for loud music and a few drinks. This club is relatively new, but it's the typical gym-rat hangout. Guys like the one she was dancing with are the type to hang out here, and they come with one thing on their mind; I already know it would have ended up with a hangover and a head full of regret for Gemma.

That's why I'm here. Figured I'd save her the trouble.

"What the hell are you doing drinking my champagne, Eoghan?" Gemma walks over to the table and snatches the bottle sitting in front of me.

"Technically, that bottle was mine," I reply as she narrows her eyes on me.

"Are you following me?" she spits, and the eyes of the man standing next to her are darting between her and me. Gemma isn't paying him any mind; her laser-focused gaze is directed squarely at me.

I raise my hands and shrug. "Happy coincidence." I shoot her a smile, and she rolls her eyes.

"Those seem to be going around lately." Her brow quirks and her gaze continues to bore into me.

The guy next to her backs up a step. "Uh, should I leave you two alone?"

Gemma shakes her head as I slowly nod. The little vixen grabs his hand and pulls him over to the couch, seating him at the far end. "Ronny, we were just getting to know each other. Don't pay Eoghan any mind."

Her smile is fake as hell. I saw her dancing with him when they were downstairs, and she was completely disinterested in the man next to her. This little show is for my benefit.

"Ronny, what do you do for a living?" she asks over the loud music. I pour her a glass of champagne and hold it in front of her. Her eyes flick to me, and she grabs it from my hand. She smiles at the poor sap sitting next to her who has yet to realize he doesn't have a shot in hell.

"Finance," Ronny replies.

A snort of derision escapes me. Exactly as I thought. Fucking typical.

Gemma shoots me another narrow-eyed look, and I simply smile in her direction.

"What about you?" Ronny asks Gemma.

"I'm the creative director for Aubine Couture."

"That's one of those fancy fashion designers, right? So, what? You look at pictures and decide what goes in magazines and stuff?" he asks.

"Something like that." Her smile is turning more brittle by the second.

"Sounds easy enough." His eyes dart around the space as though he isn't sure if he wants to waste his time here with someone who is anything but a sure thing or if he can salvage his night with someone else.

I don't miss the way Gemma's entire demeanor stiffens at his obviously uneducated comment. Not that I understand what her job entails, but I know she has a degree from Yale and is sharp as a fucking tack. If the digging I did hadn't included her college transcripts, I would have figured it out in the two brief conversations we've had because I actually pay attention. Unlike some people, apparently. Gemma is stubborn as hell, though, so she doesn't show any further outward indication that his take on her profession pissed her off. Instead, she leans in a touch closer and starts asking him inane questions about his job and where he works. If she thinks she's pissing me off, she's...right. Ronny's eyes are now focused on Gemma like she's a fucking steak and he's prepping her to be his next meal, and she's eating it up instead of tearing his balls off. Is that what this stunning creature next to me does? Dumb herself down for the attention of a guy, or is this solely for my benefit?

"Gemma, who's your friend?" an extremely attractive woman asks as she sits between Gemma and me on the sofa.

"I'm Eoghan Monaghan," I reply, holding my hand out to the other blonde woman.

"Camille," she replies, slipping her hand delicately into mine and holding it there as she stares expectantly into my eyes. Does she expect me to kiss it or some shit?

Ronny leans around the women and asks, "Did you say Monaghan?"

I nod and Gemma rolls her eyes. She seems to do that quite a bit around me. "Don't feed the man's ego, Ronny."

"I don't think there's any reason for a man like him to not have an ego," Camille says next to me as she trails her fingers over my arm.

"You run fights in the basements of your bar, right?" Ronny asks.

This dumb fuck. Like I'm going to tell him anything about what I do.

"I do a lot of things, Ronny."

He nods his head quickly and fucking winks at me like he's in on some secret. "Right, right. I get it, man."

Usually it's my brother who gets annoyed when people are overly casual with him. Tonight, it's me.

"You're a fighter?" Camille asks, leaning into my space, now rubbing my bicep with her palm.

"Like I said, I do a lot of things."

"I'd love to come watch you one of these days. See you in action." I'm getting the distinct impression she's not referring to the fights. At least, not only the fights.

Another tall woman who I've seen on billboards downtown comes over to the couch.

"Come dance with me," she says, holding her hand out to Gemma, who smiles broadly at the dark-haired woman. That's the first genuine smile I've seen from her tonight.

Camille turns to me. "Let's dance, handsome."

She stands and grabs my hand the same time Ronny gets up and follows Gemma to a mostly open area where a couple of my guys are already enjoying the attention of the other models Gemma's here with.

Instead of Ronny attempting to close the gap between him and Gemma, it's her. The closer Camille gets to me, the closer Gemma gets to the finance bro in front of her. Interesting. Am I a fan of watching another man so close to the woman I'm here to see? Hell, no. But I'm quite enjoying the challenge in her gaze every time her eyes meet mine then narrow in on Camille. She's jealous, and that means I'm more than just the annoyance she said I was last week at the gym. I'm well aware of the fact that we're playing juvenile games, but she started it.

Jesus, get a grip, Eoghan.

This push and pull between me and Gemma goes on for a few minutes as one song melts seamlessly into another. If I ran a club like this, I'd hire the DJ on the spot. But I like my bars dark with old jukeboxes in the corner and plenty of beer and whiskey ready to pour. Not saying I don't come out and frequent places like this; I'm single as fuck and always planned on staying that way. But lately...I've been dreaming of waking up to a blue-eyed woman in my bed. For once, I want more than a quick cup of coffee and a kiss on the way out with every intention of losing the number slipped to me. It's fucking weird. When I started my little fact-finding mission, I'd met Gemma all of once. Maybe it's because my brother and his bride told me she's off-limits. Maybe it's the thrill of the chase. But there's something that's been needling the back of my brain when it comes to the woman dancing feet from me, and I haven't been able to shake it.

Camille is still writhing against me, but my mind is elsewhere. Right now, I wish I was, too. I'm not a fan of this little game anymore. Camille isn't the woman I'm interested in being with tonight. She isn't the reason I came to this too-loud, too-crowded club.

I'm about to gently remove Camille from where she's attached her entire body to the front of mine when I catch Ronny's hand moving to Gemma's ass as he leans in for a kiss. She tries to shove him off, but he pulls her tighter against him. I'm about to rip his fucking arm from his body, but before I can make a move, Gemma lifts her foot and plants her spiky heel right on the top of Ronny's shoe and digs in.

He yelps and pushes her away, but Gemma has plenty of practice staying on her feet so the movement doesn't cause her to fall. That's about the only thing saving him from a bullet between the eyes right now.

Stepping away from Camille, I put myself between Ronny and Gemma.

"Fucking bitch," he spits over my shoulder at the furious blonde.

My fist lands a solid punch to his gut before I grab him by his gelled hair and wrench his head up to meet my eyes, nearly nose to nose.

"Watch your fucking mouth, asshole."

"Oh, come on, man, she was all over me."

It's the casual way he thinks he can call me *man* and I'll bro out with him or some shit that sends me over the edge. When my fist lands a punch to his nose, I think he finally realizes he's barking up the wrong fucking tree.

"I'm not your friend, Ronny. Dancing with her doesn't mean you get to grab her ass and shove your tongue down her throat."

"You're a fucking psycho, man," he cries.

I punch him again because I'm not a fan of the casual way he's still addressing me. The bouncers make their way over to us, but all I have to do is shoot them a look and they back the hell off. They know exactly who I am and what it could mean for them if they try to interfere with the little lesson I'm teaching the piece of shit in my grip.

"Apologize," I grit out, watching with satisfaction as blood runs from his nose, staining the front of his pressed baby-blue shirt.

"I'm sorry," he says to me, finally catching on to the fact that he's well and truly fucked.

"Not to me, you moron. To her." I'm still holding him by the hair. "Tell her what a slimy skeezeball you are for thinking that dancing with her means you get to put your hands all over her."

"I-I'm sorry," he stammers in her direction.

"The rest of it, Ronny," I say, tugging on his hair. Fuck, I'm going to have to wash my hands in scalding-hot water to get all the gel off them.

"I'm a skeezeball who sh-shouldn't have put his hands on you."

Gemma rolls her eyes and waves her hand as if to tell me to hurry it along.

Slapping Ronny on the face a couple times, I mutter, "Good boy. Now run along and get the fuck out of here." I shove him to the side, and he nearly topples over from the force.

He pushes his way past the two bouncers at the top of the stairs and runs down without looking back. His friends, who made the right decision by not intervening, follow him without making eye contact with me or mine. Smart boys.

When I turn my head back toward Gemma, the scowl on her face doesn't surprise me in the least. The fact that it's directed at me and not the retreating back of Ronny does, though.

"What?" I ask, rubbing the tender flesh of the knuckles that met Ronny's face. That's gonna leave a bruise.

"Seriously, Eoghan? I had it under control."

"I know you did, blondie." It's true. With all the training she's had, Gemma is perfectly able to take care of herself in these situations. "But you shouldn't have to. I didn't like seeing his hands all over you, and you didn't like having them there. I took care of it."

"Jesus Christ." Her eyes roll toward the ceiling as she lets out a deep breath. "I don't want you to take care of it. There's no reason *for* you to take care of anything. Ronny wasn't the first guy to ever get a little too handsy with me, and I've always handled it. I'm not a damsel in distress, and you sure as hell aren't my knight in shining armor."

She whirls around, stomps over to the couch where her purse is sitting and grabs the small bag before turning back to me. "Might want to have that hand looked at."

Gemma heads down the stairs, and I nod at one of my guys to follow her out. I just want to make sure she doesn't run into any trouble. And I have a very strong feeling if I tried to make sure she got to her car safely, she'd have my balls.

"She's ungrateful. I'd love for a man to fight for my honor like that," Camille says, coming up to my side and trying to wrap her arm around mine. But it's the wrong blonde, and she doesn't have blue eyes.

I untangle myself from her grip and offer her a small smile. "Make sure you get home safe," is all I say before getting the attention of Declan, one of the guys on my crew who came with me. I motion to the bar and send a text to one of my other guys who went outside for a smoke. After telling him to watch for Gemma, I realize how badly I'm in need of a shot. Also, I need to let the bartender know to keep my tab open for Gemma's friends until they're ready to leave.

Declan follows me, and I order two shots of whiskey and tell the bartender to add a thirty-percent tip for herself when she closes my tab. She's unsure, but the guy behind the bar with her recognizes me. I've seen him around Clovers, and he's been to a couple fight nights, if memory serves. He whispers something in her ear, and she shrugs before walking away.

"I'll make sure everything is taken care of," the male bartender tells me. "Shots are on the house."

I raise my glass and nod my thanks. Declan and I down the alcohol, and I relish in the burn as it travels down my throat. Fuck. This night did not turn out how I expected.

Gemma's friend, who prompted her to dance, steps next to us and throws Declan a flirtatious smile, which he returns tenfold.

When her gaze lands on me, she looks me up and down. She's not checking me out; it's more like assessing me from head to toe. "I saw what you did back there. You don't strike me as the kind of guy to step in unless you hold a personal stake in the situation."

"What kind of guy do I strike you as?" I ask, amused by her quick study of me.

"The kind who sets his sights on something and doesn't give up easily."

I incline my head toward her, and she smiles, then continues speaking. "I've known Gemma a long time, but I've never seen her so flustered by any man."

"You call that flustered?" I scoff.

"For her? Yes." She turns her head to Declan and reaches her hand out for him to shake. "I'm Sami."

"Declan." Their gazes hold and both of them are wearing smiles that make me feel like a third wheel.

"I'm going to head out. You good?" I ask my friend.

"Yup," he replies without ever taking his eyes off Sami. "I'll catch you tomorrow, boss."

A small chuckle escapes me before I head through the VIP area and down the stairs to the exit. Sean is walking in as I'm about to head out.

"She get in a car?" I ask.

"Yup. Don't think she knew I was there to keep an eye on her. She was pretty pissed and seemed a little preoccupied with whatever argument she was having with herself."

I'm sure she was.

"Thanks. Go back inside and have a drink. I think Declan's going to stick around for a while."

"What about you?"

"Nah. I'm done for the night."

Sean nods and heads inside as I walk to the street and hail a cab. Declan drove us here, but I'm not in the mood to wait around for anyone. I need a hot shower and some ice for my fist. Then I need to figure out what to say to Gemma to make up for the fact that I apparently overstepped when I taught that asshole a lesson. I thought girls were supposed to fall all over themselves when they saw a man protecting them. But I'm quickly learning Gemma doesn't react to anything the way I would expect, and fuck me if I don't find that enticing as all hell.

Three days later, I get a text from Javier at Freddy's gym. I gave him my number and told him to let me know the next time he sees Gemma. I considered having Declan or Sean trail her, but if she ever figured out what I was up to, she'd have my balls, probably run to Alessia with the information, and then Finn would have what's left of me after Gemma got through with me. No thanks. This is much safer for all involved.

When I walk into Freddy's, I immediately spot Gemma in the ring with her trainer, but she's too focused to notice I've entered. Or maybe she did and she's still salty over what went down at the club on Friday.

"Hey, boss," Javier greets me as he steps out of the locker room I'm heading into. I came straight from a meeting when I received his text, so I need to change. Fortunately for me, I typically have a bag of spare gym clothes in my trunk, so it was nothing to head over here as soon as my meeting was over.

"You on the clock?" I ask him.

"Not yet. Was going to do some weight training."

"Feel like sparring?"

"With you?"

"Yeah, Columbo, with me."

Javier chuckles at my reference to the crusty old TV detective and nods. "Sure."

After changing, I head to the empty sparring ring across the gym from Gemma. Javier is suited up in headgear and a mouth guard waiting for me. I hop in the ring and tape my knuckles, but that's it.

"Freddy wants everyone in here in protective gear," Javier says.

"I don't think it'll be a problem."

Freddy knows what kind of fighter I am and about the fights I put on. I'm all for Javier being protected while practicing, but I've never used any of that shit.

We circle each other, and Javier is the first to throw a punch. I can tell he's holding back, though.

"You're not going to break me. I've been trading blows with my brother since I was eight."

I'm not sure if it's because of who I am or the fact I didn't bother with protective gear. He nods, and before I know it, he's going full force. Mostly body shots, but the kid's got some power behind his punches, that's for sure. We go round and round. I get a good feeling for his fighting and plan on talking with a trainer I know about him. I point out some of his weaknesses and where he's pulling back when he should be going in harder. He'll make a tough opponent, that's for damn sure, but he's still green. That's okay; finding someone to work with him and bring him up to par will be a piece of cake.

After thirty minutes, both of us are drenched in sweat, and I notice Gemma finishing up with her training.

"I'll be right back," I tell Javier and jump out of the ring to make my way over to the blonde who has yet to acknowledge my presence.

"Hey, blondie," I greet when I walk over to where she's gathering her things to take off for the night. "You weren't going to say hi?"

Gemma nails me with an annoyed look. "Is showing up at my gym whenever I'm here going to become a habit?"

"Maybe." *Definitely.*

"What do you want, Eoghan?"

"Why are you so upset with me? Is this about the other night?" I figured she would have calmed down by now. It's not like the guy didn't have it coming.

"I'm not mad at you." She grabs her bag and pulls the

strap up her shoulder. "Look, I get it. You saw a woman being disrespected and wanted to step in. Hell, there's a part of me that appreciates it. But what you don't get is we"—she waves her hand between us—"can't happen."

"You're right. I don't get it."

Gemma shakes her head and holds up a finger. "One, you're my best friend's brother-in-law." She holds up another. "Two, you aren't looking for anything more than a good time, and I'm not interested in a fling with someone who, by all accounts, will be in my life in some capacity forever. And three"—she holds up another finger—"I didn't like who I was the other night. I *was* leading him on. Not saying he shouldn't have backed off the moment he realized I wasn't willing for anything to go further than dancing, but the way I was behaving isn't who I am. It wasn't my finest hour."

"Am I allowed a rebuttal?" Gemma reluctantly nods in my direction. "Okay. One." I hold up a finger. "Anything between us has nothing to do with who my family is or who my sister-in-law is. I just happened to have never met you before the wedding." I raise another finger. "Two, I never said anything about a fling. I want to get to know you, Gemma. There's a spark between us, and I'll probably regret saying this, but I haven't been able to get you off my mind. Every time I see you it's like a jolt to my chest. I don't know why, but I know it's something I want to explore." I hold up a third finger and stare into her blue eyes, which are just a little less guarded than before. "I don't regret punching that guy, but I regret not telling him to get lost the second I saw him with you, and I regret dancing with that other girl, too. It was childish and immature on both our parts."

"That's my point, Eoghan. Just because there's attraction doesn't mean we wouldn't be toxic as hell together. I think the other night proved that."

"No, the other night proved we're dumbasses." We both let out a huff of laughter. But the second the tinkling sound falls from her lips, it's as though she realizes she let her guard down and her eyes shutter and turn cold again.

Gemma shakes her head and moves to step past me. "I have to go. I'm sure I'll see you around."

I don't try to stop her. There's something here. She knows it just as well as I do. She's just so damn stubborn.

But so am I.

Chapter Four
Gemma

"YOU DON'T HAVE ANY idea what Finn got me for my birthday?" Alessia asks as we sit in her penthouse, guzzling water after our workout with Giada.

Alessia and I have been coming over and working with Finn's cousin's wife for the last couple weeks. It's a whole mess of how she ended up married to Luca, considering she's the sister of the asshole who was responsible for shooting Alessia's bodyguard and one of my favorite people on the planet.

When Alessia and I were roommates in college, Enzo was her bodyguard, so he was around a lot—as in all the time. He became less bodyguard and more brother to both of us in that time. Not that he had much choice in the matter. He learned pretty quickly he could forbid us from going out and having the college experience we were desperate for when we weren't studying or working our asses off, but that would only end up with us sneaking away. The second time it happened, he decided it was better for everyone involved if he trailed us and made sure we were safe. Not to mention, he threatened to tell her father that we were sneaking out if we didn't give him a heads-up. Even when Alessia and I were no longer roommates, I stayed in contact with him. Well, if you counted sending him random and hilarious cat videos keeping in contact. Which I do. That reminds me, I just found one the other day that I've been meaning to send. He hated the cat Alessia found next to a dumpster and insisted on adopting. When I found out he'd nearly been killed by one of Finn's enemies, I knew Alessia would get revenge. For the first time in my life, I was happy that a man would most likely die for hurting someone. I'm not violent by nature, contrary to popular belief, but if I knew where the body of the man who hurt Enzo was buried, I'd happily spit on his grave.

"He didn't ask, and even if he did, I wouldn't tell you," I reply, shaking myself out of my murderous thoughts. I've been happy to stay on the periphery of this part of my best friend's life. The part where murder and violence are a part of everyday life and hardly given a second thought. Just one more reason why getting involved with Eoghan would be a monumental mistake. I'll happily keep to my law-abiding, simple little life. *Keep telling yourself that's the reason.*

"You're no help," Alessia says, chucking a bottle cap at my forehead.

"Careful. You could have taken out an eye, asshole," I exclaim while Giada laughs at our antics from where she's sitting on the floor. "Why are you even worried? It's not as though Finn has ever gotten you anything you didn't love. Remember your first real date?"

A small smile tugs on her lips. She was so damn nervous about dating her husband who she was already sleeping with by that point. She called me in a panic when she was packing, freaking out that she was going to hate whatever plans she had. Luckily for her, her husband was a master at reading her before she realized he'd been paying attention.

"Gemma, you're coming tonight, right?" Giada asks. Tonight is Alessia's birthday dinner at the Monaghans'.

"Of course I'll be there. It's Alessia's birthday party." This will be the first time I've seen Eoghan since the last time we ran into each other at the gym. I'm still not convinced it's been all happy accidents like he tries to explain it away as. I was furious when I saw him at the club. I'd like to say it was because I hate him and want him out of my life, but that would be a lie. I was angry with myself and the visceral reaction he seemed to bring out in me. He's so damn wrong for me, but my mind won't stop traveling back to his smirk every time I try to knock him down a peg or two. That's always worked with men in the past, but it's like he purposely tries to rile me up to get my reaction. I can't stop thinking about how fucking good he looked that night when he punched Ronny in the face for being a disrespectful little shit. Don't even get me started on the two times I've seen him working out—especially when he was sparring with the kid who works at the gym. I wasn't joking when I told him we wouldn't work, but that doesn't stop the very *non*-PG thoughts from invading my mind.

I haven't said anything to Alessia about running into him a few times. I'm not sure why. Maybe part of me is afraid she'll tell Finn and he'll warn him off again. Maybe I'm afraid Eoghan will listen. I've told him nothing is going to happen between us, but it's not because I'm uninterested. I'm too interested, and with my track record, that's a red flag in and of itself.

"Ugh," Alessia groans. "Don't remind me. I'm sure there will be plenty of talk about how I'm not getting any younger, and Finn and I should start thinking about having a family. We haven't even been married for six months, and my mother and Maeve are already salivating over the thought of grandchildren."

I give my best friend a sympathetic look. "I'm sorry, sweetie. I know that's a tough subject for you." I don't elaborate since we both know why that's a hard one for her. "Well, you'll have me to steer the conversation," I say brightly. "And as long as Eoghan stays out of my way, there won't be any bloodshed." My vicious smile hides the excitement racing through me at the thought of seeing him again.

"You don't like Eoghan?" Giada asks.

"Oh, come on. Finn told you he was playing a joke on his brother at our wedding. Eoghan had no idea who that girl was," Alessia says. Finn did mention it to me after Eoghan had already told me his brother set him up to look like a jackass. So he wasn't a complete cad that night. It doesn't exactly clean up the reputation he's already garnered in Boston as being a playboy.

"Fair. But that doesn't make Eoghan a saint. I swear, every time he's around, it's like he's undressing me with his eyes."

"Does he make you uncomfortable?" Giada's concern over my well-being is rather adorable. I've been in plenty of situations where the male gaze has made me want to curl in on myself, but that's not what's happening here, unfortunately.

"She's uncomfortable because he's the exact kind of guy who she usually drools over." Alessia laughs and I send her a scathing look. Damn her for knowing me so well.

"Exactly," I say. "I'm done with fuckboys. He's all about the chase and getting what he wants."

"I think you both want it," Alessia mumbles.

"Shut it, lady. What I want and what's good for me are two very different things, and it's time I started focusing on finding serious relationships, not spending my time chasing losers."

Or guys in the Irish mob who are used to women falling all over themselves when he turns his dimpled smile on them.

"Eoghan is pretty far from a loser," Alessia comments.

"He's also pretty far from being the type to settle down and take a relationship seriously," I point out. His saying he wants to see where this goes doesn't mean he wants to settle down. He could decide he's over it next month and move on as though nothing's wrong. Then I would've wasted more time and energy on someone who I knew wasn't right from the start.

"Let's try to keep the claws sheathed. I love my mother-in-law and would hate for her to have to clean blood out of the carpets. It's such a pain in the ass."

"Okay. I'll do it for Maeve," I concede with a wide smile on my face.

The elevator doors open and Finn and Luca walk into the penthouse, smiling when they both see their wives in the living room. I'm so damn happy that Finn's cousin and his wife are here and safe within the Monaghan fold. I know Giada has her fears where fitting in with the Monaghans is concerned, but seeing the bright smiles on her and my best friend's husband's faces warms me. Even though the family is composed of people who don't exactly follow the letter of the law, there's a loyalty and bond that has always fascinated me and, at times, made me a bit wistful. I've never had that with anyone other than Alessia. When I told her I'd gladly poison her ex, I meant it. I'd do anything for the woman sitting next to me. Giada is damn lucky she gets to call these people family. It's just going to take some time for her to adjust.

After firming up plans for tonight, Finn grabs our bags, and we head out of the penthouse.

"I need to check in with the guards before we leave," Finn tells us before leaning down to kiss his wife squarely on the mouth. I'm honestly shocked they didn't start making out like teenagers in the elevator with the looks he was throwing her way. I have a small chuckle with myself over their constant PDA, considering Alessia hated him at first sight. I never thought she'd end up truly and wholly in love with the Irish mob boss, but these Monaghan boys have a way of worming their way inside your mind, the likes of which I've never witnessed. Well, Finn seems to. Eoghan...yeah, he's got the same damn charm as his older brother.

When Alessia and I are walking to my car in the underground garage, my phone starts ringing. I grab it from my bag and look at the screen. *Unknown Caller.* This is the third time I've gotten a call from a blocked number this week. At first, I thought maybe Eoghan had somehow gotten my number and didn't want me to know it was him, but I feel like he's more likely to text or at least leave a message. Eoghan isn't exactly the type to do anything under the radar, and blocking a number certainly is that. The only other person who would try to call me from a blocked number is the last person I want to talk to, so I sure as shit won't be picking it up.

"You okay?" Alessia asks when she spots the frown tugging at my lips.

"Unknown caller, " I explain, holding my phone to her.

"You don't think she's trying to get a hold of you again, do you?"

I shrug. "Anything's possible. But I changed my number after it happened the last time. Considering I haven't heard from her in nearly seven years, I doubt she somehow tracked me down now. Not like she ever has before."

I'd rather not get into all the reasons I don't want to speak to the person who could be calling. The likelihood it is her is pretty fucking slim. It's probably the one man I've been trying my damnedest not to think about but failing miserably at. He frustrates me to no end, and the fact I let him is even more annoying.

"That's not it, though. I feel like there's something you're not telling me. Listen, I know I've been spending a lot of time at the casino and with Finn—"

I cut her off before she has a chance to finish that sentence. "No, no, no, my friend. I know exactly where you're going with that line of thinking, and I'm telling you to put it out of your head right now. I've had a few things on my mind," I admit without telling her what those things are. "Once I'm ready to talk it out with you, I will." That's how we've always been. It's not that we keep secrets from each other, but there are some things we need to turn over and over in our own heads before we bring it to the other person. Alessia and I have always given each other the space to do that.

"As long as you know you can talk to me," she says.

"I know." I offer her a smile and open my car door to throw my bag in the back seat.

"Just as long as you know I'm here for you like I've always been."

"Shut it, sister." I playfully nudge her in the arm. "I know."

This is so stupid. I can't believe how nervous I am walking up to the Monaghans' front door. You'd think Eoghan and I were keeping some torrid love affair a secret from everyone the way the butterflies are rioting in my stomach. We ran into each other a couple times, but other than that, he hasn't pursued me any further. It's not like he's calling or texting me every day, and I haven't seen him since that day at the gym. Hell, I haven't heard from him once. Maybe that has something to do with my nerves, too. Maybe he's finally listened to me and has given up this pursuit of whatever he thinks is between us. That would be good—smart of him. It would definitely be for the best.

Liar, liar, pants on fire.

Jesus, I seriously hope no one is watching me as I stand out here and argue with myself. I must look like a complete moron.

Pull up your big-girl panties and knock on the door, Gemma. You aren't the type to run scared for any reason and certainly not away from the blue-eyed devil who's been starring in some very naughty dreams the last few nights.

Raising my hand to knock, the door flies open before my fist makes contact with the wood, startling me out of my thoughts.

"Hey there, blondie." Blue eyes twinkle in the soft glow of the porch light. And I know right then and there, I've been busted. "What are you doing standing out here?" Asshole.

"So, stalking me now includes spying on me? Should I tell your brother to keep a tighter leash on you?"

"Interesting you haven't already," he says with that damn perpetual smirk.

"Move," I growl, shoving past him and into the foyer of Maeve and Cormac's home.

"Let me take your jacket," Eoghan says from behind me as I slip the light coat from my shoulders.

The heat from him soaks into my back as his breath tickles the side of my neck the same time he slips the jacket over my arms. In a blink, he's stepped away from me, and I'm left standing still, my breath suddenly stalled in my chest.

"You okay?" Eoghan whispers from behind me; he's so close that if I turned my head slightly to the left, our mouths would be less than a centimeter apart.

Fine," I reply, clearing my throat and taking a step away from him. "Where is everyone?" I turn to look at him, and there's no way he misses the blush creeping up my neck. The dark-blue shirt he left open at the neck brings out the light blue in his eyes that are brimming with mischief. The urge to run my fingers through his blond hair or smack him in the face is strong, and I'm not sure which is stronger. I loathe the way I can't seem to control my emotions around this man. This isn't me at all, but Eoghan Monaghan seems to have a knack for turning my insides topsy-turvy without anything more than an almost touch. And right now, I despise him for it.

"There you are," Alessia says, coming around the corner and taking in the scene in front of her. Her dark-brown eyes dance between me and Eoghan. "Everything okay?"

"Dandy," I reply, offering her a wide smile.

"I was just helping her out of her coat," Eoghan chimes in as he walks past me, brushing his sleeved arm against mine. I look at where we made contact and notice his rolled-up shirtsleeve showing off his strong forearms. What is it about a man and his forearms that turn me to mush? Especially the ones on this particular man.

Alessia narrows her eyes at him, and as soon as he's out of earshot, her scrutinizing gaze turns to me. "What's going on?"

I laugh, but it's hollow. "Nothing." She holds my gaze until it wanders past her and into the living room, where I spot her parents. "Come on. I haven't seen your parents since the wedding."

When I walk into the large living room, Lilliana stands and greets me, kissing both of my cheeks. "Gemma, it's been too long. You look amazing. Your cheeks are so rosy. Have you been enjoying time outside of your office?"

Lilliana is always telling me I work too hard and need to enjoy the sun and fresh air rather than keeping myself cooped up. However, that's not the reason for the color in my face tonight. That reason is standing behind the bar against the far wall of the room, pouring a glass of prosecco. Eoghan walks up to me and hands me the glass of bubbly as I settle on the couch next to Lilliana, and he sits on the arm of said couch right next to me.

"Work has been keeping me busy. But I've tried to make time," I say, taking a sip of the delicious sparkling wine.

"Boston is so beautiful this time of year," Lilliana says. "Before it gets too hot. I'm so thankful I gave birth before the summer hit." She turns to Alessia, who has positioned herself next to Finn on the couch directly across from us. Alessia's gaze darts between me and Eoghan, who's made himself comfortable, perched right next to me. "I hope you don't have to endure the brutal humidity when you're pregnant, Alessia."

That grabs my best friend's attention. She offers her mother a bland smile, and Finn's hand tightens on her knee in a comforting gesture. Alessia was afraid her mother was going to bring up grandbabies tonight for...reasons.

"Lilliana, how are your rosebushes? It's been so long since I've seen your gardens," I say, taking the heat from Alessia and distracting Lilliana with one of her favorite topics. She begins to tell me about the new flowers she's planted and how beautiful the blooms have been this year. Cormac and Maeve sit in chairs off to the side, and Maeve and Lilliana begin trading gardening tips and tricks. Only a few minutes pass before there's another knock at the door. Maeve looks at Cormac with excitement radiating from her blue eyes. Though this is a birthday dinner for Alessia, this is also the first time she's seen her nephew since the first day he showed up at the penthouse a week ago with a new bride in tow. The entire family spent the last twenty-five years believing he was dead, only to find out he was alive and well, living in California under a different name. Maeve stands and rushes to the door while Cormac looks lovingly at his wife.

"Maybe you should go save them, Dad," Eoghan says, taking a sip from his beer.

"I'll give your mom a second to fuss. She's been chomping at the bit."

When Alessia told me the situation with Luca and Giada, she mentioned Finn has kept his mom from bombarding the newlyweds everyday like he knew she was desperate to do. Finally, Maeve put her foot down and insisted they were here tonight so they could finally celebrate as a family, including Alessia and the Amattos.

After a couple minutes, Cormac decides Maeve's had enough time and heads out of the room to greet the newcomers, probably saving them from the teary hugs and kisses Maeve is no doubt bestowing.

When Giada and Luca enter, there's a relief in Giada's features as Lilliana stands and walks over to the woman who had been so nervous about what kind of reception she would be walking into. I'm thrilled for my new friend and am also glad I don't have to knock skulls together if anyone says anything or makes the girl feel uncomfortable. Alessia may think my protective streak is funny, but she knows I'd go to bat for anyone in my circle, even against the Irish or Italian Mafia.

Eoghan gets up from where he was sitting next to me and offers to grab drinks for Luca and Giada.

Alessia's eyes follow him and then land back on me. I'm trying so damn hard to not give her any ideas about me and Eoghan, but the infuriating man may as well be lighting a neon sign above our heads with the way he's been so attentive to me since I got here. I swear, if I tried to move myself closer to Lilliana, I'd be sitting in her lap.

Maeve walks back into the room to let us know dinner is ready. We all head into the dining room, and Alessia has a wide smile on her face when she sees the beautiful table Maeve set up for her birthday. A centerpiece of red calla lilies sits in the middle of the table, her favorite flower that matches the red lipstick she's so fond of wearing. She turns to her husband and gives him a private smile before she places a soft kiss on his lips.

We have a seat at the table and everyone is enjoying the feast before us. Maeve went all out for her daughter-in-law's birthday. Even Giada seems to be relaxing a bit as plates are passed and piled high with food. This is family. This is what I'm so damn happy my best friend and my new friend have found with their husbands. This is also something I never dreamed possible for myself. Not that the Monaghans and the Amattos don't treat me as one of their own, they absolutely do. But this isn't how I was raised. When I was growing up, I was lucky if my mom made it out of bed before noon and stuck a candle in a Ding Dong. No one was there to make my favorite meal or anything of the sort. After a while, I stopped hoping for it. Hell, Alessia and I were friends for three years before I told her when my birthday was. Then I told her I'm not a fan of birthdays and don't like to celebrate, which is partially true. The whole truth is I didn't want to be let down if she forgot. She never did though, but old habits die hard, so I still don't let her make a big deal out of the day.

While we're clearing the plates, Eoghan walks up next to me and takes a stack from my hands.

"You were quiet at dinner," he says as I grab more things from the table.

"I was concentrating on not stabbing you with a fork. It takes a lot of effort."

I send him a sweet smile and he laughs. Laughter is a good look on him. So is his relaxed demeanor when he's spending time with his family. Not that Eoghan is ever particularly uptight, unlike his brother, but when they're in the safety of their parents' home, it's hard to picture them as anything other than two brothers who like to joke around and have a good time, rather than the criminal kingpins they appear to be to the outside world.

"So violent," he says with a smile, giving me every impression that he likes it.

"You need to back off. You're making it look like something is going on between us, and I'm tired of playing oblivious to the looks Alessia keeps giving me."

"There is, blondie. You just haven't accepted it yet."

"You're insufferable," I say through clenched teeth.

"I like to think of it as tenacious." Eoghan leans in close, and his breath on my neck causes heat to explode through my body for the second time tonight. "Have I told you that you look absolutely edible tonight?"

When he pulls back and pins me with those blue eyes of his, it takes monumental effort to remind myself to breathe.

"Yeah, there's nothing going on between us," Eoghan says, holding my stare before I break the contact and head into the kitchen with the plate in my shaky hand. I'm not going to break. No matter how much I want to feel the heat from his mouth on other parts of my body, I'm going to make the smart choice for once in my life.

After the table is cleared and reset with Alessia's birthday cake, Giada and Luca come from wherever they went off to while we were cleaning up. I can tell she's been crying, but when I shoot her a questioning look, she smiles softly and nods, letting me know she's okay. We sing to Alessia for her birthday, and she's absolutely beaming with happiness when she blows out the candles.

"Mmm," she says, taking a huge bite of her chocolate mousse cake. "My favorite."

She looks at her husband, and Finn shoots her a wink. He's filled this house with all of her favorites. I'd say she has no idea how lucky she is to have a man who pays such close attention, but she knows damn well she won the jackpot with the man sitting next to her.

"Your mom made the cake," Maeve says and Lilliana beams.

"Mama, you've always been the best baker."

"I knew this one was your favorite, sweetheart."

"I used to love making the boys' birthday cakes when they were younger, except Eoghan. He never liked cake," Maeve says.

"This is good," Eoghan says around a mouthful of the decadent dessert.

"Yeah, but you always preferred brownies. Those vanilla ones with ice cream, if I recall."

"I always enjoyed a good blondie," Eoghan says, and I nearly choke on my dessert.

Our eyes meet, and he shoots me a quick wink. My cheeks instantly feel like they're on fire as my eyes drop to my plate. When I look up again, Eoghan has turned his attention to his brother; they're talking about the new fighter he's been working with. I assumed his little nickname was about my blonde hair, not his favorite dessert. That knowledge absolutely should not be sending a thrill through me like it is, and I should be thinking about anything other than the creative ways we could use brownie batter, but I'm not.

Jesus, what the hell is wrong with me?

After dessert, it's time to head home. I have a busy as hell week ahead of me, and as fun as it is to field looks from my best friend and try to keep my heart rate at a normal pace around the smirking Irishman, I'm exhausted, and my bed is calling.

When I've finished saying my goodbyes, Eoghan follows me into the foyer and grabs my coat from the hook on the wall. He's silent, which I'm thankful for, considering everyone is in the next room, but he doesn't pass up the opportunity to ghost his fingertips over the back of my neck as he settles my coat around my shoulders.

"Drive safe," he says in a low voice that vibrates through my muddled mind.

I don't say anything as I walk to my car, but I spot him in the doorway with that damn smirk on his face. That asshole knew exactly what he was doing, and he damn sure saw the effect it had on me. As I'm pulling out of the driveway, a call comes through, causing me to jump in my seat and scaring the absolute shit out of me. It's late, so there's no reason anyone should be calling. I notice it's another blocked number. Knowing Eoghan, it's probably him wanting to give me a hard time, yet again, about sticking to my guns in regard to nothing being between us. I'm finding it harder and harder to convince myself of that the more time I spend around him.

"What do you want?" I say by way of greeting.

The raspy voice that answers is not the one I was expecting—the one I was so sure it couldn't possibly be.

"Is that any way to greet your mother?"

CHAPTER FIVE
EOGHAN

THE LAST FEW WEEKS have been an absolute shit show of epic proportions. The night of Alessia's birthday party, my cousin's wife was shot after they'd left my parents' house. We ramped up security at all of our bars and the casino, which means fight nights have been canceled until Carlo Cataldi is found. That slimy bastard has eluded us at every turn and Finn is determined to find him no matter the cost, which is why every one of our men has been tracking down even the smallest possible leads that could tell us where that asshole has been hiding. Between helping with the search and running all four of our bars, getting extra security, and installing more security cameras at the bars, I'm run the fuck down.

When I got the call from my brother after Giada was shot, we didn't know who or why she was targeted or if she was even the intended target. I called a cleanup crew to take care of the car Luca was driving and the body of the gunman Finn had taken care of, but unfortunately, it wasn't before Giada took a bullet to the shoulder. When we arrived at the scene, not even fifteen minutes after the crash, I scoured the would-be hit man's car and found a picture of Giada and one of Luca. So they were after the newlyweds. That narrowed the list of suspects considerably, specifically down to one person—Giada's brother, Carlo. He knew the two were married, and he was fucking pissed. It ruined his plans for the Russian alliance he was banking on, and desperate men do desperate things. And make stupid mistakes. Namely, hiring a hit man who would keep pictures of his targets in his car. *Fucking amateur.*

Since the shooting, I've kept someone on Gemma. It's completely under the radar. I don't want her thinking this life is spilling into hers. She's an innocent in all of this. I know she's been friends with Alessia for over a decade, so she understands certain aspects of this life, but she's always been on the periphery, never knowing the true scope of what being a part of a criminal organization entails. But Carlo is reckless and might consider hurting someone who has any connection with my family. Finn didn't agree when I brought it up to him, and I wasn't keen on the idea of being too insistent and raising his suspicions so I simply put one of my guys, Tommy, on her and told him to keep it quiet. If Finn finds out, oh well, but at least Tommy won't go blabbing to everyone about the job.

Unfortunately, I haven't been able to see Gemma much other than the few times I ran into her at my brother's house, where she was visiting Giada while she was recuperating from her gunshot wound. I could tell something had been bothering her, but anytime I tried to talk to her, she brushed me off. Not unlike most of our interactions, but this one felt different. Like she was trying to keep something from me instead of the normal annoyance she'd pretend to have at my advances.

I haven't made it to the gym either, but the trainer I lined up for Javier has been there working with the kid. Once this is all taken care of, the plan is to have Javier get a few fights under his belt at one of our fight nights, and I plan to woo the hell out of Gemma. I'm sick of dancing around this attraction, and I sure as hell am sick of letting her avoid it. We just need the dark cloud of Carlo Cataldi that's been hanging over our heads to be taken care of. Then I can focus on the feisty blonde who hasn't stopped running circles in my mind.

Yesterday, Finn called and told me they had a new lead, and he thinks this one might be it. God, I fucking hope so. I'm so tired of this Cataldi asshole having us by the balls. He's like a damn phantom menace that could jump out at any moment and try to kill someone I care about. My brother and Alessia, along with Luca and Giada, went up to Shine this morning to check out the lead. There's some old lake house Giada remembers from her childhood that wasn't in any property records, and we've been keeping surveillance on it. It's the perfect hiding spot for Cataldi since we know he's the type to stay close to the chaos and mayhem he's been spreading around.

When my phone rings and I see Cillian's name flash

on the screen, I hope to hell he has good news for me.

"Hey, Cill. What's up?"

"They found the lake house. Property records show it belonged to Giada's grandfather on her mother's side. The house hasn't been sold, and all the taxes have been paid on it since his death. Utility bills are in the name of a corporation I tracked to the Caymans."

"Let me guess; it ties back to the Cataldis."

"It doesn't tie to anything, so yeah, it has Carlo written all over it."

Offshore bank accounts are a favorite of Carlo and Francesco Cataldi. Hell, for anyone trying to hide money. Certainly works well for my family from time to time.

"Do they know if he's there?"

"Someone's there, and I have money on it being Carlo."

"When do we leave?"

"How fast can you pack?"

I look around the penthouse I keep close to my brother's safe house/penthouse. This is where I have most everything I'll need for what we'll be walking into when we finally go after Carlo.

"Won't take me long. I'm at my penthouse by the warehouses." Another perk of this place is it's situated on the same block as the warehouses where we keep our inventory. Everything we need to start a small revolution is housed only feet from my front door. Not to mention the personal arsenal I keep here. Much like

Finn's place, the exposed brick and open floor plan gives the space an industrial feel. And also, like Finn's, I keep a cache of weapons in a secure room on a lower level, though mine doesn't come with a gun range.

"I'm going to have my guy hack into the county's planning department and see if they have a digital copy of the building plans so we're not going in blind. Finn wants this taken care of tonight."

"Can't come soon enough."

Cillian grunts his agreement and tells me to be ready within the next two hours. Plenty of time to pack a couple bags of special goodies to greet that fucker Carlo with.

The drive to Shine is quiet as most times spent with Cillian are. Sometimes, I wonder if my brother's lieutenant likes me. Not that it would matter one way or the other. He's loyal to my family, and that's what's important to me. When we went after Alessia's ex, he was just as quiet, so maybe this is him preparing to take a man's life. Me, though? I have no reservations when it comes to wiping pieces of shit like Carlo from the face of this earth, and I'll be damned if I let it affect my mood like my brother's brooding lieutenant sitting next to me.

The last time Finn had me come to the clubhouse

with him was before he was married. In fact, it was when he'd finally decided to make the moves that were the catalyst for the overdue mission we're going on tonight. Carlo has been a thorn in our side for far too long. He was never going to get out of this alive, but there was a chance he could have gotten out of it without a painful death. Maybe. Okay, probably not. But going after Giada cemented the fact that he'll be in as much pain as possible before his sorry existence is ended.

When we pull up to the clubhouse, the prospect at the gate opens it for us and we park next to my brother's car and unload the bags that were in the hidden compartments in the trunk and back seat of Cillian's car. Obviously, anytime we're transporting weapons, we take extra precautions and make sure to drive the speed limit so as not to call attention to ourselves—but shit happens. If we were caught with the small arsenal we brought with us, we'd be looking at life behind bars. I have much better things to do with my time than sitting in an eight-by-eight cell until the day I die, so most of our cars also have several nifty hiding places that we put to good use.

With our hands full, the prospect jogs over and opens the door to the clubhouse for us. When we step inside, all eyes turn to us, and a round of hellos fills the space. Cillian and I walk to the bar at the far end of the room where Luca and my brother are sitting with cups of coffee in front of them.

We drop the bags to the floor and Cillian turns his attention to Finn.

"We made a trip to the warehouse. Brought a few extras just in case," Cillian says, surveying the guns and knives on the bar. "I looked into the property records for the address you sent me," he tells Finn. "It's had the same owner since the sixties. Antonio Russo. Giada's grandfather."

"It's Carlo then. You're sure it was never sold?" Luca asks my brother's lieutenant. He hasn't been around us the last several years, so he doesn't know that Cillian is the last of any of us to go in half-cocked. He doesn't make any move unless he's one-hundred-percent sure who the players are and any other little kernels of information he can glean from his sources.

Cillian shoots Luca a look that conveys my cousin just said something incredibly stupid. I have to stifle a laugh at Cillian's obvious displeasure that someone would even think to question that he isn't prepared to the point he could probably tell you every last bit of information on the property and the man inside the house.

"Of course," Cillian replies. "The taxes on the property have been paid every year from a shell account that ended in the Caymans. If I recall, the Cataldis are particularly fond of using shell companies to hide their money."

"We go tonight. Before dawn breaks, I want that fucker six feet under," Finn says. This is what I've been wanting to see and hear from my brother for months. The stone-cold determination that Carlo dies tonight and we finally show every other asshole what happens when you fuck with the Monaghans and the people we love. This is the boss that has the other families bowing to his authority.

"We have a plan?" Ozzy asks as he, Jude and Linc walk to our group. I smile at the MC president and the two enforcers as I shake their hands.

"To go in and kill Carlo and anyone else we find," Luca replies

"Sounds solid," Jude says, his lip curling into a deadly smirk. He looks down at the bags Cillian and I brought in. "And look. You brought more toys."

"Of course we did," I say, smiling broadly. "A few things for our newest shipment and some of my favorites." I open one of the bags and pull out several handguns, placing them on the bar top. "A .22, great for quick kills and easy to dump. A couple38 Specials—classics in their own right." Then I pick up a long barrel .45. "And my personal favorite, the .45." When I was a kid, I loved the movie *Dirty Harry*, and every time I hold one of these, I picture myself as the actor telling the bad guy to make my day. What can I say? I'm just a big kid at heart.

"Very nice, mate," Jude says, taking the .45 from my hand and examining it. When he places it on the bar, a short woman with long black hair tucks herself under his arm.

"Dinner will be ready in about thirty minutes. Tanya

brought some things over, so Charlie and Cece are warming stuff up, and Cece made enough bread to feed an army."

Jude's hand goes to his stomach, patting it a few times. "Fuck yeah."

The woman rolls her eyes but smiles at the tall Englishman before turning her gaze toward me. "Hi, I'm Lucy," she says, holding out her hand for me to shake.

"Eoghan," I reply.

"Shit, sorry. Where are my manners? Eoghan, I'm pleased to finally introduce you to the bane of my existence and the love of my life, Lucifer."

A bark of laughter bursts from me when Lucy takes the opportunity to wallop her man in the gut, and he releases a grunt of pain.

"Jesus, woman. I think that's a perfectly reasonable introduction."

"You would," she replies while shaking her head. "I'm glad to finally meet you, Eoghan. Jude, also known as the asshole that I share my bed with, has told me so much about you."

"Hey, what about love of your life?"

She looks at him with a bland expression on her face. "I said what I said."

He laughs and kisses her hard on the mouth. She returns the kiss with just as much ferocity, and if I wasn't so amused by their antics, I'd probably feel mildly uncomfortable.

When he releases her, she waves at me before turning

back toward the kitchen.

"Goddamn, I love that woman," Jude says, staring after his girlfriend.

"Are you sure she feels the same?" I ask with laughter in my voice.

"Aye, she does. She hated me on sight, though. Probably wouldn't have spit on me if I was on fire, but I eventually wore her down." His smile stretches across his face as though he's remembering those times with sweet fondness. It's an odd thing to see on the biker's face.

"Oh yeah, how'd you do that?" Maybe I can get some pointers to thaw the heart of a certain blonde in Boston.

"I didn't let her push me away. And damn, that woman tried," he replies, chuckling to himself and shaking his head. "How about a game of pool before we eat? Winner plays Lucy."

"Sounds good to me."

Jude and I play an aggressive game of pool as Lucy sits in one of the stools off to the side and talks shit to her man, which seems to only serve in getting him more riled up. I forgot how competitive the asshole is when it comes to any kind of game of skill. Fucker always has to try to one up everyone.

"Eoghan, how are you at darts?" Lucy asks and Jude growls.

"Shut it, Lucifer. I'm trying to concentrate."

A light laughter falls from her lips before her fingers go to her mouth, imitating a zipping motion.

When he takes his next shot, he misses and inadvertently sets me up for a winning shot.

"Better luck next time," Lucy says as I sink the eight ball in the pocket.

"Maybe I would have fared better had you kept your damn trap shut," Jude mumbles as he lays the pool stick on the table and shoots Lucy a narrow-eyed glare.

"Maybe, but what would have been the fun in that for me?" Lucy hops off the stool and walks to where platters of food have been laid out on the bar. "Soups on, and I'm starving."

She saunters away, and Jude shakes his head as he smiles to himself. I swear, I don't think I've seen the man smile as much in the last hour as I've seen in the last five years we've known each other.

After dinner everyone takes off with their women, and Cillian heads to his room that one of the ladies here set up for him.

It's late, but we plan on leaving to find that asshole in just a couple short hours. That thought alone has me wired and ready to get this shit over with so we can get back to Boston. I think about what Jude said as I sit back on the black leather sofa in the clubhouse. A couple of the guys are playing pool and some are shooting darts, but my mind is going in a million different directions at the moment, so my concentration would be shit if I tried to join them for a game.

Instead, I send a quick text to Tommy.

Me: *What's going on, man?*

Tommy: *Nothing much. Gemma has been in her apartment for a few hours. I think she's in for the night. Gonna head home.*

Tommy hasn't been on her for the entirety of the last few weeks. When she was at work one day, I had a motion-activated camera set up outside her door that would send a notification to my phone whenever it was activated. I didn't want him to have to sit in front of her building all night, every night. I'm not a monster, after all.

Me: *Okay. We'll be back tomorrow. Cataldi will be gone by morning.*

Tommy: *Bout fucking time.*

I'm sure everyone in the organization is looking forward to getting back to business as usual.

I slip my phone into my pocket and head outside. It's a clear night that we're about to make very bloody. I think about what we're walking into and let my mind wander to tomorrow when all is said and done. My family will be on top in Boston. The Cataldi organization will be dead, with no one left to resurrect the crumbling syndicate. I think about the weight that's been around our necks finally lifting. What that's going to look like and mean for me.

Grabbing my phone out of my pocket, I dial the number of the only person whose voice I want to hear.

"Hello," Gemma answers groggily, as though I've woken her up.

"Hey, blondie."

"I should have known you would call and wake me out of the best dream I've had in ages."

"I hope I was in it."

She chuckles sleepily into the phone. "Sorry to disappoint. I was making out with Henry Cavill while he was dressed as a 1900s detective."

"Most girls would dream of him in his Superman costume."

"Well, I'm not most girls. You should know that by now. I'm going to go back to my dream now." She lets loose a loud yawn.

"Wait," I say before she can hang up. "Let me take you out next week."

"Eoghan," she groans into the phone.

"Listen, blondie. I know your reasons, and I know why you think they're valid, and I'm not one to beat a dead horse." Her laughter sounds from the other end of the line. "Give me a shot, Gemma. Come on, a little date won't hurt you."

"It might end up hurting you."

"I might like it," I say with a smile on my face. "Are you scared or something?"

She scoffs. "Of what, pray tell?"

"Falling in love with me."

At that, she laughs outright, but I don't take offense. Well, not much.

"What do you say?" I press.

She groans and I know she's thinking about it. "I'm busy next week."

"With what?"

"Washing my hair."

Cheeky woman.

"I'm not hearing a no..." I let the sentence trail off.

"You're not hearing a yes, either."

"So I have a shot?"

Gemma's throaty laugh widens the goofy-as-fuck smile on my face even more. "I have to go. Henry is calling my name from dreamland. I'll talk to you next week."

She hangs up, and I think I've finally broken past the first barrier with that wildly infuriating and unforgettable woman. I've never had to work so hard to break down a woman's walls. Shit, I've never cared to. Gemma was right to be wary of me at first. I didn't gain my reputation as a playboy by sitting at home and twiddling my thumbs. But that was before she turned that hard aqua gaze in my direction. There was a shock to my core I'd never experienced before, and I was instantly addicted to that feeling, to her.

"You're shite at picking women up."

I whirl around and catch Jude blowing out a puff of smoke before his lip tips in a smirk.

"Honestly, mate. My eighty-year-old grandfather would probably have better luck with whoever you were on the phone with."

"Fuck off, prick," I reply with no real heat behind my words. "I'm laying the groundwork." What he doesn't know is this is probably the furthest I've been able to get with Gemma. She didn't tell me to fuck off outright. That's progress in my book.

"So little Eoghan's gone and found himself a girl. Could it be true love?" The sarcastic British asshole asks.

"Could be, my friend. It definitely could be." It's the truth, and I'm not going to deny it.

"Well, buckle up, then. You're in for the ride of your fucking life."

I sure as fuck hope so.

Sneaking in is the easy part. When I was a kid, I decided I wanted to master picking locks. I don't really know where the urge came from, but once I get something in my head, good luck trying to get it out. Naturally, in my family's line of work, it's come in handy a time or two. Carlo only had one guy in the house with him, who Cillian quickly and effortlessly disposed of. Having Carlo fire a shot at my cousin nearly has me unloading my .45 into the man's chest as I stand behind my brother, my gun staying trained on the slippery motherfucker as he bleeds from the bullet wound in his arm courtesy of my brother.

"You think killing me is going to somehow save your sorry ass?" Luca asks Carlo, raising his gun to Carlo's forehead.

"No. But if I'm going to hell, I'm taking you with me, you fucking rat bastard."

This asshole doesn't know when to shut up. It's obvious he's trying to get out of the painful death that awaits him at our hands, and he almost gets his wish by the look on Luca's face. Hell, I'm ready to end his existence this second until the MC president walks in the room, smiling at Carlo like we've delivered an early Christmas present to him.

"Now, now, boys. Don't kill him too fast," Ozzy says, walking up to the bed. "I haven't had my fun with him yet." The MC president digs his gloved finger into the bullet wound Finn gave Carlo, and it takes every bit of strength in the soon-to-be-dead man to not scream out in agony.

"You fucked up, Carlo. You went after what's mine. Twice."

Ozzy whips out a hunting knife from his belt and plunges it into Carlo's stomach. Sweat pours down the soon-to-be-dead man's face as he tries to hold back his scream. I have to give him some credit. A wound like that has got to be excruciating.

"Hurts like a bitch, don't it? Funny thing about stab wounds to the stomach. It takes a few minutes for them to kill you, but it'll be the most painful last minutes of your life. I bet if I keep the knife inside you, it'll buy me and my friends some extra time."

"You all have no idea what's coming for you," Carlo says, his wild eyes darting to everyone in the room as sweat pours down his face. "You think you've won? I'll see you all in hell before long."

"Maybe, but it won't be today." Luca raises his gun to Carlo's forehead and fires.

Pride flares in my chest as I watch my cousin stare at the prone body of the man who nearly killed his wife. It's been a long time coming for Luca to finally be able to exact the revenge he came to Boston for. Even though I was angry when Finn told us of Luca's existence and what they'd been up to the last several years, there's a peaceful calm that washes through me and the entire room as we stare at the dead man who terrorized my family and people I cared about for far too long. I've said it before, and I'm sure I'll say it again, no one fucks with the Monaghans and lives. We can now put this chapter behind us and move forward as the family I've always been proud to be a part of.

By the time we get back to the clubhouse, the sun is high in the sky. My brother and Luca got back hours ago, but I went with Cillian, Knox, and Cash to a pig farm an hour outside of Shine. Apparently, the farmer likes to keep his pigs well fed, and when the need arises for the Black Roses to dispose of a body, they get fed extra well. Cillian wanted to check out the guy's setup in case we find ourselves in need of an alternative form of cleanup, and I wanted to see what they could do.

I'm not going to lie; I kind of wish I hadn't. To be honest, I'm going to have to tell my mother she's no longer allowed to make her Sunday pork roast ever again. To Cillian's credit, he simply looked on with mild interest then took the guy's number before heading back to the truck. That man was completely unfazed like he is with most things in life, it seems. He's a fucking psycho if that didn't have at least some effect on him.

When we walk inside, it's dark, everyone having already gone to bed, probably exhausted from pulling an all-nighter. My head is finally quiet enough to go back to the little room Ozzy offered me earlier. After taking the shower I was in desperate need of, I collapse onto the queen mattress, not even bothering to get under the plaid comforter.

The last thoughts I have are of striking blue eyes and a wicked smile that would scare the piss out of most men.

Fuck, I can't wait to go home and see my girl.

CHAPTER SIX
GEMMA

JUST WHEN I THOUGHT Eoghan had given up on his ridiculous idea of giving him a shot to prove the chemistry between us is more than a fleeting attraction, my phone rings in the middle of the night. I'm not sure why I answered Eoghan's call. It's not like the last time I answered the phone from an unknown caller it went well. Though as annoyingly persistant as Eoghan can be, I'd much rather hear his voice on the other end of the line rather than the woman who gave birth to me.

I've been out of sorts since the night I heard from my mother a couple weeks ago. She needed money, which was no surprise, and it was the reason I'd changed everything about myself after leaving Virginia Beach. Hell, I even made sure the way I spoke had no Virginian accent that could give people an idea of where or how I grew up. When I was accepted into Yale, I changed my name. I wanted a fresh start, and I wanted Jennifer Wilkins to be nothing but a distant memory. So Gemma Dalton took her place.

No one knows who I used to be, not even my

best friend. How my mother found me is a complete mystery. She could have probably hired or fucked a PI, so he would do some digging. She knew I went to Yale, but I never told her I'd completely transformed myself. Cutting ties to her was harder than I thought in the beginning, hence why, during my freshman year, I still answered her phone calls. But those calls were nothing more than her wanting money and to bitch about her life being a dancer and how I abandoned her for some rich pricks in Connecticut. The last conversation we had when she called me a "spoiled little bitch" sealed the deal. That woman never once did anything for me that could be construed as "spoiling." I changed my number that very day and left all remnants of my past life in the rearview—including her.

Imagine my surprise when I answered the blocked number, and it was none other than my mother. Pure shock was the only thing that stopped me from hanging up the phone when she muttered her greeting.

"Is that any way to greet your mother?" my mother says in a low, raspy voice that tells me she's probably been smoking at least two packs a day since the last time I spoke to her ten years ago.

Hearing her voice nearly stuns me stupid. Good thing I recover quickly, considering I'm driving.

"What do you want? How did you get my number?"

"Aren't you happy to hear from me, Jennifer? Or should I call you Gemma?" The scorn in her voice makes my skin crawl. It's the same way she spoke to me throughout my

childhood. Every time she would berate me for wanting even the simplest of necessities, like something other than canned meat for dinner, she'd ask why I thought I was some special little princess. Meanwhile, my mother was never short on whiskey or any of her other coveted substances.

"I'd prefer you didn't call me anything, Mother." Not Angela, as she preferred I call her when I got a bit older so she could try to pass me off as her younger sister instead of her teenage daughter. "I'll ask again: What do you want?" I didn't bother asking her how she got my number. I doubt she'd tell me anyway.

"Well, sweetheart,"—Oh, this shit is going to be good—"it's been a little rough here the last few months. My husband, your stepdaddy, well, he lost his job. He worked with a PI who used to investigate insurance fraud, and the asshole made up some lies about Reggie taking bribes and fired him. Can you believe it?"

I can believe it. I do believe it. Plus, I have no idea who this Reggie guy is. My mother was single when I left for college, so the fact she thinks I'd care about a stepfather I've never met proves how delusional and desperate she is.

"Are you working?"

"I would, but I hurt my back about two years ago. It's so painful for me to dance, Jenny. The doctors don't know what the hell they're doing around here."

The idea that my mom is even under medical care is laughable. My guess is she tweaked it, they gave her some pills, and she decided she hurt it worse than what she actually did to try to manipulate the health care system into supplying her addiction.

"That's too bad," I tell her. "But unfortunately, I don't have any money to send you."

"Right. I'm sure you must be so broke if you can afford a place in Boston."

"How do you know where I am?"

"Your daddy's a PI."

"Okay. First off, he's nothing to me. He's your husband, and I've never met the man, nor do I plan to. Second, I'm not sending you money, Angela. I'm sure you can do something other than dancing, and your husband can get off his ass and find a job, too. I'm not in the habit of supporting you anymore. Figure it out."

"You ungrateful little bitch. What if I'd told you to figure it out when you were little, huh? You would be nothing without me," she yells into the phone. "I'm sure you have some fancy job, and you're just living it up in Boston. There's no reason you can't help me out a little 'til I get back on my feet."

"I have every reason to not help you. Namely, you never did a damn thing for me when I was a kid. I owe you nothing."

"You're going to regret this, Jennifer. And real fucking soon."

With that, she hangs up, and I can't even call her back to ask what the hell she's talking about, considering she called me from a blocked number. I'm sure I could *track her down like she did me, but Angela's threats have always been hollow, just like her soul.*

The memory of that conversation plays over and over in my mind, like it has for the last two weeks, as I try to fall back to sleep. So fucking typical of her. Every time she pulled a stunt like this when I left home, I would ruminate over our latest conversation for days on end, working my stomach into knots with guilt. Then, one day, I decided enough was enough. I'd never felt more free than I did the day I trashed my old phone along with my old life. Now, here she is again, trying the same tired bullshit. The difference is I'm no longer the little girl who just wanted her mom to love her. Now, I'm Gemma Dalton and refuse to take anyone's shit—including my egg donor's.

Three days pass before I hear from Eoghan again while sitting in my office going over some ad copy for the campaign we're launching next week.

Eoghan: *Are you free Saturday night?*

Me: No.

Eoghan: *What are you doing that you can't possibly tear yourself away from?*

Me: *Washing my hair.*

Eoghan: *I'll let it slide this time because I know it's short notice. How about next Saturday?*

It is short notice, but that's not why I can't go out with him this weekend. I just don't want to give him the real reason.

Me: *I'll pencil you in.*

Eoghan: *You can write it in with permanent marker, blondie. I'm taking you out next weekend.*

Never in my life have I had a guy try so hard to break through my walls. I've given him no reason to think it's ever going to happen, well, not on purpose. I'm still not a hundred-percent sold on the idea that starting anything with Eoghan isn't going to end up in flames with my heart in ashes, but against my better judgment, that man has worn me down, at least somewhat.

However, this Saturday, I have a date with one of the few straight men in the fashion world. On paper, we're a perfect match. He's a photographer who understands the demands of the industry. As far as I can tell, he's not some playboy you would expect from someone in his position, taking pictures of beautiful women for a living. He's sweet and tripped over his words when he told me he would be in town for the week and was wondering if maybe I'd like to have dinner with him. Of course I said yes. He's so far from the guys I typically date. And that's exactly what I'm looking for.

But then why did I tell Eoghan I'd go out with him next weekend? *Because you've never been able to resist a bad boy, so why start now?* that infuriating voice in the back of my mind likes to remind me. *Shut the hell up,* I say to that incessant voice and tilt my head down to get back to work.

The next day, after I've showered, shaved, and slipped into a new sapphire-blue dress with a low V-neck, I feel like one of the models Stephan normally shoots with. The urge to wear something simple was strong, but that's not how I would usually dress on a first date. But for some reason, I didn't feel particularly compelled to put in the effort I usually do. That does not bode well for the evening ahead.

When I pull in front of the upscale restaurant, the valet opens my door for me, and I hand him my keys. Stephan is waiting by the front door. Walking to him with a smile on my lips, he leans in and kisses both of my cheeks.

"You look stunning, Gemma."

"Thank you. You look great, too." He's wearing a white, collared shirt with a tweed blazer and brown slacks. He looks respectable and charming. Though, I would have expected a bit more...I don't know...something, considering the industry we work in. I'm not saying he looks like some sort of troll or anything, but he kind of looks like he raided his dad's closet for an outfit.

You're being a fashionista bitch. Knock it off.

Stephan leads me into the dimly lit restaurant with his hand at the small of my back. And I feel nothing.

No *zing*, no warmth traveling from the spot where his hand is connected to me. Just a big old nothing. Not like when...

Nope, not going there.

The restaurant is beautiful. There are cream tablecloths, votive candles illuminating each table, and the faces of smiling couples as we follow the hostess, who is wearing a simple black dress. It's tasteful and sophisticated—your classic Bostonian elegant affair. After the hostess seats us, I smile at her as she hands me my menu. It strikes me just how bland this place is. Beautiful, yes. But so, so bland. So typical. *Unlike that little Irish pub in downtown Boston run by a man who is anything but typical.* I groan inwardly at the thought of Eoghan and plaster a smile on my face, directed at the man sitting across from me, attempting to focus my attention there and nowhere else.

Our waiter comes over with two glasses of water and asks if we would like to start with a bottle of wine.

"Yes," Stephan answers. "We'll have a bottle of the 2018 pinot noir." He hands the wine menu back to the waiter and nods before turning his attention to me. "You'll love it. It's the one I get every time I'm here."

"You come here often?" I ask with a chuckle and try not to be irritated with the fact that he didn't ask if I like red wine.

"Every time I'm in the city," he replies without picking up on my joke.

"It's a beautiful restaurant. I've never been here." I

open the menu and scan the contents. "Oh, the rib eye sounds good," I say and set my menu down.

"It's okay, but the linguine with clam sauce is what you should get."

"I'm not really a fan of seafood."

"Trust me. It's the best you'll ever find, and it doesn't have that seafood taste."

I never understood why people say that. *Oh, the fish is delicious. It doesn't taste like fish,* or *Oh, the venison is amazing. It's not gamey at all.* That's exactly what it is. Fish is fish and game meat is gamey.

When the waiter comes back with our bottle of wine, he uncorks it and pours a small amount into Stephan's glass. He does the whole swirl, sniff, sip thing that I've always found so damn pretentious before setting his glass on the table and nodding toward the waiter again without even a simple thank you. That's another thing I've always found annoying as hell in places like this. No one can manage to mutter a polite *thank you* anymore.

"We'll both have the linguine with clam sauce and an order of lobster rolls for the appetizer. And two Caesar salads to start," Stephan says as he hands the waiter his menu.

I stare at Stephan as though I'm seeing him in an entirely new light. Seems the shy charm I found so endearing when I accepted the date has flown out the window, replaced with whatever the hell this is.

"I'm glad you came out with me tonight, Gemma. I've been wanting to get to know you, but it's rare I'm in

Boston for more than a night or two." And he's back to being sweet. This back and forth is starting to give me a head rush—and not in a good way.

"You spend most of your downtime in New York, right?"

Stephan nods. "Between there and a studio I have in San Francisco. But my real love is traveling. I've visited Thailand and Sri Lanka recently and was honored to stay at the Buddhist temples. It was life-changing. The oneness, the connection you feel with the very grass you walk on. You won't be able to look at the world around you the same after that."

I've always appreciated people who can find that kind of peace in their lives. It's not something I've ever been able to achieve, that's for sure.

"I swear, it's what keeps me going when I have to do those god-awful shoots with vapid models. I can't wait to get out of the fashion industry," Stephan continues with a small shudder. "I'm sure you can relate."

Okay, I'm getting the distinct impression I made a mistake coming here tonight. I'm just about done trying to be nice enough to give this guy a chance when a head of dark-blond hair and blue eyes lasering in on me catches my attention. My eyes track Eoghan as he walks to the bar on the other side of the restaurant and orders a drink from the bartender, having a seat on one of the stools. The bartender hands him a glass of what looks like whiskey, and he turns his entire body in my direction, sipping from the glass. His gaze is piercing, and he doesn't look particularly amused seeing me here with Stephan.

"Gemma, are you listening?"

I shake my head and turn my attention back to Stephan, trying not to bristle at the eyes I feel staring a hole through me. "Sorry. I thought I saw someone I knew. What were you saying?" Oh right, he was trying to talk down the industry I've spent my entire professional career working my ass off for.

"I was saying that the fashion world is nothing but smoke and mirrors, and people put too much stock in the pretty pictures. Life isn't pretty. It's gritty and layered, not shallow and shiny like what the magazines would have you believe."

Well, that's certainly an opinion. "Or you could say the industry highlights artistic expression because, at its core, that's what fashion is. Whether it's expensive couture pieces or a look that you put together with what you find at a secondhand store, it all falls under the umbrella. There's nothing wrong with wanting the pretty shiny things, Stephan. And it's a bit shallow to think that because people like those things or are attracted to a certain lifestyle that's showcased, that they're somehow vapid creatures who only care about beauty. I don't apologize for liking what I like, and I certainly don't shit on the industry that provides not only beautiful things for people to wear and feel good about themselves in but has provided *both* of us the means to support ourselves. Studios in San Francisco aren't cheap, after all. And it costs a pretty penny to take those *life-changing vacations* you were yammering on about." I take a sip of wine and stand from the table. "If you'll excuse me for a moment."

Without waiting for a reply, I turn on my heels and head to the restroom. I don't look in Eoghan's direction, but I can feel his gaze on me as I walk across the restaurant. When I shut the bathroom door behind me, I walk over to the sink and look at myself in the mirror. Are nice guys just assholes in sheep's clothing? Stephan always seemed so sweet and down to earth. Turns out he's just a judgmental prick who works in an industry he disdains but has no problem collecting a paycheck from. Another pretentious dick who has more in common with the other hot assholes I've dated without even knowing it.

Jesus, am I some sort of universal magnet for these guys?

The door to the restroom opens and Eoghan walks in, that damn signature smirk of his playing on his lips. When the door closes behind him, he turns the lock, and the room seems to heat at least ten degrees.

"Having fun?" he asks. I'm sure he could tell that within the last two minutes of me and Stephan's conversation, I was ready to reach over the table and throat punch him.

"What are you doing here?" I ask without answering his question.

"Having a drink. Imagine my surprise when I walked

in and saw you with another man. The way I see it, he hijacked the date we were supposed to be on."

I shake my head at his ridiculous claim. "Why on earth would you think...you know what? Never mind." Only Eoghan would decide that this is somehow *his* date—that I'm somehow his.

"You're lucky I'm not a jealous man," he says, prowling toward me.

My eyes roll toward the ceiling. "And here I thought you've been trying to convince me you weren't a liar."

"I prefer to call it a little fib."

"So you are jealous?"

He stops less than an inch from my back as I watch his reflection, watch his gaze drink in the low front of my dress and the way the satiny sapphire material hugs all of my curves.

"You look absolutely edible, Gemma. Fuck yes, I'm a jealous man if you wore that dress for someone else."

"You think I should have worn it for you?"

I feel the brush of his black shirt against the exposed back of my dress as his right hand grips the edge of the vanity we're standing in front of, and his left hand sweeps my hair behind my shoulder. He leans in close, runs his nose up the column of my neck and stops at my ear. "If only I could be so lucky," he whispers and locks his blue gaze with mine. His eyes are so dark they nearly match the color of the deep-blue dress I'm wearing.

My breath hitches in my chest. Before I can think better of it, or talk myself out of it, I turn my head.

Eoghan stares at my red lips for a beat before crashing his mouth to mine. The kiss is frantic and desperate. His teeth bite my bottom lip, and I open my mouth on a gasp or a breathy moan; I'm not quite sure what noise that was. He plunges his tongue inside, swirling it roughly with mine. The hand he'd had resting next to me now presses against my belly, pushing me into his front before spinning me to face him without breaking the kiss. When my fingers claw at the back of his shirt, Eoghan lets out a growl of need and frustration, like he's cursing the thin material between us. I'm completely swept away in the feel of his body pressed to mine and the way his muscles are coiled so tightly beneath my fingers. His fingertips dig into me as though he wants to grab tightly to my naked flesh, not the soft material he's liable to shred at any moment. It's clear he's still fighting with himself about taking the kiss further or reining himself in—the same feelings I'm struggling with at the moment.

Before either of us can make a decision, there's a knock at the door. That's enough to shock me out of the haze of lust I allowed myself to succumb to.

"What the hell am I doing?" I mumble as I pull away from him and release the grip I had on his shirt. Eoghan's hands drop from me, and when he pulls back, my red lipstick is smeared across his mouth. Grabbing a couple paper towels, I hand him one and use the other to wipe my mouth—to wipe the taste of him from my lips.

His gaze finds mine, and there's a self-satisfied smirk playing on his lips.

"This was a shitty mistake," I say, and he gives me a flat look. "I'm on a date with another man, for Chrissake." I shake my head, disappointed that I got swept away so easily. Granted, the date is going horribly, and come to find out, Stephen is an asshole, but still. Making out with another man in a bathroom before the appetizers have even reached the table is low.

"Your date looks to be about as bland as wheat toast," Eoghan says, tossing the paper towel in the trash. He hasn't moved from his spot, his body still caging me against the vanity.

There's another knock at the door.

"Someone's going to find a key any minute."

"I don't give a shit. Let me take you out of here. We'll go grab a steak and find a bar with live music. We'll drink and dance and have some fucking fun. This place is stuffy as hell."

"Then why did you come here for a drink?" There's no way he didn't somehow find out I was here.

He lets out a long sigh, closing his eyes for a brief moment before meeting my gaze again. "After Giada was shot, I put a guy on you."

My mouth pops open and I stare at him for a few beats. "You *what?*"

Eoghan opens his mouth to speak but stops himself as though he's thinking better of whatever was about to come out of his mouth. He decides to stay quiet. Smart move.

"I *cannot* believe you put someone on me without telling me. I can't fucking believe I was in danger, and you didn't think to let me know. And now you're what? Using your guy to spy on me? What kind of bullshit is that, Eoghan?"

"In my defense, we really didn't have a reason to think the threat extended to you. I wanted to play it safe, though. If I'd thought for sure you were in danger, I would have had you at the house with Giada and Luca."

"Oh, so you not only give me a secret bodyguard, but now you think it's okay to dictate where I live? Let me be very clear, Eoghan Monaghan." I lower my voice into that *don't even think of interrupting me* tone. "I did not grow up in the same life as you or my best friend. None of this behavior is normal or acceptable to me. It's pretty fucked up that you decided to keep me in the dark, Eoghan."

Another knock sounds, and I shove Eoghan away from me; he finally backs the hell off. Spinning toward the door, I unlock it and wrench it open, my gaze finding three very pissed-off women on the other side. "And call off your guard dog," I spit at the man standing silently in the bathroom before shoving past the women with scandalized looks on their faces when they see the six-foot-two man I just yelled at.

I make my way back to the table and Stephen looks up from the lobster roll he was just about to shove in his mouth.

"I'm going home. Enjoy the seafood that I told you I hated." Grabbing my wineglass, I finish the remains—the only good thing about this date—and slam the glass back on the table. "And lose my number."

I turn on my heels and head to the exit, not deigning it necessary to turn around and check if I'm being followed. The valet takes my ticket, and my car is parked in front of me within a minute. As I'm pulling away from the curb, I catch sight of Eoghan walking out of the restaurant, staring after me as I pull onto the street. The frustration is clear on his face—as are the fists tight at his side. Oh, he's pissed? Well, la-de-fucking-dah. Let him stew in the shitstorm he created. I've got better things to do with my time than give Eoghan Monaghan one more damn thought.

CHAPTER SEVEN
EOGHAN

GODDAMNIT. I FUCKED UP. I shouldn't have told her about Tommy. Or maybe I shouldn't have done it in the first place. No, *fuck that.* I did what felt right. She wasn't in danger at the time, and I wanted to make sure it stayed that way. Cataldi wasn't the sort of man I wanted to underestimate. My brother and Ozzy did, and it nearly got their women killed. I wasn't going to allow that with Gemma.

She's not your woman, you numpty.

Yeah, fuck that little voice, too. She might be pissed right now, but there's no denying the heat that exploded between us was unlike anything I've ever felt before, and I damn well know she hasn't either.

I grab my phone out of my pocket and dial Tommy's number as I watch Gemma's car make a right turn onto the next street.

"Hey, boss."

"You have eyes on Gemma?"

"Yup." I watch his car follow her onto the street.

"Okay. Make sure she gets back to her apartment then you can take off."

"You sure?"

"Yeah. Cataldi's out of the picture. There's no reason for you to stay on her." That's been the case for the last couple days. I should have called him off earlier...but I didn't. Part of me liked the idea of knowing he was keeping an eye out for her. The other part knows my light stalking is wrong and *blah, blah, blah.* I rarely listen to that voice, so I don't see the point in starting now. Gemma is most likely on the lookout for a tail, and honestly, I don't wish her wrath on anyone. If she spots Tommy, I have no doubt she'll have some very choice words for him, and then me, as soon as she's done filleting the poor guy.

"Whatever you say, boss. I'll meet you at the bar tomorrow?"

"Yeah. Time to get fight nights back up and running."

"Okay, have a good night," he says and hangs up.

I was on my way to having a great night until I opened my fat mouth and decided to try that whole "honesty" thing my brother is always going on about. That sure bit me in the ass in spectacular fashion.

Instead of stewing on the events of the evening, I decide to make my way to Clovers for a nightcap. The bar is busy as hell when I walk in. Good for business, but not so great for my mood. Instead of making the rounds and shaking hands with some of our regulars, I head to my office and sit behind my large oak desk. There are expense reports stacked on my desk that need my attention, but the bottle of Irish whiskey in the left bottom drawer is what's calling my name right now.

My phone alerts me to movement outside of Gemma's apartment, and I pull up the camera feed to see her walking inside. A moment later, I get a text from Tommy telling me she's home safe and that he's heading back to his place. I thank him and let him know tomorrow afternoon would be a better time to meet than in the morning. Tonight, I'm drowning my idiocy with whiskey.

Staring at my phone, I think about why Gemma was so pissed. I'm not stupid. I'm well aware of the fact that having Tommy on her was an invasion of privacy—just like having a camera pointed at her door so I can monitor who comes in and out or tracking her credit cards falls under that umbrella. Thank God I didn't mention that part. Do I regret what I've done? No, not particularly. I wanted information on her and what she was doing. It's not like I'm doing any of it to be creepy. Just curious.

Curiosity killed the cat, dumbass.

Jesus, my inner voice is really fucking rude tonight.

Since some people are apparently touchy about privacy and all that shit, I pull up the app that's connected to her camera and log out. There. Now she can't get mad at me for spying on her anymore. Not that I would tell her about it in the first place. Not after her reaction over Tommy.

I take a swig of whiskey directly from the bottle. Gemma can have her opinions about what she finds acceptable, but like she said, she didn't grow up in this life. If there's even a chance her life could be in danger because of her connection to the Amattos or my family, I'll do whatever the hell I think is best, regardless of her opinion on the matter. She doesn't understand this life—not fully. I'm not going to make any apologies for caring about her safety. Now, my obsessive tendencies with the camera and tracking her credit cards? Well, I'm not going to go down that road.

The fucking abyss I found myself falling under when I touched my lips to hers is playing over and over in my mind. Though I relish in the burn of the whiskey as the next swig travels down my throat, I'm suddenly angry that it's washing the taste of her from my mouth. I need another. And not of the alcohol grasped in my hand.

Screw it.

I put the cap back on the bottle and shove it into its place in my desk drawer, slamming it shut for good measure. My body bursts from my chair, causing it to slam into the wall behind me, and I make my way across my office. Yanking open the door that leads to the small hallway, I shut off the lights, lock the door behind me, and set the alarm. Then, with sure steps, I make my way back through the bar and to my car with one destination—and one need—in mind. Another taste of her mouth. That's the only thing that will calm the swirling in my gut that no whiskey in the world could touch.

When I pull up to Gemma's apartment building, the

lack of security irritates the hell out of me. I know, thanks to her bank statements, that she makes plenty of money; she could live in a safer building. Not that she's in a bad neighborhood or anything, but there's no doorman, for Chrissake. Anyone who knows the code—like I do—could have access to her building anytime they want. I'm here proving that very point as I punch the code in the small vestibule to gain entrance to her building.

See, anyone could do it.

I pull my phone from my pocket and dial Gemma's number as I make my way up the stairs to her apartment on the third floor.

"What do you want, Eoghan?" she asks when she answers.

That's a loaded question. "To apologize."

She remains silent on the other end.

"You still there?"

"Yeah. Sorry, I was stunned speechless."

"Cheeky woman," I growl into the phone. "Look, I'm sorry I didn't clear it with you when I called Tommy to keep an eye on things while I was busy with....stuff." Alessia has said before that Gemma doesn't know details about the world we live in and prefers it that way. "But Gemma, I'm not sorry I did it." I'm not entirely sure what her heavy sigh means because her face is on the other side of the door I'm now standing in front of.

"Eoghan. There are so many reasons why this is a bad idea. Why that kiss tonight shouldn't have happened.

You thinking it's okay to put a protection detail on me without telling me is just one."

"You have a lot of ideas about why this is wrong, but that kiss was anything but a bad idea, and you damn well know it. That kiss..." I let my voice trail off. "When your lips met mine, I nearly cried from relief. All the feelings, all the attraction we've been dancing around for weeks, finally boiled over in that bathroom. It was inevitable and unexpected at the same time; you know what I mean? Even I wasn't prepared for how perfect you fit against me, or how delicious your mouth tastes." She doesn't say anything, but I hear her breathing on the other end of the line, so I know she hasn't hung up on me. "I went to my bar after I left the restaurant. I figured, since you ran out on me, I'd drown my mood in whiskey."

"So you're drunk? That's why you're calling me?"

"Far from it. I stopped drinking after two shots. Ask me why," I command.

She's silent. Of fucking course she is.

"Ask me why, blondie."

Her huff of annoyance brings a smile to my lips as I take a step closer to her front door.

"Fine. Why did you stop drinking?"

"Because it washed the taste of you from my mouth. I need another, blondie."

"Eoghan," she says with a groan.

"Open your door."

I hear her footsteps and watch the shadow fall over

the peephole of her door before it disappears just as quickly.

"Open the door. Please." I'm practically begging at this point, but fuck. I'm desperate for her, and knowing she's just on the other side of this slab of wood is killing me. She disconnects the call, but for several long moments, there's no movement on the other side. If she thinks I won't stand out here all night, she obviously knows nothing about how far I'll go or how long I'll wait to have her mouth on mine again.

Gemma finally takes mercy on me, and her door opens, revealing her in a white silk robe, her full breasts heaving against the thin fabric. Her hair is tied up in one of those messy buns on top of her head, and her cheeks are free of makeup; they're rosy, as though she was either soaking in a warm bath or she can't hide her body's reaction to me. I like to think it was the latter.

I drink her in. The way she's staring so openly at me. It's in her eyes. The same need that made it impossible for me to not come here tonight and knock on her door. Or beg for her to open it. Whatever. I can admit that I'm not always a proud man, and there's something about Gemma Dalton that has me throwing all that bullshit out the window.

"Hi," she says, still holding the door.

"Hey, blondie."

Standing there in her doorway feels monumental somehow. Like this is a do-or-die moment.

Luckily, I'm a doer.

I step toward her and wrap my arm around her waist, yanking her body to mine. She lets out a small gasp at the sudden movement, and I don't waste another second as I crash our mouths together, immediately tangling my tongue with hers. I shuffle forward a bit and she moves back, giving me room to kick the door closed with my booted foot. The scent of jasmine invades my nose, and I taste red wine on her tongue before I pull away and look her in the eye.

"How much have you had to drink?" She doesn't seem to be intoxicated, plus she's only been here for forty-five minutes tops.

"Half a glass. Are you the sobriety police all of a sudden?"

Her brow arches as I bring my right index finger to the edge of her robe and slide the soft material from her shoulder. My mouth replaces the silk that was just there, and I trail kisses across her skin to just below her ear, grinning at the goose bumps left in the wake of my lips.

"There's no doubt in my mind that, at some point, you're going to try to make excuses for why you let me into your apartment—into your body." My left arm glides down her perfect, round ass, and I press her closer to me so she can feel what she does to me. "Alcohol will not be one of those reasons."

"You're expecting me to have regrets already? You're not really hyping this up very well."

I lift my hand from her ass and bring it back down

against her covered flesh. Hard. I expect indignation, but instead, lust dances in her ice-blue gaze.

Interesting.

"Do you ever shut that mouth of yours? Maybe I should take this sash and tie it around your mouth."

"You love my mouth," she says before her breath hitches as I trail my other hand to the front of her robe and quickly undo the knot at her waist. Her robe parts and I skate my fingertips from her navel, watching her muscles ripple as I trace a light line up her belly, then between her breasts, circling my hand around her soft neck.

"You're absolutely right, blondie. Now give me another taste."

I yank her to me again and devour her mouth, whimpers and moans sounding as I plunge my tongue inside and battle with hers. Her hands find the buttons of my shirt, and she begins undoing each one while we greedily take and take from each other in a rough, claiming kiss.

When she finishes unbuttoning my shirt, Gemma breaks the kiss and practically rips the material from my body. I don't miss the way her eyes travel over every hard plane of my chest and over the swirls of ink I have marked there and down each arm to my elbows. I may or may not tighten my abs and pecs while she examines the tattoos before her nails score over the hard flesh of my chest.

"Fuck," she says, appreciating the hours of work I've

put in to make my body the machine it is.

"Your turn," I say as I remove the robe from her body. This is the first time I've seen Gemma completely naked, and holy shit, I might fucking pass out. Her pale skin offsets the rosy color of her hard nipples. There's a small beauty mark on the side of her left breast, and I immediately decide I need to taste it. When my mouth goes to that spot, Gemma's hands tangle in my hair, pulling at the short stands. I lick my way to her peaked nipple and swirl my tongue around the bud before pulling it into my mouth and sucking hard. Her fingers tighten in my hair, and my cock feels as though it's about to punch itself straight out of my jeans. Goddamn, this is going to be over before it starts if I'm not careful.

Lifting my head from her sweet skin that tastes like whatever she was soaking in, I take her mouth in another bruising kiss. Gemma's hand goes to the belt at my waist and she makes quick work of my zipper before her hand delves into my boxer briefs and squeezes my hard cock. My forehead is pressed to hers, and a hiss at the sensation of her hand around me escapes. Her soft chuckle vibrates through me before I grab her hand and rip it out of my pants then lift her by the waist, wrapping her legs around my middle. It takes five long strides to get to the couch on the other side of her living room, and I bend down before dropping her on the soft cushion. I sink to my knees and spread her muscular thighs, eying the place I want to be more than anything in this world. When my finger lightly trails up her center, her entire body shudders with the contact.

"Fuck, Gemma. I need to taste you before I bury myself inside you."

"Then do it," she says before biting her lower lip and staring at me in a challenge.

When I throw her legs over my shoulders and grab her thighs to pull her to the edge of the couch, she lets out a loud laugh. But as soon as my tongue parts the lips of her pussy, that laugh turns into a deep moan, bringing a wide smile to my face as I flick my tongue over her swollen clit in quick movements. Her hands grasp the cushion on either side of her hips, and I hear threads snap as Gemma writhes on my mouth. When I look up to her face, her head is thrown back with her mouth open as moan after moan falls from her lips. She's right; I do love her mouth too much to ever do anything that would make it hard to hear her moaning my name with the occasional *fuck, that feels so good* sprinkled in.

It's when I slide two fingers into her tight channel, curling them to graze that spot inside, that her words become incoherent, and her body seizes as she tips over the edge into ecstasy. I continue to lick and pump into her. My gaze stays on her face the entire time, and when she finally comes down from her orgasm, it takes monumental effort not to bang my chest and prance like a peacock. I did that. I put that look on her face. The stone-cold princess who said she would never give me a shot in hell just came in my mouth, and I fucking loved every second.

Gemma is a mess of satiated desire on the couch, practically melting into the cushions with a blissed-out smile spread across her pink lips. But I'm not done. My hands untie the laces of my boots, and I yank them and my socks off before standing to my full height. After shucking out of my jeans and boxer briefs, I pump my cock a couple times in my hand. The look in Gemma's eyes tells me she hasn't had her fill yet either. She sits up and wraps her lips around the head of my dick and my hand tangles in her hair, my eyes rolling to the back of my head at finally feeling her hot mouth on my cock. She then swirls her tongue, making me nearly lose my shit and shoot down her throat.

"Fuck, babe. I'm not coming in your mouth before I get the chance to see those perfect tits bounce in my face while you ride me."

I grab a condom from the pocket of my discarded jeans. What can I say? Luck happens when preparation meets opportunity, so I make it a point to always be prepared.

Sitting on her soft, gray couch, I lean over her and grab her by the hips, hauling her onto my lap. She lets out a small squeal, which I cut off with a kiss. Soon, she's writhing wildly on top of me. The feel of her wet pussy sliding over my length along with her tits pressed into my chest as I devour her mouth is getting me so damn worked up I'm ready to say fuck it and slam inside her.

But I refrain. I am a gentleman, after all. And neither of us is in the right headspace for that conversation.

I break the kiss and grab the condom sitting next to me. Gemma lifts her weight from my chest and settles herself on my thighs, giving me ample room to slide the condom down my length. My hand tangles in her hair again before I pull her close for a kiss as she lifts her hips, placing her drenched opening over the head of my cock. Our moans mingle in our kiss, and she slides herself down until I'm fully inside of her tight heat.

"Fuck," she groans out as she lifts herself again and glides back down. Over and over, she rolls her hips on top of me and takes me deeper inside her delicious body. She's controlling her pleasure, but there's one thing missing as she rides me with her head lifted toward the ceiling, her eyes squeezed shut.

"Look at me, Gemma. Give me your eyes."

When her wild blue gaze collides with mine, it's as though a charged current snaps in place.

"Do you feel that?" I ask, pressing my forehead to hers as I continue to pump in and out of her from below.

"You feel so good, Eoghan." Her eyes stay connected to mine, and though I want to watch her pussy take me over and over, I can't look away from her blue depths.

"I'll never get enough of you," I growl, slamming my mouth to hers.

Her whimpers fill the room, and I know she's close. Thank God, because I don't know how much longer I can hold off.

When her walls tremble and clamp down around me, I let out a shout as my cock jerks, and I release myself into the thin latex. Gemma's body goes taut, and her nails dig into the skin on my shoulders. I watch her fall over the edge with a high moan that's music to my fucking ears.

As her breathing slows and the remnants of her orgasm have subsided, she realizes her nails have left grooves in my skin.

"Sorry about that," she says, kissing the marks in an uncharacteristically tender gesture.

"I'm not." My hands trail up and down her sweat-slicked back while I'm still seated inside of her. When she moves to get off me, I band my arms around her waist.

"I'm all sticky," she says with a laugh, trying to get away.

"I don't care. I like you like this."

"Naked and thoroughly fucked?"

A chuckle vibrates through me. "Yeah. That. And here. With me."

Gemma lets out a hum of agreement and settles back against my chest. We lie there for a few moments until I hear her phone vibrating somewhere in the distance.

"Ugh," she groans out. "I'm not ready for the rest of the world yet."

"Ignore it," I say as I kiss the side of her head, smelling her sweet shampoo. "Fuck, I love the way you smell."

She laughs. "That's a first. I swear I don't think I've

ever had a man sniff me as much as you do."

"What can I say? It's the one sweet thing about you."

She laughs and half-heartedly slaps my chest. "I need to go empty my bath. I'm sure you have to get home soon, too."

The way she says it isn't so much a statement as it is a question. As though she's trying to gauge my reaction and how this is going to play out now that we've scratched the itch.

"Or," I say, running my hand through her blonde locks, "we empty the bath, fill up your tub again, and I make you come a couple more times before I have you so thoroughly exhausted that you pass out in your bed. And then in the morning, you let me take you out to breakfast."

Gemma shrugs her slim shoulder with her head still on my chest. "That sounds like a good plan, too."

There's no controlling the victorious smile that takes over my face. It could be the two orgasms or the fact she's finally stopped fighting me, but I'm getting to see the soft underside of my blondie, and I have to say, I really fucking like it.

"Okay," I say, tapping her ass with my hand. "Show me the way."

We both groan a bit when she lifts off me, and I slide from her body. When Gemma walks over to where her phone sits on her kitchen counter, I shamelessly ogle her naked form. The way she casually stands without a scrap of clothing with the confidence of someone comfortable in their skin is waking up parts of me that were completely spent moments ago. I reach over to the small table next to the couch and grab a couple tissues, using them to remove the condom from my already half-hard dick.

The way Gemma's jaw tightens when she looks at the screen on her phone doesn't escape my attention.

"Everything alright?"

She looks over at me and pastes a smile on her lips. "Yup, just work stuff."

There's no reason to think she's lying, but I haven't gotten where I am in life by not being able to sense when people aren't being one-hundred-percent honest.

That's the thing with Gemma, though. She may have let me into her body, but letting me into her life is going to take a hell of a lot more work and isn't going to be accomplished in one night.

Good thing my father taught me the rewards of hard work always pay off in the end.

After breakfast at my favorite little diner that serves the best Belgian waffles on the planet, I leave Gemma with a kiss at her doorstep and head to the bar to get some work done. Tommy meets me for lunch, and we go over the plans for a fight night in a few weeks. I'm sure Javier will be ready to get in the ring by then, judging by the reports from the trainer I set him up with. Kid's got talent and is going to make himself and my family a shit ton of money.

I'd like to say I'm able to concentrate better on the paperwork that has been sitting on my desk. People may think bars practically run themselves or that I'm only interested in the fight nights and having my own personal watering hole. But the bars my family owns make a lot of money, legal or otherwise, and I'm responsible for it all. My brother is the face of what the Monaghan organization has turned into, with our lucrative gun business and a successful underground casino, but we started in the booze business, namely bootlegging and speakeasies. Though what I do is a far cry from how things were run when liquor was outlawed, I like to consider myself as the one carrying on part of our family tradition. It's no walk in the park, but it's always suited me and I'm happy with my role in our organization.

When I lift my head from the last invoice and sign the check to the distributor, the clock on my wall says it's seven o'clock on the dot. The thought crosses my mind to pick up takeout and head home, but there's somewhere else I'd rather eat and rest my head tonight, and it isn't in my lonely apartment where a certain blonde won't be.

I knock on Gemma's door, wondering if she'll hear me over the loud music playing in her apartment. I wait.

Then, I knock again and wait some more. When I knock for the third time, the door finally opens, and Gemma's flushed face greets me.

"What are you doing here?" she asks, eying the bag of takeout and the bottle of wine.

I hold up both items and smile. "Dinner."

"I didn't know you were coming over." She hasn't moved or opened the door farther.

"Because I didn't tell you. It's called a surprise. You're familiar, no?"

"With the concept in general, yes."

"Jesus, blondie, are you going to let me in, or am I going to have to get on my knees and beg?" I shoot her a wicked smile. "Not that I'm opposed to getting on my knees for you."

She rolls her eyes and steps out of the way.

"Good call." I walk through her doorway and lean down to give her a quick kiss. "Where are your plates?" I ask as I head into the kitchen, leaving her standing by her door with a slightly stunned and slightly confused expression on her face. She shakes her head and closes the door before following me and opening a cabinet in her small galley kitchen, pulling out a couple plates and two wineglasses. I've never been a fan of wine, but I know she is, so I figure I'll give it another shot.

"We have Mongolian beef, kung pao chicken, fried rice, and shrimp lo mein," I tell her as I pull each box from the bag.

"Yes to everything except the shrimp lo mein," she

says, pulling spoons and a couple forks from her drawer. It doesn't escape my attention how domestic and right this feels as we move around each other, piling our plates before we head over to the small dining table next to her kitchen.

"You don't like shrimp?" I ask, looking for any kernel of her life that I didn't dig up myself.

"I hate seafood, especially shrimp lo mein."

"Bad experience?"

"You could say that." She doesn't offer anything further, and I don't push. Gemma is many things. Fiercely loyal to her friends, brilliant and sexy as all hell. But the one thing she isn't is an open book.

"What did you do today?" I ask before taking a bite of rice.

"What I do every Sunday. Cleaned and caught up on laundry."

"Do you always blare music while you clean?"

"Better than being in a quiet apartment." She spears me with a questioning look as she takes a sip of the chilled white wine I brought. "Why did you bring me dinner?"

Leaning over to kiss her, I pull back with the taste of Gemma and wine on my lips. "Better than being in a quiet apartment." She quirks her brow, and I shoot her a wink before digging back into my food. "We used to eat take-out Chinese every Friday night. It was the one night my mom didn't cook, and my dad would come home with bags full of nearly everything on the menu from a place down the street from Clovers." I smile, remembering sitting at our dining room table and slurping noodles with my brother and Cillian. Or seeing who could stuff the most spring rolls in our mouths at one time. "When we got older, my parents insisted on me, Finn, and Cillian being at the table every Friday night. I think it was their way of having one night where we made sure to be together as a family."

"You grew up with Cillian?"

"Yeah. His mom went through a rough couple years, and my dad took him under his wing. He's practically an honorary Monaghan."

"He's lucky he had your family." There's a hint of melancholy in her voice that makes me curious about how she grew up.

"What about you? Any brothers or sisters?"

Gemma scoffs and shakes her head. "No, thank God. It was just me and my mother." The way she says "mother" tells me there's a lot more to her story and it isn't a happy one. Again, she doesn't elaborate, and I don't push. That's not the way I'm going to get her to break down her walls. It's going to take more than some takeout and sex for her to let me in. Though patience was never my strong suit, something about Gemma tells me it's going to be so damn worth it when she finally opens up to me.

We finish our meal and have a seat on her couch; Gemma leans back into the cushions, her hand resting on her belly.

"God, I'm stuffed. Thank you for bringing me dinner."

My fingers wrap around a lock of her bright-blonde hair, playing with the soft strands. "You done with your cleaning?"

Her head tilts toward me. "I just have to make my bed."

I hum, considering her statement. "How 'bout I make you a deal?"

Her soft lips tilt in a small smile. "What?"

"I'll help you make it if you let me sleep in it."

"Just sleep?"

"I mean, if that's what you want—"

Before I finish my sentence, she throws her leg over me and straddles my lap. "It's not."

"Just to be clear, this isn't why I came over."

Gemma's brow quirks when she feels the reaction my body has to her being pressed against me. "So you don't want to take me to bed?"

"I sure as hell didn't say that."

"Eoghan?"

"Yes?"

"Shut up and kiss me."

"Yes, ma'am."

Though I didn't come over with the intention of anything more than dinner and a night spent in Gemma's company, I'm sure as hell not going to pass on spending another night making her scream my name. Only a saint could resist the blonde currently grinding herself on my hard cock, and that's something I'll never claim to be.

Chapter Eight
Gemma

THE LAST WEEK AND a half has been...unexpected. That night when I went on a date with Stephan, I certainly didn't expect to see Eoghan there, and I didn't expect for him to corner me in a bathroom—or to kiss me. Well, I think that first kiss was me, actually. Then, when he told me he put a guy on me without telling me, I was so damn angry with him. But still, there was no denying the intense pull I felt toward him. And when he showed up at my apartment later that night, everything I'd kept bottled up inside exploded, just as I knew it would.

I didn't know what to expect when he dropped me off at my place after breakfast and gave me a toe-curling kiss and devastating smile before heading to his bar, but it wasn't that he'd show up that night with a bag of takeout and a bottle of wine, that's for damn sure. And every night that I've gotten home from work and a knock sounds at my door with Eoghan on the other side has been just as unexpected. I'd be lying if I said it doesn't make my heart flutter every time I open the door for him, and I'd also be lying if I said that doesn't scare me. We haven't fully defined what's happening. Honestly, I have a feeling Eoghan doesn't want me thinking too hard about the turn of events, considering how hard I fought him and the idea of the possibility of an us. But just because I haven't voiced my concerns or insecurities doesn't mean they aren't sitting under the surface, waiting to rear their ugly little heads.

Sitting at my desk while going over the numbers from our latest campaign, I'm trying to pack in as much work as possible before lunch so I can take a half day. Giada and her husband are leaving for Italy today. She wants to introduce Luca to her Italian side of the family. They don't have a return flight booked yet, deciding to stay in Italy indefinitely, so I have no idea when I'll get to see her again.

So far, I'm pleased with the results and the minor tweaks we've had to make throughout the launch. Marketing isn't something that's ever finished. It's constantly changing and evolving, and you have to roll with the waves or get swept under the current. That's something I excel at. I have a certain knack for seeing the pieces that aren't working or can be made just that much better, even in the craziness of a launch. It's a talent that I've always been proud to possess, and Natalie has often recognized it as well.

The knock on my door startles me out of the numbers haze I've been drowning in for the last three hours.

When Natalie peeks her head in, I offer her a smile. "Come on in."

She shuts the door and pulls a bottle of champagne from behind her back in one hand while holding two champagne flutes with the other.

"Girl, I just got off the phone with one of the biggest high-end department stores on the East Coast. They ordered five thousand units of the new line. We need to celebrate," she exclaims as she walks to my desk and sets the glassware down so she can uncork the bubbly.

"Drinking on the job? How scandalous. What would my boss say?" I joke as I add a mental reminder to add the new figures to the campaign's cost analysis.

"She would say you did a kick-ass job and deserve to take a little champagne break."

Laughter escapes us both as she hands me the filled glass. "Have I ever told you I have the best boss?"

"I think she would agree."

We toast and sip from our glasses, the bubbles tickling my nose.

"I knew from the minute you walked into this building you were going to be amazing. I love it when I prove myself right." Natalie grins, and I dip my head in appreciation.

We chat a bit about some long-term marketing ideas. I have to keep the buzz going over the first ready-to-wear line Aubine has ever released. When Natalie moves to pour me another glass, I shake my head. "I have to get this work done so I can get out of here in a few. A friend is having a little honeymoon send-off party, and I told her I'd be there."

"Good for you. You work too damn much. And that's coming from a workaholic." Her brow arches in that knowing way.

I shake my head with a smile on my face. "But they say if you love what you do, you never work a day in your life."

Natalie stands from the chair across my desk. "Do you love it?" she asks, studying my expression.

"It's what I grew up wanting with my entire heart. Of course I love it. I wouldn't be here otherwise."

She nods with her lips tipped up at the edges. "Good. That makes me happy to hear." She grabs the bottle and her glass. "I'll let you get back to it so you can get out of here. Great fucking job, Gemma. I'm proud of you."

I preen a bit at her compliment. Natalie is a tough boss who expects the absolute best from her team, so when I hear that from her, it means that much more.

She heads out of my office as my phone dings with an incoming text.

Eoghan: *When are you getting here? I miss your mouth.*

Me: *Jesus, you're so damn needy.*

Eoghan: *Yes. I am. And I'm not afraid to admit it. Hurry the hell up, blondie.*

Me: *Well, stop texting me so I can get back to work, then.*

He sends me a text with a little yellow emoji face with a zipper for a mouth.

I shake my head and lay my phone next to my laptop.

We've spent every night together, except yesterday when he had to work late and cover for one of his bartenders who had a sick kid at home. He told me he'd come over after he closed the bar, but there was no way in hell I was going to wait up for him that late. He pouted over text, but I held firm. Plus, I needed a minute to catch my breath.

Sex and feelings were easy for me to separate in college. I didn't have much time for a social life, but I dated around, kept my options open, and when the mood would strike, I'd go home with a guy. But I was laser-focused on getting a degree, and that took precedence over a college romance. When I moved to Boston and started working, the amount of time I spent in the office was rarely short of sixty hours per week, more if we were launching a new line. I went on a few dates and finally found someone who I thought understood the demands of my job. He was working on his own internship in finance law. He was a few years older and had a smile that charmed the panties right off me. I thought I was the luckiest woman in the world. I was working my dream job, had a boyfriend who was so far from the losers my mom dated when I was growing up it was laughable, and he loved me.

Then, one night, I decided to bring him and his colleagues a late dinner at his office. I understood working insane hours to impress the boss, and it was the first time since I could remember that I was out of the office before him. Turns out that charming smile worked on his boss the same as me. I looked up to her as a woman who made it in a man's world. She was successful and didn't need a husband and kids to make her feel fulfilled. No, she preferred for my boyfriend to *fill* her—at least, that's what she was screaming about when I opened his office door. The look of shock on his face didn't surprise me. Neither did the look of victory on hers. I knew women like her. I'd met plenty in college. They liked fucking another girl's boyfriend for the simple fact that they could. I threw the container of shrimp lo mein at him and left the office as fast as my four-inch heels would carry me.

Alessia came and stayed at my apartment that weekend. When Richard, my ex, came banging on the door, she opened it with that shark smile she'd really honed to perfection throughout the years I'd known her. He argued with her because she refused to move out of his way.

Then, in a voice that held all the authority befitting a Mafia princess, she looked him dead in the eye and asked him, "Do you know who my father is?"

Richard visibly swallowed and nodded. The Amatto name was whispered in certain circles in Boston, and being that Richard was going into finance law, some of those circles occasionally overlapped.

"Then you know that the man standing behind you will make sure you eat through a straw for the next six to eight weeks with one word from me. The fancy lawyer bitch you were fucking won't come to rescue you. In fact, Richard, piss me off enough and I'm sure my father can call some of his contacts and have her disbarred, and you put under investigation for a slew of crimes. I suggest you leave and never come back. Do not test me, Richard. I don't make idle threats."

When he turned, Enzo was so close Richard had to take two wide steps to the right to move out of his way before he could tuck tail and run. If I wasn't so heartbroken, I probably would have laughed outright at the petrified look on my ex's face.

When Enzo looked at his retreating form, he shook his head. "I could follow him and break his nose if you want," he offered.

I just shook my head and sighed.

"How about some ice cream then? Still like rocky road?"

I nodded and that's when the tears started again, and Enzo looked wholly uncomfortable. That was the day I decided he was my honorary big brother, and I would never date a man who worked in law or had that charming of a smile again. That's why I'm feeling all kinds of fucked up with my Eoghan situation. The man oozes charm and has disarmed me more than once when he turns that smile on me. As far as the law part, he's the exact opposite, but there's no denying his past as the perpetual bad-boy bachelor, brother of the head of the Irish mob, and player extraordinaire. Maybe that's why I haven't told my best friend that we've been sleeping together for almost two weeks. Hell, I haven't told her anything about Eoghan. The last time he was discussed, I said there was no way in hell I would go there.

But I did.

Many, many times.

An hour later, I'm shutting down my computer and grabbing my bag to head to Clovers where everyone is meeting to give Giada and Luca a send-off. The place is pretty empty, but considering it's midafternoon, I'm not surprised. The only time I've been here was during a fight night, and obviously those are busy as hell.

When I walk through the front door, Alessia waves to me from her seat at the table toward the back, where the Monaghans can be found taking up residence anytime they're here. Giada is sitting next to Luca at the large round wooden table, nuzzled into his side, with Cillian sitting between her and Finn. I can tell all of the hesitation she had about being around the Monaghan clan has vanished as she says something to Eoghan, and he tips his head back in laughter with her chuckling along with him. Luca lovingly places a kiss on the top of her head, and a gooey feeling warms my chest; those two are so in love and happy after everything they went through to get here.

Shit. Eoghan must be turning me into some sort of

softy.

Yeah, we'll go with that.

Alessia stands from her seat and envelops me in a quick hug. "You finally made it," she says, and then releases me so I have a chance to greet everyone else at the table. I give Eoghan a bland hello, and I can tell he's a little disappointed with the lack of enthusiasm in my greeting. What does he expect, though? To kiss him senseless in front of the entire table before I've even mentioned to my best friend that we've been spending time together? Or maybe I'm reading too much into the look on his face. I don't know. I don't know how to handle any of this if I'm being honest with myself. The feelings, where we are with each other, keeping it a secret without necessarily meaning to—all of it. I sit next to Alessia in the only empty seat between her and Eoghan. There's no doubt in my mind he placed himself there on purpose, and if the look Giada is giving me is any indication, she knows it too.

"You want something to drink, blondie?" Eoghan asks, and I give him a withering look when he uses my nickname.

"Watch out. She's emasculated men for less," Alessia says with amusement lacing her tone.

"Nah. She likes me too much," Eoghan replies.

I arch my eyebrow and tilt my head to the side. "Careful, Eoghan. That confidence is going to get you in trouble one of these days."

"Oh, are you going to spank me? I've never been into

that type of foreplay, but I could get behind it."

Finn clears his throat, shooting Eoghan one of his signature *you're on thin ice* looks. So, he hasn't said anything to his brother about what's been going on between us. Good. Although, if he had, there's no doubt in my mind I would have received a very angry phone call from Alessia about why her husband found out about anything before she did.

"If you consider getting a swift kick to the balls foreplay, then by all means, keep talking." I shoot him a smile that's all teeth and zero warmth.

Eoghan laughs and stands from his seat. "Yeah, I'm good on that, thanks. But I'll still get you a drink even though you're threatening my manhood."

I look at Alessia's glass of white wine. "Whatever she's drinking will be fine."

Eoghan nods and heads to the bar, returning with a glass filled to the brim. When he hands me the glass, our fingers brush for the slightest moment before I bring it to my lips and take a healthy swig of the cold wine. I knew this was going to be hard—pretending like it's business as usual between me and Eoghan—but I wasn't going to miss the opportunity to spend some time with Giada—or my best friend—before she left. But I swear to God, if Eoghan doesn't stop giving me those private looks that tell me he's counting the seconds before we can be alone, I'm going to fucking combust at this table. Every time I take a sip of my wine, I catch him staring at me from the corner of my eye as though he wishes my lips were somewhere else—somewhere not fit for the general public. At one point, when everyone is engrossed in their own conversations, I turn my head to Eoghan and give him that wide-eyed look that says *knock it the hell off.* The smirk he gives in return tells me he has no intention of toning it down.

Oh my God, we've turned into that couple that talks with their eyes. When the hell did that happen?

An hour passes, and Eoghan refills all of our glasses. Giada tells us about everything she's excited to show Luca in Italy, along with all the food and shopping she's excited about. Luca looks on with utter devotion in his gaze as his wife talks, continuously stroking her arm as though he can't stand to not touch her.

"Any idea when you two are coming back?" Finn asks his cousin.

"Not a clue. I've spent the last seven years as someone else. Maybe I'll spend the next seven being a nomad with my wife."

"As long as you know you always have a home with us. Both of you," Finn tells him.

Giada smiles at her husband then Finn. "Thank you. We'll be back, though. I promise. I think I want to take some college classes."

"Oh," Alessia chimes in. "What are you thinking?"

Giada starts telling us about her ideas and interests. Maybe something in the restaurant business, but she isn't sure. Her mom and grandmother were amazing cooks, and Giada inherited their love of baking and cooking. When she was living under her father's roof, she was never allowed the opportunity to pursue any higher education or have any sort of career. She was basically raised to be a housewife to a high-ranking man in whichever family her father wanted her to marry into. I don't think the Monaghans were the one he had in mind, though.

I lean over and let Alessia know that I need to use the restroom before standing from my chair. The glazed smile from my best friend tells me she's definitely feeling the effects of the wine. She's always been a lightweight.

After washing my hands, I step out of the bathroom and back into the dimly lit hallway when a hand grasps my wrist and pulls me through another door. Before I can even let out a yelp of surprise, demanding lips meet mine in the dark room. Familiar lips that have spent the last week and a half tracing every inch of my naked body.

When Eoghan releases my mouth and trails his tongue down the column of my neck, a needy moan escapes my throat.

"What are you doing?" I whisper. "Everyone is right outside."

Eoghan flicks the light switch on, and a soft glow illuminates his office—or what I'm assuming is his office since I've never been inside this part of the building.

"I couldn't sit next to you for another second and not touch you," he whispers hotly into my ear.

"This is going to look suspicious," I say as I run my fingers through his short, blond hair.

"Yeah, I can tell you're really worried."

"Shut up." I pull his lips back to mine and practically climb his body as I delve my tongue into his mouth. God, one night away from him, and I'm so damn desperate to feel him again, I'm willing to throw caution to the wind and take whatever he can give me before heading back out to meet our friends. Hopefully, what he plans on giving me is at least two orgasms.

My legs wrap around his waist, and Eoghan carries me over to his desk, setting me on the edge before he sits in his chair directly across from me.

"I missed you last night," he says, running his hands up my covered thighs.

"Me or my pussy?" I ask as his fingers undo the button of my black slacks, and he lowers the zipper.

He stops and looks me straight in the eye. "You, Gemma. Always you." His mouth quirks up in a devious smirk. "But your pussy is a close second."

I chuckle, trying to dispel the heavy feeling that settled in my chest when he said he missed me. I missed him too. And that thought alone should have me walking out of this room right now. But it doesn't. Instead, I lift my hips from the desk, allowing him to slide my pants over my hips and down my legs before he removes my heels and pants in one fluid motion. Eoghan places both of my feet on the armrests of his chair, opening me up to his heated gaze.

"Fuck, blondie. Fisting my cock to the memory of you last night doesn't even compare to seeing you in the flesh." He dips his head toward my center and takes a long lick over my panties. "Not even fucking close."

Before words have a chance of forming on my tongue, he pulls the thin, lacy material to the side and dives in, licking at me furiously.

"Holy shit," I breathe out as his mouth begins its mission to destroy me in the best possible way.

When he pushes one, then two fingers inside of me and immediately finds that spot, my walls begin to tremble with my impending orgasm. Eoghan groans into my pussy, feeling the same thing. He works double time as his finger massages over my G-spot, bringing me to the edge faster than ever before. I come completely undone, trying to keep my voice down in case anyone comes looking for me, but a high-pitched cry manages to escape.

When I come down, Eoghan takes his mouth from my center and looks up at me with unbridled need in his gaze. "Fucking hell, Gemma. Take your top off," he says while standing from his seat. He quickly unbuckles his belt, pulling his pants down to release his hard cock. "I want to suck on your tits while I fuck you on my desk."

He opens his desk drawer and finds a condom before sheathing himself while I rip the light sweater from my body and drop it next to me. I unclasp my bra and discard it on top of my sweater. Eoghan looks up from his task and mutters something before attaching his mouth to my pebbled nipple and sucking hard. When he releases me, he lines his cock up to my pussy and slams in. It's fast and frenzied, and I absolutely love it. I lean back on my elbows, arching my back to give him better access to my breasts, which he wastes no time taking advantage of. He laves one nipple, then the other, nibbling and sucking while he pumps into me over and over. We're both so wrapped up in the glorious sensations of him being inside of me that it takes a moment to register the incessant knocking on his office door.

"Eoghan," a voice barks from the other side. "Get out here. The Russians are here."

"Fuck," Eoghan gripes before calling to whoever is on the other side that he'll be right there.

"Who was that?" I ask as he pulls from me and rips the condom from his still-hard dick.

"Cillian."

Oh shit, oh shit, oh shit. There's no way he doesn't know what we were doing in here.

"Get dressed," he says, pulling his pants up his legs before he tucks himself into his jeans. I put my bra back on with shaky fingers and tug my sweater over my head. Eoghan helps me back into my pants and slips my shoes back on my feet before opening the drawer to his desk and pulling out a gun.

"I take it the Russians aren't friends of yours?" I ask as he tucks the gun in the back of his pants and covers the butt with his shirt.

"Not by a long shot. Stay behind me." He opens the door to his office, and we both walk out to the bar.

I spot Alessia and Giada by the jukebox, staying out of whatever is going on with the three Russians and the rest of the Monaghans. Luca glances at us briefly, then fixes his attention on the strangers standing at our table.

"That's what he wanted you to know," the stranger in front says to Finn. I have no idea who *he* is or what they were talking about before we came out here, but judging by the tension visible on everyone's face, it isn't good. "His plans to make his way into Boston have been put on hold."

"Tell him he'd better keep it that way. I'm not open to any new alliances with him or anyone from New York," Finn says, his cold eyes never leaving the man he's speaking to.

The man nods in Finn's direction, then his attention turns to me and Eoghan, who's wound tighter than a drum, standing slightly in front of me.

"You look familiar," he says to me, staring at me like wherever he knows me from is right on the edge of his memory. "Have you ever lived in New York?"

"Nope. And never plan on it," I reply, crossing my arms over my chest. I don't feel bad for the attitude radiating from me right now. These guys obviously aren't friends of the Monaghans.

"Hmm. Could have sworn I knew you." He turns and meets Eoghan's hard gaze, then Cillian and finally Luca and Finn, who are still sitting at the table. "I'll let you get back to your celebration. Have a good night."

The three men turn and leave the bar. The interaction took less than a minute, but something inside me is left unsettled.

"That was fucking ballsy as hell," Alessia comments when she walks back to the table. "For all they knew, you could have shot them on sight."

"That's probably why Nikolai sent Andrei. He knows if Luca sees his face, he might do just that. And in Irish territory, he'd definitely get away with it," Cillian mutters, his dark stare focused on the door they just exited through.

Andrei. I don't think I've ever met an Andrei in my life. I've only been to New York a handful of times, usually for Fashion Week with Natalie. For some reason, this Andrei guy doesn't seem the type to attend runway shows.

Alessia and Giada return to their seats next to their husbands, and Alessia tucks herself into Finn's side before looking in my direction. There's something in her eyes that's giving me the feeling she knows exactly where I've been and what I've been doing. She just shakes her head a bit, and the conversation resumes at the table for a few minutes before Giada and Luca stand to say their goodbyes. I know for a fact their plane doesn't leave for several hours, but the way Luca is looking at his wife, I have a sneaking suspicion they aren't going home to pack.

"I'm going to miss you," I say, pulling Giada into a hug.

"I'm going to miss you, too." When she pulls away, her mouth is right next to my ear. "Your sweater is on inside out," she whispers quickly before releasing me then turning to her husband. "Ready?" Luca nods, and they both wave as they walk out of the bar into the afternoon sun.

"I'll be right back," I say to no one in particular as I haul ass to the bathroom.

"Son of a bitch," I mutter when I see my reflection and the state of my clothes. I rip the sweater off and fix it before slipping it back over my body. I'm positive that's why Alessia gave me that look. She saw me standing next to Eoghan and undoubtedly put two and two together. Hell, everyone in the bar probably figured it out.

When the door opens, I don't have to look up to know that my best friend is standing behind me. I turn around to find her standing in front of the door with her arms crossed.

"I'm not going to ask you to explain this second even though it's killing me not knowing everything this instant. But I know whatever's going on with you and my brother-in-law, you've kept under wraps for your own reasons. I get it. But just know I'll be showing up to your apartment very soon with a bottle of wine, expecting all the details."

I nod. "Fair."

Alessia has always been good about not pushing me

on anything. There are things she doesn't know about my past simply because I'm no longer that person. She never insisted on having my entire life's story, just as I didn't insist on having hers. There are things about her life I'm not privy to, and vice versa. That's always been okay between us. I don't think that's going to be the case here, though.

And that only gives me a few days to figure out what the hell I'm going to tell her and everyone else. Whether Eoghan and I like it or not, our bubble has burst, and it's time to face reality.

Chapter Nine
Gemma

"What the hell am I going to say to her, Eoghan?" I ask after telling Eoghan about the conversation with Alessia. We've just gotten back to my apartment from Luca and Giada's going away party, having left in separate cars ten minutes apart. Though I'm not sure what good trying to keep up pretenses is doing at this point.

After Luca and Giada left the bar, the mood was still sour, thanks to the Russians. Not to mention, I felt a bit weirded out by that Andrei guy who thought I looked familiar. The way he eyed me like he knew exactly who I was but was asking to see if I would admit it was fucking strange. The last thing I want is attention from the Russian Bratva for any reason whatsoever.

There was also the way Alessia kept eyeing me. Thank God no one else noticed my appearance. At least, I hope they didn't. I'm not prepared to have that conversation, especially since I'm still wondering what the hell is going on with Eoghan myself. The sex is absolutely phenomenal; there's no way in hell I could or would deny that. It's the feelings part I'm having a hard time with. The first time we slept together, we were just scratching an itch. At least, that's what I told myself. But every night after that? I haven't been able to reason that out.

"What do you want to tell her?" Eoghan asks, opening a bottle of wine from my fridge and pouring us each a glass. After bringing them over to where I've settled into the corner of my couch, he takes a seat at the opposite end. His body is turned toward mine with his arm thrown over the back of the couch like he doesn't have a care in the fucking world.

"You seem way too casual about this. I believe it was your brother who told you to stay away from me."

Eoghan shrugs and takes a sip of wine, then makes a disgusted face. "I really need to bring over some beer or a bottle of whiskey, at least." He sets the wine on my coffee table, then leans back into the couch.

"I don't like beer. Or whiskey."

"I do. And I'd like to enjoy both of them while I'm here. Unless you'd like to start spending our nights at my apartment. I'll make sure to pick up some of your favorite wine."

"You honestly expect me to spend the night in the bed where you've had countless women before? No thanks." That was a bitchy thing to say, and honestly, I'd like to suck the words back in my mouth as soon as they're out, but Eoghan barely blinks an eye at my comment.

"Blondie, contrary to apparently popular belief, I have never had a woman spend the night at my apartment.

Never wanted anyone in my personal space."

Well, shit. I can't deny that his statement doesn't spark something in my chest, but it doesn't change the fact that our little secret is now out in the world before I've had a chance to wrap my head around it. Now there are going to be expectations. Instead of being Gemma Dalton and Eoghan Monaghan, we're going to be Gemma and Eoghan, like *Finn and Alessia* and *Luca and Giada.* People are going to lump us together like the couple I'm not sure we are.

I let out a huff of annoyance, but he ignores me. Instead, he leans forward and unwraps my legs from the cross-legged seated position I'm in and pulls my feet onto his lap.

"Eoghan, I don't think you're really understanding the gravity of the situation. My best friend's figured out there's something going on between us. The same best friend who's married to your brother. You remember him? The head of the Irish mob who forbade you to pursue me."

Eoghan tilts his head back and forth. "I think 'forbade' is a little strong. He just told me to stay away from you."

"And what does that mean to you exactly?"

"It means he was warning me off from messing around with his new wife's best friend and fucking things up for him. Since that isn't the case, I'd say there isn't an issue."

My eyes stay fixed on his relaxed smile for a few beats. Are we actually having the *where do we stand* conversation? Why isn't he freaking out? I'm freaking out a little. Or a lot.

"Why aren't you jumping up and running out of my apartment like your hair's on fire?" That's more along the lines of the reaction I would've expected from him. Never in a million years would I have imagined Eoghan as the *let's talk about our relationship* type. In fact, I've never pictured him *as* the relationship type. Then again, I thought I had found the perfect man once who told me all the right things, and look where that got me.

Eoghan tilts his head back and laughs. I mean, I'm well aware of the fact that I'm a funny person, but that question wasn't actually a joke.

"Listen, blondie. I don't care what you tell Alessia, and I care even less about what my brother has to say about it. Tell her whatever you're comfortable with. You want to tell her I'm just some lucky bastard you're fucking until you get tired of me? Fine. Whatever you want."

"Is that what you are? I mean, is that what you see this as?" I'm just going to ignore the knot in my chest as I wait for his answer.

When Eoghan speaks again, he doesn't have the same laissez-faire attitude from moments before. He looks me square in the eye before opening his mouth. "What do you want me to say, Gemma?" Uh-oh. He's using my actual name. Why did I open my big mouth? "The last thing I want to do is have you run scared with the idea of this being more than the fling you keep trying to tell yourself it is."

"You don't know what I tell myself."

Eoghan rolls his eyes. "You don't think I pay attention? It's not like the only thing we do when I come over is fuck then roll over and go to sleep. We've had plenty of conversations, Gemma, and for the most part, you keep them as surface level as you can."

I don't say anything because he's right. I'm good at making jokes and giving him a hard time, which he likes to give right back. But so far, I haven't tried to get to know him on a more personal level. Which is insane, considering I let him into my body every chance I get. God, I've been treating him exactly how I was afraid he was going to treat me before we started this thing between us.

Letting my guard down has never been easy for me. How could it be? I tried with my ex, though at that point, we were so young and driven by our need to prove ourselves in our respective careers. I didn't let him in, not entirely. Though his boss had no problem letting him between her legs. Even though it hurt like hell in the moment, I suppose it was for the best. But this thing with Eoghan feels different, or maybe I'm different with him. He's managed to slide through my defenses, and the sneaky bastard has done it without me realizing just how deeply he's embedded himself there. Now that I've realized it, the question remains: Do I let him stay there? If I do, he has the potential to shatter me, but if I don't? Well, I'd be hurting myself before he has a chance to. I'm not keen on either one, but if I don't take even the smallest of chances here, I know I'll regret it.

"Why do you stick around then? It sounds like that isn't necessarily what you're looking for," I say.

"Because there's no other way I can see to break through whatever barriers you've erected around your heart. I want to get to know you. I want to be the man you turn to for anything and everything. Whether it be someone to let you carry some of the weight I sometimes see in those devastating blue eyes or a couple orgasms to help you forget whatever darkness occasionally shadows your beautiful face, I'm here for it. I don't know how else I can show you I care except to keep showing up, even if I'm worried that one day you're just going to disappear on me."

"Like you'd ever let me do that. I'm pretty sure I tried to shake you a couple times."

"I'm nothing if not persistent," he replies with a tilt to his lips. "So, tell Alessia whatever you're comfortable telling her. I'll follow your lead. But you're right. Trying to ghost me would probably be completely futile on your part, so you should just accept you're stuck with me."

"Like...how stuck are we talking here?" I ask before removing my feet from his lap. Eoghan pouts, but as soon as I change my position to move closer to him so I can kiss him, he relaxes and smiles against my lips.

"Crazy glue stuck, blondie."

I lay my head against his chest as his fingers comb through my hair. Neither of us says anything for a few long moments, but I keep thinking about what he said about seeing the darkness in me sometimes. The first night he was here, my mother was trying to call. I think it was her, at least. It was from our old area code, and since I never kept in touch with anyone back there, I can only assume it was her. Not that I'm answering her calls ever again if I can help it. But maybe I'm not as unaffected by it as I thought. Or Eoghan is just that good at reading me, which doesn't scare me as much as I would've thought.

"I didn't have the best childhood," I start. I'm about to tell him things about my past even my best friend doesn't know. Sure, Alessia knows it was shitty, but I never gave her details. "My mom was a dancer in Virginia Beach. And not the kind that performs ballet. She was never really single when I was growing up; more like our apartment was a revolving door for whatever boyfriend she had for a few weeks or months. Some of them weren't the greatest." I let out a resentful scoff. "Most of them, actually." Eoghan's hand moves from playing with my hair to rubbing small circles on my back. "I don't remember a time when I felt like she liked me or liked being a mom. I was an afterthought. I don't think she ever loved me." It's a fucking blow to admit, but it's a truth I came to accept a long time ago. "I studied my ass off in school and worked from the time I was fourteen. Paper routes, yard work, babysitting—whatever I could do until I was old enough to get paid legally. Then I had a job at a convenience store, which I ended up getting fired from because my mom came in high off her ass and walked out with a bunch of alcohol under her arm. The owner knew who she was and thought having me there was a liability. Of course it was. I should have called the cops, but I didn't. I didn't want my mom arrested. I got a job at a car wash after that. Thank God there was nothing she wanted there."

"Did any of her boyfriends..."

I look into his tortured gaze and watch as his jaw tics with anger. "Hurt me?"

His head jerks in a tense nod.

"No. There were a couple that tried. I guess that was the one thing she did right. If they 'accidentally' came into my room, I would start screaming my head off. She'd storm in, but these assholes told her they just got confused about what room they were walking into. They were usually drunk or high, along with my mom, and she would believe their flimsy excuse. They never got more than a squeeze in here and there."

"Jesus fucking Christ, Gemma. That's still too much. The fact that anyone touched you at all is too much."

I suppose, over the years, I watered down the events in my memory. It stopped before it got too far. It was one of the many things I left in Virginia Beach when I took off. I wasn't the girl who was molested by her mom's slimy boyfriends. I became Gemma Dalton, the kind of woman who would have no problem kicking someone's ass for trying. But I still can't sleep by myself without that damn light on.

"You're right. I just don't allow myself to think about it too much. I'm not saying it's the healthy way to deal, but it's how I coped when I finally got out of there. I shut out that part of my life. I even changed my name."

I look up from my spot on his chest to see his eyebrows nearly up to his hairline.

"What? Your real name isn't Gemma?"

"My real name is Gemma. But it's not the name I was born with."

"What name were you born with?"

I scrunch my nose in distaste. "Jennifer Wilkins."

Eoghan's eyes narrow as he studies my face. "Nope. Doesn't fit you."

I roll my eyes but smile at him. "Agreed."

"Does Alessia know all of this?"

"Not the details, just that I grew up in a crappy situation and I don't talk to my parents. Not that I ever knew who my dad was, but I cut my mom out of my life sophomore year of college. Alessia never really pried."

"I guess if you grow up the way we do in this life, you allow others their secrets since you're keeping so many of your own," Eoghan comments.

When Alessia told me who her family really was, I didn't pry further either. I only cared about her as a person, not as the daughter of a Mafia boss. She was just my friend and vice versa.

"That's what you picked up on. My mom found out who I am now and called me a few weeks ago. She wants money. Again."

"I hope to hell you told her to fuck all the way off."

I smile at the gruffness in his tone. "Of course I did. God, it's like you don't even know me," I joke.

"Oh, blondie. I may not know everything about you yet, but I'd say I'm having a hell of a time figuring you out."

I wake the next morning to Eoghan putting on his pants and let out a groan of disappointment.

"It's too early. Come back to bed," I say with a yawn.

He turns his blue eyes to me and gives me one of his sweet smiles. "You have no idea how bad I want to."

I pull the blanket from the upper half of my body to give him a little tease of what he could be doing instead of getting dressed. The tortured groan that releases from his chest makes me laugh.

"Goddamn, blondie, you're fucking killing me right now." He leans down and places a light kiss on my lips, which I attempt to take further, but he pulls away with a growl.

"Evil temptress."

A wide smile covers my face, and I flutter my eyelashes.

"I have to get to one of the bars. My opening manager called, and there's a problem with one of the walk-in fridges. Then I have to head to Freddy's and check out some of the progress Javier's made with the trainer. Then I'm going *back* to the bar to close it down for one of my other bartenders who has the night off for his little sister's graduation."

"Okay, fine." I sigh and pull the blanket back over me.

"I have Sunday brunch with my family tomorrow, but how about I come over afterward? We can have a lazy Sunday together, just the two of us. Unless you want to come to brunch."

"Oh, no," I say, shaking my head. "I'm not ready to face Alessia yet."

"You chicken?"

"Hell yeah, I am." I'm not, but it's a pretty big jump from fucking like rabbits to going to Sunday brunches after not really figuring out where you stand, but you know it's more than just the fuck-buddy scenario you were trying to convince yourself of. There still might be a few things I need to unpack before I see my best friend.

"I'll give you time, blondie. But think about what you're going to say to Alessia. I want to introduce you to my family."

"I know your family."

And there's another one of his smiles. "But they don't know you as my girlfriend."

"That's something you usually ask a girl, not just declare it so."

"Huh. Well, it doesn't change the fact that you are, so

we'll just have to agree to disagree."

"I haven't even agreed to anything to begin with."

"No need. It's already been decided."

"Eoghan, you can't—"

He cuts me off with a deep kiss, and before long, I'm not the one trying to take it further this time.

Then his damn phone rings.

He pulls away with regret in his gaze when he answers. "Yeah, I'm on my way now. I'll be there in thirty." He hangs up and kisses me briefly before standing from the bed. "I really do have to go. I'll call you later."

"We aren't done talking about this," I tell him as he walks out of my bedroom.

"Didn't think we were," he calls back, then I hear the door close behind him.

I let out a perfectly ladylike growl of irritation and rise from my bed, throwing on a robe before walking to the kitchen to start the coffee. Just as it's finished brewing there's a knock at the door.

"What did you forget?" I ask, opening the door and expecting Eoghan because no one else would be showing up unexpectedly, especially this damn early on a Saturday.

Only it's not Eoghan on the other side.

An older man in a suit is standing at the threshold with a stony expression on his weathered face. Immediately, I take in the other two men behind him, recognizing one immediately. It's that man from the bar—Andrei.

"Hello, Gemma. I'm Viktor Petrov," the man in front introduces himself. "I believe you met my associate, Andrei, yesterday."

I stare at the man and nod faintly, shock warring with the intense urge to slam the door in the man's face. And what? Jump from my fire escape?

"May we come in?"

"I'd rather you didn't."

The man obviously isn't used to hearing the word "no" and pushes past me; the other two follow him, one shutting the door once they're all inside.

"This won't take long," Viktor says, completely nonplussed that I asked him not to come in. "I spoke to your mother."

My head rears back, shock ricocheting through me. "How the hell do you know my mother?"

A knowing smirk crosses Viktor's face. "We had a fling back in New York when she was younger. A little over thirty years ago."

A little over thirty years ago means he could be...no. No, absolutely not. But I study his features, in particular his bright—yet cold—blue eyes. My mom has brown eyes, dulled by years of alcohol and drug abuse. His high cheekbones and straight nose are also familiar. Much different than my mother's round face. *More like mine.*

"Your mother hasn't changed much since I knew her. Still looking for her next big score. My wife wasn't fond of the whores I kept around. The one agreement we had in our marriage was I would never father another woman's child. It only came up a time or two, but those women were...shall we say, disposed of. Seems your mother decided not to tempt fate and ran away before I knew she was pregnant. Probably the only smart move she's ever made."

Can't fault his logic there.

"She called asking me for money in exchange for information about you. Family is important in my life—having not only a son to carry my name and legacy but also a daughter to marry into a powerful family. My wife was only able to give me one son. Seems your mother was able to give me a daughter."

What the actual fuck?

"I'm not your anything, Viktor. And you sure as hell are no father to me."

He takes three long strides to me, and when his palm collides with the side of my face, the urge to claw his eyes out is like nothing I've ever felt. The only thing stopping me is the two other men inside my apartment—and the bulges I see under their suit jackets.

"You'd be wise to not push me. I realize you weren't raised in my house, so that was your warning. Your only warning.

"What do you want?" I don't cower or cover my face. I'm not going to fall apart with him standing in front of me.

"I saw the Monaghan scum leaving your apartment

this morning. Considering your involvement with the Monaghans, I'm willing to make you a deal."

I stay silent, but what I really want to tell him is he can fuck right off with whatever deal he thinks he's going to be making. Self-preservation is the only thing keeping my lips firmly together.

"I want Boston. The Monaghans are in control of Boston, and after that fuckup Cataldi screwed up, the Monaghans have no interest in any sort of dealings with me."

Somehow I doubt Finn would have rolled out the red carpet to them regardless. Not that I would know since I've always purposely kept away from any and all details of anything in the criminal life. Guess that's all changing now.

"You're going to be my mole inside the family. Worked well for Finn when he planted his cousin in the Cataldi organization, so I think I'll take a page out of his book. And before you ask, no. You don't have a choice. I will make sure your mother suffers before I kill her, and I'll make sure you disappear where no one will find you. The Monaghans are powerful, but they don't have the ties to Russia that I have. And my comrades do enjoy breaking pretty little things like you."

"How do you expect me to get any information? I'm not involved the way you think. I don't know anything about the Monaghan's business dealings."

"You're a smart girl. I'm sure you can figure it out. You did graduate from Yale, after all."

Yeah, with a degree in marketing, not espionage.

"My son, Nikolai, will be your liaison to my family. It will be a nice little brother-sister bonding exercise."

The sickening smile on Viktor's face tells me everything I need to know about his son.

"Nikolai will be here in the morning to give you the rest of the details." Viktor turns toward the door as Andrei opens it for him. Before crossing the threshold, he turns his penetrating stare back to me. "If you think running to the Monaghans is going to save you, think again. If Nikolai thinks—even for one second—you're betraying our family, not only will you and your mother pay the price, but I'll finally let him have the Cataldi girl. She's in Italy with her new husband now, yes? And then there's Finn's beautiful wife. I think I'll give myself some time with her before gifting her to my men."

I think my heart has actually stopped beating.

"I'm willing to let them live, Gemma. This doesn't have to get bloody. That is one-hundred-percent dependent on you."

With that parting shot, he turns and walks through the door, and I sink to the floor. It takes the briefest second before tears are pouring down my face.

What the hell am I going to do?

The answer to my question comes from the most unlikely source the next morning when I open my door to find another stranger on the other side.

"I'm Nikolai Petrov. If we play this right, our father will be dead by the end of the year."

Chapter Ten

Eoghan

"YOU LOOK TIRED, SON," my mother says as we walk down the stone steps of our church. My mother insists on Sunday mass followed by brunch at her house every weekend. The only time there was an exception to her rule was when Finn was first married, and he and Alessia were still "figuring things out." At least that's what my mother said when I complained about it. Now that they have, they're expected every Sunday as well, which is why they're currently only a couple of paces behind us.

"I had to close the bar last night. We didn't get out of there until after four in the morning."

"And you still made it to church on time. You're a good son, Eoghan Monaghan."

I preen at her compliment—and not only because my brother is walking behind me. "Of course, Mom. I'm your favorite son for a reason."

"For fuck's sake," my brother mumbles behind me, but not quiet enough for my mom not to overhear.

"Language, Finn," she snaps at him. "We just left church, for God's sake."

"He's full of sh—"

My mother's cutting glare stops Finn midsentence.

"That's enough, boys. Your mother loves you both equally," my father chimes in, shaking his head at the same old argument we've been having for decades.

Alessia shakes her head as well with an amused grin on her face. It's quite the improvement from the *if you hurt my best friend I'll castrate you* looks she's been shooting me all morning. What she doesn't realize is, it's Gemma who's steering this ship. If anyone is in danger of getting hurt here, it's most likely me. That's definitely not a position I've ever found myself in. Before Gemma, the most important woman in my life has always been my mother. I've never had a serious girlfriend, never wanted one, but everything has changed with the blonde vixen I left in bed yesterday morning.

"Why don't you go home and get some sleep? You look ready to fall over from exhaustion," my mom says.

"You've got to be kidding me," Finn grouses. "I'm threatened with imminent death if I miss brunch."

Mom turns her shrewd gaze to my brother. "Is it so painful for you to spend one day a week with your mother?"

"Of course not, Mom. It's just—" She quirks her brow, and I can tell whatever he was about to say dies on his tongue. "You're right. Eoghan deserves some rest."

She smiles. Then, when Finn steps around me to open the car door for his wife, I see our mom shoot Alessia a conspiratorial wink. Alessia laughs as she gets in the car, and I turn to give my mom a kiss on the cheek.

"I love you. I'll see you next week."

She nods. "You absolutely will, son. Get some rest."

Rest is the last thing I have in mind.

I punch in the code for Gemma's apartment building. We really need to have a conversation about her moving into a building with a doorman. These electronic keypads are great for keeping out any Joe Schmoe, but they're incredibly easy for someone like me to hack. At least with a doorman, random assholes wouldn't have access to the apartment.

Instead of taking the elevator, I decide to jog up the three flights of stairs. Considering it my workout for the day since I don't plan on leaving Gemma's apartment until tomorrow. I knock on her door, and she opens it, but barely a crack.

"Hey, you're here early," she greets without a smile on her face.

"Yeah, I was released from brunch," I reply with a hand on the door to push it the rest of the way open, but her grip on the wood stops me. My head tilts to the side. "What's going on?"

"I'm not feeling very well. I don't think today's the best day for you to come over."

I don't know what bullshit she's trying to sell, but I'm

not buying it. "That's okay. I'll make you some tea, and we can watch a movie or something." She's freaking out about the discussion we had. That's what this has to be. Maybe telling her she's my girlfriend now was a step too far too soon. But like hell I'm going to let her run from me. I told her she was stuck with me, and I damn well meant it.

"Eoghan..."

"Let him in. He needs to know about everything, too," I hear a man say from inside of her apartment.

Rage—red-hot, boiling rage—washes over me. Whoever that voice belongs to on the other side of the door is about to wish he never spoke up.

"Yes, Gemma. Let me in." My voice has that deadly calm tone that is usually my brother's go-to.

I can't tell if it's fear or regret I see in her blue eyes, but she closes them before I have time to figure it out and opens the door the rest of the way for me. My eyes don't leave her face as I take a step inside, but as soon as I get an eyeful of the man standing in front of her couch, my muscles tense as I ready myself for a fucking fight.

"What the fuck are you doing here, Petrov?" I seethe out.

Nikolai Petrov, the fucking Russian scum who nearly got his hands on my cousin's wife, the man who was helping that asshole, Carlo, is standing in my girl's living room.

Is she your girl, though? that nasty little voice in the

back of my head asks.

"After you left yesterday, I got a visit from a man who says he's my father," Gemma says, closing the door behind her. "Remember when I told you I never knew my dad?"

I nod but don't take my eyes off Nikolai, who is standing stone-faced as he holds my stare, probably so he doesn't miss a beat when I decide to attack him.

"For some reason, I always assumed she didn't either," Gemma continues. "She never mentioned him, and the one time I asked, she just shrugged and didn't say anything further. Turns out my mom is from New York. And guess who daddy dearest is?"

You've got to be fucking kidding me.

"When my mom realized she was pregnant, she ran to save her ass. Seems Nik's dad is a sadistic asshole who murdered any of his mistresses who got pregnant."

"Nik?" I ask snidely, turning my gaze to Gemma when she comes to stand between the two of us.

Gemma shrugs off the remark. "When Viktor showed up yesterday, he threatened everyone I care about if I didn't help him with his plan. Apparently, my mother called him and literally sold me out to that piece of shit. She was afraid of him killing her when she was pregnant but had no qualms about him getting his hands on me now to try to force me into marriage. Sounded like she figured she would get a cut of my dowry or some shit. I don't know what the hell she was thinking, to be honest. I haven't talked to her yet."

My eyes keep jumping between Gemma and Nikolai, not willing to give her too much of my attention just in case this is all a ruse to get me here alone and unarmed.

"When he saw you leaving yesterday, his plans changed. He wants to use me to get information on you and your family. He wants Boston. He said it was my decision if it's a bloody war or not."

"You can't possibly believe that bullshit, Gemma," I say through a clenched jaw. "He'd gladly see every person in my family bleed out. Including your best friend."

"I fucking know that, Eoghan!" Gemma yells. "He was very clear that Alessia and Giada would pay the price if I failed or if I ran to you with this."

"You should have called me *last night* and told me what was going on."

"I probably should have, but you know what? I've never been in this position before. You know, where some Russian mobster threatens my best friend's life if I don't comply. Or threatens to sell me to the highest bidder so they can break me for funsies. Excuse the hell out of me if I'm not handling it how I'm supposed—"

"My father is a ruthless man," Nikolai cuts in. "There's no doubt he'll follow through on any of his threats. But he made one fatal mistake."

My eyes narrow on the man talking. "And what's that?"

"He put me in charge of this little operation. And he hasn't figured out I'd rather see him six feet under than help him with any of his designs on Boston. Or any other power moves he wants to make."

So, little Nik and daddy don't see eye to eye.

"But you were more than willing to take Giada from us. You let Carlo trade her for protection."

"That was my father. I never had any intention of hurting her or her husband when they ran. I told my father that I would catch them and make them pay. I simply whispered in a few ears to make it seem like I was angry. I couldn't care less that she got away. And contrary to popular belief, I'm not the monster of my family."

"Well, you certainly play a pretty convincing supervillain, Petrov. Why the hell would I believe anything you say now?" This almost seems too good to be true. Is it really possible that the demise of Viktor Petrov begins and ends with his own son?

The man shrugs, not seeming to care one way or another if I believe anything coming out of his mouth.

"He was about to explain everything right before you knocked," Gemma says.

"Then by all means"—I wave my arm in front of me as if to say he has the floor—"please proceed."

"You don't have to be a dick, Eoghan," Gemma chastises.

My stony gaze turns to the woman currently standing between her brother and me. *Her fucking brother.* "I don't have to do a lot of things, Gemma. Just like I don't have to be willing to hear him out instead of leaving right now and telling my brother that Petrov is a problem and he needs to be handled immediately. I'm willing to listen to the man, though, and then I'll decide what I'm going to do with the information."

Nikolai takes a seat on Gemma's couch. Bold move when you're facing down an enemy. But maybe this is his way of showing he doesn't want this conversation to be contentious. Or that's what he wants me to think. I'm a hell of a long way off from trusting the Russian pakhan's son.

Two leather chairs sit opposite the couch, with a low coffee table separating the space. When Gemma sits in one, I take it as my cue to sit in the one beside her. I'm still not convinced anything that comes from Nikolai's mouth is going to be true, but at least I'm here to call bullshit if I think he's sucking my woman into a web of lies so we can help him take over his father's empire.

"Our father rules his organization—and his family—with an iron fist. He was never a man who cared about anything other than gaining and keeping the power he had, even to the detriment of his children. I wasn't given a choice in who I was to become. He decided that for me before I was born. My mother isn't much better. She was all too happy to turn a blind eye to the brutality he raised me with. I killed my first man when I was twelve years old. Held a gun to his head and pulled the trigger. When I cried in my bed that night, my mother told my father, and he beat me bloody for being some sort of 'pussy' as he called it."

The look of disgust on Gemma's face mirrors the one I wish I could show on mine.

"I turned off a part of myself that day, and my father thought he'd succeeded in turning me into the heartless killer he reveled in being himself. It wasn't until I met Sylvie that an ounce of emotion bled through my carefully constructed walls. She was a waitress in a little diner a block from one of the casinos we own. I'd often go there after work and have breakfast before going home. She had this infectious laugh that instantly made everyone around her want to laugh with her."

I see the moment he's no longer sitting here with us. Instead, he's back in that diner, hearing her laughter. It's just a few moments of silence, then I watch his entire demeanor shift and stiffen.

"We fell in love, she got pregnant. I went to my mother and begged for her help. I should have known better. Sylvie did something to me. Made me forget that the people who were supposed to love you didn't always hurt you. At least, that had been my experience. I thought my mother would be happy to have a grandchild. That she would make my father see reason. I should have ran with Sylvie." Nik looks down at his clasped hands on his lap. "I should have known better," he repeats in an almost whisper.

There is no faking the pain in Nikolai's blue eyes, or the fact that he blames himself for what I know is going to come next.

"My mother said she would go to my father, that she would smooth things over." No emotion is on his face as he tells the next part of his story. "The next day, there was a drive-by shooting at the diner she worked at. I was told she was dead before the ambulance arrived."

Gemma covers her mouth with her hand, the shock written in her eyes.

"Seems we both have mothers who would have no problem selling us out to our father," Nikolai says, looking at Gemma's devastated face. "I'm no fool. I knew my father ordered that hit with the information my mother gave him. I had a choice to make. Kill my father right then and there and most likely die myself, or be patient. Wait for the opportunity to take everything from him the way he did to me and make him suffer. Then, when the time was right, end his existence. I chose the latter, and the time is now."

"Say I believe you," I start, and Gemma whirls her head to face me.

"Eoghan—"

"Blondie, it's not as though I knew any of this. As far as I've *ever* known, Nikolai has been as ruthless as his father, so excuse me if I'm not willing to just buy his story hook, line, and sinker."

"He's correct, Gemma. He would be a fool to believe me outright, and unfortunately, I don't have much proof to the contrary of the image I've always maintained. You can look up the police report. The shooting did happen, and Sylvie Ramos did die. There's nothing connecting me to her except this." He pulls two pictures from his pocket and sets them on the coffee table. One is of him kissing the cheek of a smiling woman with golden, tan skin and dark curls framing her excited face. The other photo is of Nikolai on his knees; he's kissing her still-flat stomach while her hands are in his dark hair, cradling his head.

"These were taken the day she told me she was pregnant. I was scared to death about what my father was going to say, but I was so damn excited. I never thought it would have the outcome it did. That was my first mistake."

"She was beautiful, Nikolai," Gemma says, looking from the pictures to her brother. "I'm so sorry."

Nikolai nods in her direction and then looks at me. I pick up one of the pictures and take note of how young he is in them. Not everyone in this life was born some broken monster like Carlo Cataldi or Alessia's ex, Orlando. Some were made. And some have played the role so well that we assumed they were the devils they'd always led us to believe. I think Nikolai falls somewhere between the last two.

"What did you have in mind?" I ask, handing the picture back to Nikolai.

"You're going to convince my father you're in a serious relationship. Shouldn't be too hard since he saw you leaving the other morning. I'm going to feed him false information and tell him I'm tracking down everything Gemma tells me. He has his hands full with upcoming deals in New York, which is why I'm handling Gemma. We're going to start small. Hit him where it hurts—his wallet. Then we're going to sow seeds of doubt regarding his competence with the other families."

"How?" I ask.

"Steal shipments. No one wants to do business with a man who can't deliver what he promises. I'll start whispering in ears. It won't take too long for people to start second-guessing the power my father possesses. I've already been working toward planting those seeds."

"And what do you want when all this is over and your father is disgraced?" There's always an endgame.

"I'm going to kill him then take over his organization. I'm going to dismantle his human trafficking rings and the brothels where he sends the girls he buys. I'm going to continue with the guns and illegal gambling. And anyone who has a problem with the changes I make will find themselves staring down the barrel of *my* gun before they take their last breath."

It's the stone-cold determination in his words that sway me to his side.

"I want my mother protected," Gemma tells him.

Both of us whip our gazes to her.

"She sold you to that monster, blondie. Why on earth would you care what happens to her?" I ask, completely disgusted with the woman she calls her mother.

Gemma blows out a breath and rolls her eyes as though she's arguing with herself and not me for once. "She's a horrible mother. Hell, at this point, I don't even consider her that, more like an egg donor. But she got out of New York and kept Viktor away from me when I was a kid. God only knows what would have happened otherwise. I just…I owe her this one thing. If he figures out we're scheming against him, he'll go after her. I don't want that on my conscience."

I reach over and squeeze my hand on her leg. "You're a better person than me, blondie."

"I'll make sure it happens. It would look suspicious if one of your men went down there. I can pass it off as keeping an eye on her if Gemma betrays us," Nikolai says to me.

"Fine," I concede. It may be an asshole thing to say, but if this is all an elaborate ruse on Nikolai's part and he's really working with his father, I won't lose any sleep if Gemma's mom meets her maker.

Her brother—that's fucking weird to think—stands from the couch, obviously ready to leave. "I'll be in charge of making sure you're doing as you're told, Gemma, but I don't put it past my father to send one of his own men every once in a while to check on things. It's important to make sure you play the part in public. Both of you."

"That won't be a problem," I say as Gemma and I stand, and my arm wraps around her waist.

I can't quite decipher the look she gives me as Nikolai opens her front door.

"We'll speak soon," he says, then shuts the door behind him.

Gemma disentangles herself from my hold and starts pacing the apartment, shaking out her hands as she walks back and forth.

"What the actual fuck? How the hell is this my life?"

"Blondie, come here." I open my arms, but she doesn't step toward me. *Fine.* I walk over to her and take her in my arms. Gemma is stiff as a board. It's been a hell of a twenty-four hours for her, and she's used to having to deal with everything on her own.

And that's part of the problem in front of us.

"Two things. One, you should have called me the second Viktor left your apartment."

"Eoghan—"

"No, Gemma. I don't give a shit what he told you. Your first phone call should have been to me. There's nothing that asshole can throw at us that we can't handle. You're mine, and I don't ever want you to doubt that I can protect you."

Her face says she wants to argue, but she nods her head once, and I continue. "Second, we need to bring Finn in on this right away."

She lets out a long breath. "I know."

"Good. Then get ready to leave."

"Where are we going?"

My lips quirk up in a smile. "Brunch."

CHAPTER ELEVEN
EOGHAN

G EMMA LOOKS UP AT me, eyes wide and not at all excited.

"Eoghan, you have got to be kidding me. The last thing I want to do is go to your parents' house for Sunday *fucking* brunch. I just found out my father is a sadistic killer, and my mother sold me out to him. And oh yeah, I have a brother I never knew about who wants our father dead. I don't think I have enough time to get ready, wrap my head around the fucking hellscape my life has turned into and sit down to eat a roast with your family."

"I get it, blondie. But I need to go over everything with my brother, and I'm not leaving you here alone. The sooner we talk to him and get Cillian to check out Nikolai's story, the better."

"You don't believe him?" There's a vulnerability in her eyes when she asks me that question.

She's had to fight on her own her entire life, but she has so much love to offer, even if she doesn't see it. All anyone has to do is look at her relationship with Alessia and Giada to know she considers the two women sisters and would protect both of them with everything she has. Now, to find out she has an actual brother who essentially grew up in the same kind of heartless household has to be messing with her on some level. There's sure to be some sense of camaraderie there, and that could be dangerous for her. She may pride herself on always being the one to solve her own problems, but now she has me, and I'll be damned if I allow anyone to hurt her, blood or not.

"That's not what I'm saying. But I'm also not about to blindly put my faith in a man who, up until twenty minutes ago, had a target on his back as far as our family was concerned."

Gemma chews on her bottom lip, worry creasing her brows.

"What is it?" I ask.

"I've never wanted the details of this side of Alessia's life—or yours, for that matter. Now, I'm finding myself smack-dab in the middle of a war. This is just a lot, Eoghan. Everything I knew, or at least was okay with *not* knowing, has blown up in my face."

I have no idea how she feels, so I'm not going to pretend I do. She's always been on the periphery of this life, and she's right. She's now front and center. I don't blink an eye at this world of violence and revenge. Haven't for a long time. I grew up knowing who my family is, though they're nothing like the Petrovs, thank Christ. But Gemma never asked for any of it. She's being thrown into the deep end with the sharks without knowing how to swim, and it twists me up inside, knowing she essentially has no choice in this.

"It's not fair to you, I get that. But this isn't going to touch you any more than it already has, Gemma. You aren't used to being a part of this life, but I am. So are Alessia and Giada. Alessia is lucky to have the father she does, but Giada's father is much more typical as far as the men in this life are concerned. They have no respect for women, daughters or not. But what Alessia and Giada do have in common is men who will lay down their lives for their women. Who will not only stand in front of them when danger comes but will stand beside them and support them. That's not something Viktor Petrov knows the meaning of. You have a shit family, babe. There's no two ways about that, but you have your friends who you consider family. It's time to lean on them the same way you've always been there for them to lean on."

"That's a hell of a lot easier said than done." She lets out a humorless laugh. "I know what family means to you and yours, Eoghan. And I just found out I'm part of one who yours hates. One who had something to do with almost kidnapping my best friend and nearly killed another friend."

"Let me and Finn worry about Petrov. As far as I'm concerned, I don't care who your father is, and I'm sure Finn and Alessia won't either."

"Alessia, sure. But your brother? I don't know about that."

"Just trust me, yeah? We'll figure it out."

She stares at me for a few moments, turning something over in her head, but she eventually nods in agreement. "Let's get this over with."

Gemma is nervous and quiet as we drive to my parents' house. I'm not used to this side of her. She's a ballbuster. A take-no-shit and handle business type of woman. This side isn't one I've seen before. She needs to find her fight and hang on to it with everything she is. That's how you survive in this world.

"You okay?" I ask, keeping one hand on the wheel and reaching over with my other to take hers.

She hums noncommittally but wraps her fingers with mine. Progress.

"So what's the story when we get there?" she asks, finally turning her attention to me.

"What do you mean?"

"What's our story? Why were you at my apartment?"

"Um, I'm your boyfriend and wanted to spend time with you? When I got there, Petrov was there, and you two told me what Viktor had planned."

At least that's what I told my mother when I called to let her know Gemma and I were coming over for brunch and to talk to Finn and Alessia. Well, the first part. I didn't mention Petrov, just that I was bringing my girlfriend over.

"So we're going public? You just asked me to be your girlfriend, and we're announcing our relationship to the world?"

"I mean, I didn't really ask. But that's what you are."

Gemma rolls her eyes, and that brings a small smile to my lips. I fucking love her attitude.

"And it's hardly the world. It's my family."

She huffs out a laugh. "I'm sure this is all a little more than you bargained for when you told me we were in a relationship now. Hell, it's more than I bargained for when I opened my eyes yesterday."

"I knew you were going to be a challenge the first time you walked away from me."

"I think *challenge* is putting it mildly. How many times did I tell you to fuck off?"

I shrug my shoulders. "To-may-to, to-mah-to."

"Have you always made it a habit to tell a girl you're in a relationship instead of asking like a proper gentleman?"

"Since I've never considered myself a gentleman, no. And since I've never been in a relationship before, also no. You would be the first. And look," I say, nodding to our linked fingers. "It worked."

She's trying to contain that smile of hers that I love so much, but her blue eyes are dancing with delight.

"What made you decide I was going to be the first?"

Do I tell her it was the fire I saw behind her icy-blue eyes? That she captivated me from the first time she opened her mouth to speak? That every time she told me to fuck off, I fell just a little harder? There has always been something about her that called to me. Told me she was the one to keep me on my toes and wouldn't roll over because of my last name and everything it represents.

"Your ass," is what I tell her instead of all that.

"My ass?" The deadpan look she gives me makes me want to laugh, but I hold it back.

"It's a great ass, blondie. I knew I needed to nail it down."

"You're a pig."

I lift her hand to my mouth and kiss the top of it. "Oink, oink."

She rolls her eyes again—she seems to do that a lot in my presence—and I shoot her a wink. That earns me a smile, and the mood lifts until we pull up to my parents' house and Gemma's nerves skyrocket again.

"Here we go," she says as she opens her car door.

I hurry around the hood and grab her hand as we walk up the front steps. "Jesus, blondie. You aren't on your way to your execution." Opening the front door, I lead Gemma into the kitchen, where my mom is.

"Hey, Mom," I greet, still clasping Gemma's clammy hand. She turns to us, and a wide smile stretches across her face. "You remember Gemma."

My mom rolls her eyes—why do all the women in my life keep doing that?—and walks over to give me a kiss on the cheek, then leans into Gemma and does the same.

"Of course I do. She was just here, not even a month ago, for Alessia's birthday. I may be getting old, Eoghan, but I'm far from senile."

"Whoa, whoa, whoa. I never said anything about your age." Women definitely don't like that. Even I'm not that stupid. "I just wanted to introduce you to my girlfriend."

My mom blinks at me then smiles at Gemma. "Well, I hope he doesn't comment on your age. I don't know where I went wrong with him. Please be patient with him. He's a good boy, I swear." She shakes her head long-sufferingly as though she's spent years enduring my inadequacies.

Gemma laughs next to me, and my mother breaks character and chuckles along with her. And they wonder why I've never brought a girl home. I mean, obviously, I've never wanted to or seen the point since none of them were the woman standing next to me. But had I known my mother was in the mood to mess with me, I may have waited until Finn was back home and driven out to his estate for this conversation.

"Thank you for having me, Maeve."

My mom smiles and shoos us out of the kitchen. "Finn and Alessia are on the patio with your father. We'll be ready to eat in a little bit."

"That went well," Gemma comments as we make our way to the patio doors. There's a lightness to her tone that she certainly didn't have when we got out of the car. Leave it to my mom to make her feel more welcome than I ever could with a warm smile and by fucking with me.

"I told you; you have nothing to worry about. My mom obviously already loves you. If she didn't, I imagine she wouldn't be so keen on giving me shit. And Alessia is your best friend. Your parentage isn't going to change that."

I open the French doors leading to the backyard and spot my brother and sister-in-law sitting across from my dad and Cillian.

"You weren't at church today," I say by way of greeting to Cillian.

"I worked late last night," he replies with a shit-eating grin. "Maeve was fine with it."

Cillian has been like another brother to me and part of the family since we were teenagers. Because of that, he's required to attend mass with us every Sunday. He doesn't miss it unless he's out of town on business.

"That's bullshit," I exclaim. "I worked late last night, and I still made it."

"Must be hard living up to being the 'favorite son,'" my brother chimes in.

"Jesus, Mary, and Joseph. Can we not start this argument again?" my father says, standing from his seat and grabbing another chair for Gemma as she gives Alessia a hug hello. "Can I get you something to drink, sweetheart?" he asks.

"White wine would be great. Whatever you have."

Gemma and I have a seat across from Finn and Alessia, and I immediately place my hand in her lap and link our fingers together. My dad notices before he turns to the outdoor wine fridge to grab a bottle. He catches my eye and nods once. And that, ladies and gentleman, is Cormac Monaghan's stamp of approval.

When he returns with her wine, I look up and give him an offended look. "What about something for me?" I ask.

"You know where the beer is. Get it yourself."

Finn and Cillian have a laugh at my expense, and I shake my head. "You're a terrible host, Dad."

My dad shrugs and rolls his eyes. "I could be having a relaxing Sunday afternoon watching baseball, but your mother insists on having you lot here." He blows out a breath and shakes his head, but the smirk playing on his lips gives him away. My dad loves being surrounded by family as much as our mom does. "I'm going to see if your mother needs help in the kitchen."

When he leaves, Finn pins me with his gaze. "Tell me everything."

"I found out who my father is," Gemma says, looking at Alessia. It's her story to tell, so I let her continue. Not like I could or would stop her. "It's Viktor Petrov."

Alessia inhales a sharp breath as she stares at her friend. "Are you sure?"

Gemma nods. "He knows my mom. They had an affair, and she ran before I was born. It was so fucking weird, Alessia. He showed up at my apartment, and for the first time, I saw all the parts of myself that didn't match my mother in someone else. There's no doubt it's him."

"Oh, honey," Alessia replies with the tenderness and love that is a result of their years of friendship. No judgment, just empathy.

"I'm assuming this wasn't a happy little family reunion. What did he want?" Finn asks.

Gemma turns her attention to my tense brother. "He wants me to spy on you. He wants any and all of the details about your life that someone on the 'inside' can get. He wants to use everything he can against you so he can take over Boston. Said it was up to me if it turns bloody or not. He also said if I didn't comply, he would hurt Alessia and Giada."

Finns sits back in his chair and narrows his eyes. "Fucking Russians. No respect for women."

Cillian stays silent on the other side of me, absorbing everything being said around him.

"That means Nikolai Petrov is her brother. His father is putting him in charge of the operation. He was at her apartment when I showed up this morning." That part still stings. Even though it was her brother and not some random man at her place, it's taking a hot fucking minute for that knot of pain in my chest to unravel.

"Fucking Petrov." Finn is still stewing on the information, his eyes darting between Gemma and me.

"Turns out Nicky Boy hates his father. Wants to help us bring him down. Wants the kill shot, too. He said he had nothing to do with what happened with Alessia and Enzo, and he never intended to take Giada from Luca. His dad was the one who was working with Carlo, not him."

"You believe him?" Finn asks.

"I do," I reply with a nod. "He had a pretty convincing story to back up his hatred, but I think Cillian should still check out the particulars."

Cillian nods. "Tell me where to look."

I give him the name of Nikolai's dead girlfriend and tell him the story he told me.

When I turn to face my brother, he's eying Gemma with his scrutinizing gaze. My hackles rise as he leans forward and rests his elbows on his knees. To her credit, she doesn't look away.

"You had no clue who Viktor Petrov is? Like, say when you went to Yale and just so happened to share a dorm room with the daughter of a Mafia boss from Massachusetts?"

"Finnegan Monaghan," Alessia says, snapping her head to him. "Don't you fucking dare."

"Watch it, brother. That's my woman you're trying to accuse of something."

"Convenient timing for that, too." Finn is watching Gemma, and I'm ready to rip his tongue out of his mouth, Sunday brunch or not.

"Trust me, nothing about your brother is convenient. Especially not our relationship. As far as knowing who Alessia was when we moved in together, I had no idea. I grew up in Virginia with a junkie mom." Gemma holds Finn's eyes, refusing to cower from his hard gaze. "I didn't exactly have any connections to Massachusetts or know anything about the criminal underworld. I was focused on surviving and getting the hell out of there. Trust me when I tell you, the last thing I wanted was to get mixed up in any of this. No offense."

"None taken, sweetie," Alessia says. "And in the spirit of honesty, I've known about your past. My father told me years ago. Since you never brought it up, I didn't want to say anything. It never mattered to me where you came from or what name you used to have. I knew if you needed to talk about it, you would come to me. But I also understand wanting to move on from a painful past."

Finn glances from Gemma to my sister-in-law. "Her name?"

"I changed it when I went to Yale," Gemma answers for Alessia. "I left everything about my past in my rearview, including my name."

"Why didn't you ever tell me that?" Finn asks his very annoyed-looking wife.

"Because it's none of your fucking business, Finn. You think my father was going to let me move in with anyone off the street when I was nineteen years old?" She turns back to Gemma. "I would have taken your secrets to the grave. I hope you know that."

"I know," she replies and smiles softly at her best friend.

Though I'm mad as hell that my brother was not so subtly insinuating my girlfriend has been lying and scheming for the last ten years of her life, I feel a tad bad for him when his wife turns her angry glare on him. I do not envy him and their ride home.

"And I understand why you feel the way you do," Gemma says, turning her gaze back to my brother. "I'd kill anyone who I thought was a threat to the people I love. I get it. And I don't fault you for it."

I let out an irritated grunt. She might not fault him for his suspicions, but I do. "Gemma had no idea about any of this. She's as much a victim in this situation as your wife was. But I'll be damned if you look at her with anything less than the respect she deserves. She's been a hundred-percent honest with me about everything since finding out."

"I had to ask, Eoghan," Finn says, trying to defend himself.

"It's okay," Gemma says, placing her other hand over our joined ones. "In all honesty, I would have been questioning things too. Your brother was right to ask." She turns to Finn. "I hope you know I love your wife like she's my sister. I would never hurt her or your family. Viktor has no idea who I am or what I grew up with. He's not the first monster I've faced. And he has another thing coming to him if he thinks I'm going to lie down and do his bidding."

There's my fucking girl.

"So, Finn. Tell us," Gemma starts. "How the hell are we going to make it out of this goddamn mess?"

CHAPTER TWELVE
GEMMA

BRUNCH WENT ABOUT AS expected. Finn reacted exactly how I predicted. Hell, if it were me, I probably would have been just as suspicious. I can't blame the man for that. He's got a wife, a family, and an organization to protect. I was a little taken aback by Alessia's revelation about knowing my life story and the fact I'd changed my name, though I shouldn't have been. Of course her father would've had me checked out. It's not like I went out of my way to cover my tracks. It never occurred to me that anyone would care to look. I suppose that worked well for me in the end. Made my story more believable to Finn. I also wasn't prepared for the way Alessia reacted to Finn. She looked about three seconds from jumping from her seat and plowing her fist into her husband's face. There's no denying there were a few moments I wanted to jump up and do the same myself. I don't like being called a liar. It's an insult that was thrown at my mother by various boyfriends and wives throughout the years. I vowed to never be like her. But I also understood his position, so I bit my tongue.

After Eoghan told Finn the plans Nikolai had, they decided that I wasn't going to be staying at my apartment alone. It makes sense as far as what Viktor wanted. He wants me in with the Monaghans, so if he were to send someone other than Nikolai to check on me, it looks like I've basically moved my boyfriend in. It puts Alessia's mind at ease, knowing I have Eoghan staying with me too. She wanted to take me to their estate and keep an armed guard or two on me at all times, but I said no. That would definitely tip Viktor off. Of course, Finn has Enzo doing double time now that the threat of the Russians has resurfaced. In the last week since brunch, Enzo hasn't had a single day off, and he won't be getting one anytime soon. I've been sending him videos of cats jumping when they see a cucumber all week to keep his spirits up. I know he appreciates me.

Rolling over in bed, I find the sheets cold. For someone who has always struck me as a night owl, Eoghan seems to get up early quite a bit. It's my day off, and he's already making me feel lazy for not being up and at 'em by...whatever time it is.

When he walks into my bedroom from the shower and drops his towel, I decide I don't care what fucking time it is. The defined planes of his hard chest that are still damp from the shower are capturing all of my focus at the moment. And when I let my gaze travel over his delicious six, no eight-pack, to that V of muscles I love running my tongue over, I begin rubbing my thighs together, feeling all the tingly things seeing him naked does to me.

"Don't look at me like that, blondie. I have shit to take care of before the fights tonight."

Eoghan turns and grabs a pair of boxers from the drawer I emptied out for him and pulls them up his legs before finding a pair of dark jeans and sliding them up his body. He leaves the top unbuttoned when he walks toward the bed and kisses me good morning. My attempts to pull him closer by the waist of his pants are thwarted when he pulls away with a chuckle.

"I have to go," Eoghan says on a groan.

"But it's Saturday." When did I turn into this whiny person? Oh, right, when I got used to Eoghan sliding inside me first thing in the morning like he's been doing all week. I swear on everything holy, it's a better pick-me-up than any cup of coffee.

He kisses the tip of my nose, and I scrunch it in distaste, making him laugh outright.

"You're a fiend." His smile is bright as he pulls a shirt over all the skin and muscle I so enjoy ogling. "I have to make sure everything is set for tonight and do a quick inventory of liquor after last night to make sure I don't have to grab anything. Then I want to check in with Javier and make sure his head is right before tonight."

Eoghan has been working with one of the kids who works at Freddy's. We've gone over there a couple times together in the last week to get our workouts in. I'm one of the few women who go to that gym, but I swear to God, Freddy's female membership has probably doubled since Eoghan started going with me on a regular basis. I can't help but snicker when I see women practically drool over him working out with Javier or lifting weights while I work with my trainer. What those women don't realize is that trying to pose pretty in front of him isn't going to steal his attention. Now, if they were in the ring boxing and putting more than minimal effort into their workout, he might throw them a passing glance. Well, before me that is. Now he only has eyes for my form when I'm in the ring, even going so far as to offer suggestions, which my trainer finds oh so amusing.

"Are you excited about tonight?" he asks while he grabs his phone and reads a text. "Nice. Jude and Lucy are coming, too." He sets his phone on the nightstand and looks at me expectantly.

"A chance to see some boxing and hang out with a bunch of your biker friends? Hell yeah. And Finn is bringing Alessia, too."

"Oh, I know. I had to beg three of my guys to work overtime tonight because he refused to come without extra security. Though, now that I think about it, Jude did make mention of wanting more security there if Lucy were to ever come to a fight."

"Jesus, you guys act like we can't take care of ourselves," I say, shaking my head.

"He insinuated the security was for anyone who decided to step out of line with his woman." Eoghan laughs and looks at his watch. "Shit, I have to go." He leans down and gives me one more quick kiss on the mouth. "I'll be back later to pick you up. We'll go to the bar early and have a couple drinks, yeah?"

"Sounds good."

Eoghan turns and walks out of the apartment, leaving me wholly unsatisfied and frustrated as hell. As soon as I hear the door slam, I reach over into the drawer of my nightstand. I'm not about to spend my day riled up with no relief until Eoghan and I get back tonight. I could possibly talk him into a quickie in his office again, but I don't want to wait that long either.

Grabbing the pink rose toy from my nightstand, I kick the blanket off my naked body. I slide my hand to my center, slipping a finger in and rubbing the moisture there around my clit. It doesn't take much more than my featherlight touch to know this won't take long. Seeing Eoghan just out of the shower is the stuff fantasies are fucking made of. My eyes shut, and I press the vibrator to my clit. The tiny piece that mimics the flick of a tongue immediately makes me jolt with pleasure. A hiss escapes me as my hand cups my breast and my thumb and forefinger begin to twist and pull at my hardened nipple. The vision of Eoghan naked in the middle of my room, giving me that cocky look that says he's going to wring every ounce of pleasure from my body and turn me into a puddle of orgasmic goo, has me letting out a little moan. In my fantasy, though, he doesn't step toward the dresser to grab clothes. No. In my mind, he grabs his hard length and strokes himself in long, slow movements, teasing me, making my mouth water as he prowls toward me, writhing on the bed, needy as hell and ready to be filled by him.

"What's going on in here?"

My eyes pop open, and standing at my bedroom door is the star of my little fantasy with a smirk on his face and blazing heat in his eyes.

"What does it look like to you?" I ask. I don't remove the toy from between my legs; instead, I widen my thighs a bit to make sure he sees exactly what he's missing this morning.

"It looks like I'm going to be fucking late," he replies and whips the T-shirt from his body before toeing off his shoes and undoing the top button of his jeans.

"Don't stop," he says, stalking toward me and never taking his eyes off the rose between my legs.

Eoghan positions himself between my thighs and pushes them farther apart, his short nails scraping over the sensitive flesh of my inner thighs.

"Goddamn, Gemma. Does that feel good? Having that toy against your clit?"

Arching my back in pleasure, I release a long moan. "So good. Almost as good as your mouth when you eat me out. Fuck." I feel the orgasm creeping up on me slowly at first, but as soon as Eoghan thrusts a finger inside me and curls it so he hits that spot inside, I see fucking stars as the orgasm I've been chasing rushes through me, soaking his hand as I come with his name falling from my lips.

Eoghan grabs the rose and pulls it from my hand before attaching his mouth to my pussy, licking and sucking on my sensitive clit, drawing out the euphoric feeling. His groans as he eats at me sound absolutely ravenous and delicious. He lifts his head, and a wet, wide smile covers his face.

"Fuck, I could eat your pussy all day and never get tired of it."

"Don't let me stop you."

He prowls up my body, the denim of his jeans scratching across my overly sensitive skin. When he reaches my face, he thrusts his tongue inside my mouth, and I taste myself in the kiss. Then he's off me in a flash, hurriedly ridding himself of the rest of his clothes before he reaches into the nightstand drawer and pulls out a condom. He places the edge of the wrapper between his teeth and rips it open. The sight of him rolling the latex down his rock-hard length has the muscles of my lower abdomen tightening with excited anticipation.

Eoghan grips my hips and flips me over onto my stomach before grabbing a pillow and shoving it under me, lifting my hips a few inches. I turn my head in time to see him reach into my nightstand drawer once again and he pulls out a little bullet vibrator. This isn't the first time we've played with toys, but it's the first time he's caught me pleasuring myself without him. I haven't needed to since he moved in, but hey, he's the one who ran out on me this morning. What's a girl to do?

"I don't think it's fair that you were playing without me, Gemma," he growls in my ear as he turns the bullet on.

"You shouldn't have left me without fucking me, Eoghan."

His low chuckle rumbles from his chest into my back.

"You're right. That wasn't good boyfriend behavior. Fuck, I'm so glad I forgot my phone."

I look over to the nightstand, and sure enough, there it sits.

"Lucky you," I say as his hand slips between the pillow and my pussy, where he presses the tiny vibrating apparatus against my clit.

"Fuck yeah, lucky me."

He lifts himself from my back, then slides into me in one thrust. "God, I love fucking you when you've just come. You're so fucking tight and wet for me." He begins thrusting in and out, pressing harder into me, which causes the bullet to sit firmly against my clit. It's so much, Eoghan being so deep inside me with the vibrations on my clit; I know I'm not going to last long.

"Jesus, you're so deep like this." I bury my face in the pillow and let out a loud moan, but Eoghan fists his hand in my hair and pulls my head from the pillow.

"Uh-uh, blondie. I want to hear you scream my name while I fuck you."

The walls of my pussy begin to flutter and tighten around his length, my orgasm mere seconds away.

"That's it. Strangle my cock. Let me hear you, Gemma."

"Fuuuuck, yes. God, right there."

He continues to pound into me, sweat slick between our bodies as my second orgasm rockets through me. Every inch of my skin feels like it's vibrating from the impact of the pleasure coursing through my body, setting my blood on fire.

"Ahh," Eoghan bellows and I feel his cock jerk inside of me as he loses himself in his own climax. After several deep breaths, the hand in my hair begins to rub my scalp as he pulls himself out of me and reaches under me to grab the bullet. Eoghan peppers kisses down my spine, causing me to let out some very girlish giggles.

"I've never been so fucking thrilled to be running late in my entire life."

I laugh outright at that and turn onto my back after he lifts off me and disposes of the condom. He stands next to the bed and bends over, taking my nipple in his mouth and sucking hard.

"Don't start something you can't finish," I warn.

"Dammit, you're right," he says in a disgruntled growl while staring at my chest. "I'll come back to you beauties later."

"Were you just talking to my tits?"

He shrugs and grabs his boxers, sliding them back into place. "I fucking love your tits and don't spend nearly enough time with them."

"You see me naked every night."

He quickly pulls his pants back on and grabs his T-shirt, throwing it over his head. "Blondie, there will never come a day when I get enough of you. I don't care how many times I get to see you naked, eat your pussy, or make you come on my cock. It's never enough."

"That was almost sweet."

"It's the truth. I told you—superglue." He leans down and kisses me again before grabbing the phone he forgot and sliding it into the pocket of his jeans. "See you in a few hours."

Eoghan may not be the most romantic man on the planet, but when he says shit like that, I get a little gooey on the inside. I laugh into the empty room, wondering how the man who used to annoy me to no end has wormed his way inside the parts of me I swore no one would ever touch. And for the first time in my life, that thought doesn't scare the hell out of me.

The bar is packed when we get there. It's the first fight night in several weeks, and the crowd is ready for some bloodshed. We still have about an hour before they start, so Eoghan and I are sitting at our table with Alessia and Finn, Enzo perched just a few feet away.

"You could have given him the night off. It's not like there isn't a shit ton of security here," Alessia says to her husband.

"I'm not taking any chances. You know I hate having you here with this kind of crowd."

Alessia rolls her eyes at her overprotective husband. "It's almost as though you think I can't take care of myself."

"I said the same thing," I grumble into my cocktail.

"It's not you I worry about," Finn starts, and Alessia gives him a flat look. "Okay, obviously that's part of it. It's the poor asshole I'll have to teach a lesson to if he thinks he can touch you, wife. Bad for business and all that."

Alessia leans in and gives Finn a sweet kiss on the mouth. "That's fair."

A few months ago, Finn had to teach that lesson to a man who grabbed her while he was in the ring. We thought we were so smooth, coming to a fight night without telling her husband. I'd always wanted to come to a fight night at Clovers, but I can admit it wasn't my smartest idea, especially without Alessia mentioning it to Finn. I like to think because of that night, I had a hand in them getting closer to admitting their feelings for each other, in my own twisted way.

"Oi!"

I look over and see a tall blond biker with chin-length hair wearing a Black Roses MC cut. As he makes his way to our table, a short woman with long black hair and eyes that promise mischief has her hand clasped in his. What can I say? Like recognizes like. Another man is behind them; this one has dark features, and he's holding the hand of a woman with deep-brown hair and bright-blue eyes.

"Hey, you fucking wanker," Eoghan says as he stands to give the guy in front one of those backslapping hugs. He then shakes the hand of the man behind him with a wide smile on his face. "I'm glad you guys could make it." Eoghan turns to me and introduces the new group. "Gemma, this is Jude and his old lady, Lucy." He points to the blond man and the woman he's with. "And this is Linc and Charlie," he says, nodding to the other couple.

I shake everyone's hands while Eoghan signals to the waitress for a round, and we all take our seats around the table. Well, all except for Lucy, who is promptly pulled into Jude's lap.

"Jesus, why don't you just whip it out and pee on me, asshole," the raven-haired beauty says to her boyfriend.

"Listen, Lucifer, I'm not taking any chances with you starting a bar fight in here if one of these overgrown frat boys tried to hit on you or cop a feel."

"Hey, I run a respectable establishment here," Eoghan grouses in mock offense.

"And I bartend for a living. Taking care of drunk assholes is practically a requirement of the job," Lucy argues.

"I'd like to have a nice evening out with my friends and old lady, so I'm covering my bases. Now stop squirming. You're making my dick hard."

Lucy smacks him in the chest. "Asshole."

"Demon wench."

I turn to Charlie, who's chuckling next to her man, tucked into his side. "Are they always like this?"

"Oh, this is nothing. If they really decide to get in a fight, watch out," she replies.

Our waitress comes over and drops off a round of beers and several shots of whiskey. She sets down a vodka shot for me since Eoghan knows I don't like whiskey, and I send him a small smile of thanks.

"Gemma," Jude says, turning to me. "It's nice to put a face to the name."

"I never told you her name," Eoghan says.

Jude turns his gaze to Eoghan. "You didn't have to. It's clear as day this is the woman you were panting after the last time I saw you." He looks back at me. "He's shite at picking up women. Good thing you put him out of his misery, love."

"Well, he can't be that bad. It obviously worked," Alessia says from across the table. "I'm not going to lie; it's still a little weird to see you two together. I swear you hated him," she says to me before taking a sip of her whiskey.

"Isn't that the start of all great love stories?" Jude asks, kissing Lucy's shoulder in a surprisingly tender moment.

Finn and Eoghan nod. "I'll cheers to that," Finn says, lifting his shot glass. We all clank glasses and down the alcohol.

An hour passes, and it's time to go downstairs so Eoghan can take care of his hosting duties. As soon as he steps away from me, Jude steps closer with his arm around Lucy when Eoghan goes to check on Javier, who is the first fight of the night.

"You playing my protector while my boyfriend works?" I ask the Englishman.

He nods. "He'd do the same."

Lucy leans around him and smiles. "I find it's easier to let them think we need protection. You know, so as not to hurt their precious egos."

"Yes, what would our little egos do without you," Jude says in a dry tone.

"So, is this like sanctioned fights with headgear and gloves," Charlie asks from the other side of Lucy.

I shake my head. "Nope. They just tape up their knuckles."

A wide smile stretches across Lucy's face. "Extra bloody. I like it."

This girl is bloodthirsty, like my best friend. No wonder I like her so much.

Eoghan enters the ring and pumps up the crowd while introducing Javier and the other fighter. When Javier jumps in the ring, there're no nerves on his face, just singular focus.

They tap fists and the bell dings. Javier studies the fighter as they circle each other, throwing a few punches here and there to test the other's reflexes. Then the real fighting begins. His opponent charges in and throws a punch combination that catches Javier in the ribs. Javier deflects the uppercut and retaliates with several of his own punches, plowing into the guy's ribs and right flank. I have to say, I'm pretty impressed with how far he's come since Eoghan has been working with him.

The bell dings, signaling the round is over. Javier goes to his corner and nods at whatever his trainer is saying. I catch sight of Eoghan, who's keeping a straight face, but I can tell he's as nervous as a mother hen watching Javier. It's in the way he's chewing on the corner of his thumb. He doesn't have many tells, but I've been around him enough to know that's a small chink in his otherwise tough armor.

The two meet again in the middle of the ring, and this time, Javier wastes no time and goes after his opponent, throwing blow after blow. The bell dings again after a couple minutes, signaling the end of round two. Eoghan is still trying to play like he's unaffected, but I see the anticipation on his face when the third round starts. This time, the other guy is a lot slower on his feet and has lost the steam he started with. He's favoring his right side, and Javier notices it, too, before going in hard. Finally, Javier throws a punch to the man's face, and he rears back, falling to his ass. When the guy's head hits the mat, Javier's trainer jumps in the ring, grabbing his hand and raising it in the air. *Holy shit.* He got a knockout and barely has a scratch on him. Half the crowd goes wild because they just won a shit ton of money betting on an untested fighter, and the other half walks off to get a drink from the bar to drown their sorrows over losing.

Eoghan comes over to me with a grin on his face. "Damn, that kid is good."

"Hell yeah, he is," Linc comments. "You been working with him?"

Eoghan tells him a bit of the story of how they met and the trainer he's had working with him when a man comes over and taps Eoghan on the shoulder. "We have a situation."

Eoghan turns his attention to one of his security guards. "What's going on?"

"Someone spiked Kenny's water bottle. The kid can barely stand."

"What the actual fuck?" Eoghan spits.

"Yeah, we have those test strips, and he was definitely drugged."

"Do you think it was someone with Roman?"

"If he's too sick to go up, it's a forfeit, so he stands a shot at winning a shit ton of money," the guard replies with a shrug.

"Goddamnit. Okay. Get Kenny out of here."

"Someone drugged one of your fighters?" I ask, shock lacing my words. What kind of stupid moron would try to throw a match run by the Irish mob?

Eoghan looks to his brother in question. Though Eoghan is in charge of the fights, Finn is the head of the Monaghan organization.

"This is your domain. How do you want to handle it?" Finn asks.

Eoghan thinks about his question for a moment, then a sinister smile appears on his face. "I'm going to send them a message." He leans over and kisses me square on the mouth. "Stay over here with everyone. I'll be right back."

Eoghan walks away from me, and I see him say something to one of his security guards, who begins talking on his radio. When he jumps in the ring, the crowd starts cheering again, ready for the next fight.

"There's been a slight change in plans. Kenny isn't fighting tonight." The crowd boos, but I spot three other guys trying, and failing, to hide their smiles.

"Calm down, calm down," Eoghan says into the microphone. "Bets are placed, so instead of canceling the last fight of the night, I'll be stepping in for Kenny."

The crowd goes absolutely wild at Eoghan's announcement, and my heart drops into my stomach.

I look at Finn, who's wearing a small grin.

"He's going to fight instead? Is that even legal?"

Finn laughs. "None of this is legal, but no one is going to argue with a Monaghan."

"Jesus Christ," I breathe out, turning my attention back to the ring.

Eoghan has removed his T-shirt and is taping up his knuckles. When he eyes the fighter in the other corner, I see the unquenched thirst for bloodshed on his face. Someone messed with one of his fighters, and he's not about to let it slide.

Standing in that ring isn't the man who opens doors

for me and makes it to church on Sundays with his family. No, standing in front of me is a man who's about to show everyone in this room why you don't fuck with the Monaghans and think you can get away with it.

CHAPTER THIRTEEN
EOGHAN

THE FACE OF THE motherfucker standing across from me in the ring is slack-jawed as I announce that I'm going to be fighting instead of Joey. Roman and his crew are a bunch of assholes, but I didn't take them for stupid. Jokes on me, I guess.

The rules of betting on fights here are once the bets are placed, the fighters can't back out. No shots at second guesses. If you forfeit a fight for any reason, you lose. I've never had to enforce it, but rules are rules. Have I ever inserted myself on the ticket? No, but like hell I'm going to let these guys run away with the money because they decided to try to use my rules against me.

I glance at Gemma standing with the bikers and their women, making sure she's where I told her to stay. Shit could go down with the other fighter's crew, and the last thing I want to deal with is having to bury a body if my woman gets hurt. My brother is next to them with his wife, and Enzo stays behind the group, scanning the crowd for any signs of a threat. Then my gaze travels to the security guards who are inconspicuously making their way to the other three guys who came with Roman. I've never liked these guys, but I let them fight here. This is the last time any of them will be allowed within a hundred yards of the building.

Roman and I meet in the middle of the ring and bump fists. The smirk on my face tells him I know exactly what's going on, and the look of fear in his eyes makes me fucking excited to spill his blood. He's not going to back out, though. He'd lose face in front of a crowd of already irritated people who've been drinking. If I don't tear him apart in the ring, there's no doubt it would happen if he tried to leave.

When Declan rings the bell for me, I take a step back and Roman and I circle each other. I don't plan on this taking long, but I'd like to give the crowd somewhat of a show. That's what they're here for, after all.

Roman steps toward me and throws a combo, but my quick weave to the right has him punching air when he aims for my face. I return the blows and get in two good jabs on his left flank. He grunts from the impact but doesn't stop moving; instead, he advances on me again. I let him get a punch in on my left. The goal is to get him feeling a bit cocky—as if he has a shot in hell.

He doesn't.

I take a step back and look him in the eye. "You fucked up, Roman."

When I advance, it's not with any trained moves. I unleash on him like I would some asshole on the street. There are no rules here, and my punches hit precise and with maximum force. I'm not trying to save my energy.

I'm going to give him the beatdown he deserves.

My fist flies to his temple, and he stumbles before I land another two blows to the side of his head. He falls to the mat, but he's still conscious. This is the point where the bell would be ringing and the fighters would separate. But not this time. I continue to rain blow after blow into his face, and when I hear the satisfying crunch of the bone in his nose, I deliver a powerful punch to his jaw and watch with sick satisfaction as it dislocates. That should have him sucking meals through a straw for some time.

Grabbing his sweaty hair, I bring his blood-covered face to mine.

"Let me be very clear. You will never step foot within a hundred yards of my bars again. You fucked with the wrong person, asshole. You're fucking done fighting in Boston. Now get the hell out of my sight before I decide to snap your fucking neck for trying to steal from me."

I drop his head, and he lies on the mat instead of moving. I decide to help him along by kicking him in his bruised ribs.

"Go!" I bellow, then nod to my security guards, who have his crew surrounded. Roman tries his best to scurry to the edge of the ring, and when he gets there, he nearly falls onto the cement floor. Eight of my men grab the four assholes who thought they could get away with some bullshit and drag them out the back door. I hop out of the ring and Declan walks over to me, handing me my shirt.

"Think they got the point, or are you going to go out there and make it more clear?" he asks, nodding to the door.

"Nah, go have your fun without me. I'm about to buy the crowd a round, so I need to hop behind the bar to help Bridget."

Declan shrugs and heads toward the door. My eyes find Gemma, and when our gazes collide, there's heat in her blue stare as it travels the expanse of my naked torso that's speckled with that asshole's blood. So, my girl likes it when I get dirty. Good to know. Not that I thought she would run screaming, but Gemma can be mercurial in the best of times. This is a reassuring development.

"You okay?" I mouth to her from across the basement.

She nods and shoots me a devastating smile, the heat in her eyes making me want to run out of here right now to take her to my office and finish what we started all those weeks ago.

"Round of drinks on the house!" I yell to the crowd, and the cheers nearly deafen me. My gaze returns to the woman who has stolen the heart I didn't think I possessed, and I point to the bar that's quickly becoming crowded. Gemma nods, catching my intention to help out my poor lone bartender who's having drink orders hollered at her.

I jump back there, quickly wash my hands and grab a towel to wipe the blood from my chest and arms before putting my black T-shirt back on. "Hold your horses.

Everyone will get a drink," I call to the crowd and quickly start pouring shots and opening beers. A few women cast me sultry glances, wanting more than the alcohol I'm offering—the only thing I'll ever be offering anyone else again if I have my way.

Once everyone has a drink in hand, they start to make their way upstairs to keep the party going. Fights are done for the night. After checking in with Declan to make sure those four assholes were handled and off the fucking property, I head over to my woman standing in our group of friends and family.

"Everything taken care of?" Finn asks as I loop my arm around Gemma. Most of the sweat has dried from the fight, but Gemma doesn't skip a beat as she leans into my side, her arm going around my waist.

"Declan and the boys took care of the other three while I was helping Bridget."

"Damn, Monaghan, I wasn't expecting to see you in the ring tonight. Can't say I'm disappointed, though," Jude says, clinking his beer bottle with the one I'm holding.

"I promised you a good show." I share a smile with Jude and Linc.

"You promised me something too, if I recall," Gemma whispers into my ear.

A grin spreads across my face, and I set my bottle down on the tall table pushed against the cement wall.

"I think we're going to call it a night. I should probably take care of this hand," I say to the group, holding up my swollen knuckles.

"Yeah, I'm sure that's what you're leaving to do." Alessia snorts out a chuckle.

"Shut it, you." Gemma laughs as she leans in and gives my slightly intoxicated sister-in-law a hug.

"I already let the bartender know to put you on the house's tab," I say to Jude and Linc.

Though I was planning on staying for more drinks after the fights, I think Gemma's offer is much more appealing. I do have promises to keep, after all.

We say our goodbyes and head into the warm evening to the back lot where I parked earlier.

"That was fun," Gemma says after we've settled into the car and pull onto the street. "Lucy and Charlie are a good time. Alessia and I got their numbers so we can get together in a few weeks. Maybe have some drinks and complain about the men in our lives."

Jesus, those women together spell trouble for the rest of us. Good thing I like Gemma's brand of trouble.

"Too bad you won't have anything to offer in that particular conversation. I'm practically perfect."

Gemma lets out a huff of laughter. "Keep telling yourself that."

"What? I make you coffee every morning, and I've even made you breakfast in bed."

"You must be thinking of someone else. You've never made me breakfast in bed."

I pretend to ponder her statement. "Oh, you're right. I ate my breakfast in bed this morning." I will never forget the sight of walking in on her this morning with that toy pressed to her clit or the taste of her orgasm before I sank deep inside of her. Fuck, I'm getting hard just thinking about it.

"You're ridiculous."

I grab her hand and kiss the back of it. "And I'm yours."

Gemma smiles and leans over the center console, kissing me below my ear. "Well, you may want to hurry home. I'm in the mood to return the favor." She tugs my earlobe with her teeth, and I hit the gas pedal hard on the way back to her apartment. Her tinkling laughter fills the small space as I race home, excited as hell to find out exactly what she has in mind.

The next morning, my ringing phone wakes me from a dream where Gemma and I are lying in bed, naked and wrapped in each other. I open my eyes and look down at my chest to see a head of blonde hair resting on it. *Nope, not a dream.*

I reach over and grab the offending device from the nightstand.

"Hello," I answer quietly so as not to wake the gorgeous and very naked creature tucked into my side. She needs more sleep after the night I had with her.

"It's Nikolai. There's a shipment coming in tonight from Russia. It's the perfect opportunity for you and your brother to start helping me sow some seeds of doubt."

"A little late with the heads-up, Petrov."

Gemma's head pops up from my chest and her sleepy eyes find mine.

"This is war, Monaghan. Sometimes, we have to think on our feet. Are you capable of doing that?"

This motherfucker. "Send me the details. We'll handle it."

I hang up the phone without saying goodbye because fuck him. What does he think? That we're over here in Boston with our thumbs up our asses living the good life without ever having to fight to keep our power?

"What's going on?" Gemma asks.

I lean in for a kiss, debating on what to tell her. Does she want all the details? Would that put her in danger, or should she know so she can make sure to be extra vigilant while Finn and I take care of this shipment? Gemma has been thrust into this side of our life without her consent. She's made it clear she was perfectly happy not knowing details and not being any sort of accomplice.

"How much do you want to know?"

Her eyes narrow as she considers my question. "All of it," she finally says, her gaze staying locked to mine. "I want to know everything. Trying to stay removed from anything isn't an option for me anymore."

My finger swipes away the hair that's fallen across her forehead. "I'm sorry you're tangled up in this."

Gemma shrugs. "It was inevitable, no? Alessia knows everything about her husband's business. It's not crazy to think I wouldn't eventually find out everything about what you guys do."

"But Alessia grew up in this life. She chose to be a part of this life. You didn't."

I ignore the hope that bubbles in my chest when she refers to Alessia knowing everything about her husband's business, like maybe Gemma is considering our relationship becoming just as permanent eventually.

"Well, turns out Alessia and I have more in common than we thought. Only difference is, I didn't know about my ties to the criminal underworld."

I fucking hate that she's been thrown into this. That I couldn't protect her. Not that Gemma has ever needed protection, but this was the one thing I could have done for her. My mom has successfully kept herself out of the details of this life. As far as I know, at least. My father could have shared things with her behind closed doors, but she isn't involved like Alessia or Gemma now. My father has always been able to protect my mother from the dangerous part. Viktor threw Gemma right into the thick of it.

"There's a shipment coming in tonight. Since part of the plan is to make Viktor look incompetent with the other families, the best way to do that is to steal it. It'll make them think he can't protect his product. No one wants to rely on someone who can't make sure his shit doesn't get stolen. It will also make them suspect that his crew isn't as airtight as he leads people to believe."

"Won't that make Viktor suspect he has a mole somewhere?"

I nod. She's too damn smart sometimes. "It will, which is why it's important to make sure it looks like business as usual around here. Viktor said Nikolai is in charge of dealing with you, but I wouldn't put it past him to have other people coming through Boston to check on things." Which is one of the reasons I took Gemma to the fights last night. We need it to look like no one is worried about the Russian threat because, as far as Viktor is concerned, Gemma is the only one who knows anything.

Gemma sits up and scrubs her hands over her face. "I hate this. I hate putting you in danger."

"Whoa," I say, sitting up myself and leaning against the white leather headboard next to her. "You're not doing this. Viktor is. We had a feeling the Russians wanted to find a way into Boston when we found out who was helping Carlo. Then, when we found out that Giada was promised to marry Nikolai, we knew a war with them was inevitable. This was going to happen one way or the other. Finn didn't want to take it to their doorstep, but Viktor practically broke yours down, and now we're handling it. That's not on you."

She turns to me with a sad smile on her face. "It figures my father would be as big of an asshole as my mother. The two people who brought me into this world just want to take everything they can from me."

I wrap my arm around her and pull her into me. I can't relate to what she's going through or what she went through with her mom. My family is as close to perfect as one can get, considering we're leaders of a criminal empire, but there's always been more than enough love to go around. Family is the most important thing in our world. Gemma never knew that kind of love from her parents or family, and nothing I say or do can erase the hurt she dealt with growing up and is still dealing with to this day.

But the one thing I can do for her is hold her close and do my damndest to make her feel like she has people in her life who would move heaven and hell to make sure she's safe.

After a lazy hour of coffee and breakfast, I have to leave Gemma's warm bed to meet with my brother and Cillian to go over the plans for tonight. I call Declan and Tommy to meet us at my brother's penthouse, too. I also instruct them to pick up a few things before they meet us.

The goodbye kiss I leave Gemma with is lingering with promises of more when I come home. And I will be coming home. This is going to be a quick in and out. When Nikolai sent me the text with the information about the shipment coming into the New York harbor tonight, it included the shift-change information for the security at the docks. And low and behold, his father's crew was given the wrong information about where to be tonight. While they're twiddling their thumbs on the wrong side of the harbor two hours later than when the shipment actually gets there, we'll be long gone.

"So, we're set," Finn says as Cillian rolls up a map for the harbor. It's not a port we've used in the past since the Italians and Russians in New York have kept a tight grip on it. But leave it to Cillian to have all of the schematics, including aerial photos, so we aren't going in blind. I swear the man has never met a *t* he didn't cross or an *i* he didn't dot.

"Let's load up then. We have a long drive ahead of us," I say before turning to Tommy. "We'll put the presents in the crates, then you and Declan can take the van. Cillian, Finn and I will be in my car."

Declan and Tommy nod, heading to the garage.

Finn's brows draw down. "Presents?"

A smile stretches across my face. "It'll be great."

The ride to the harbor is long and fucking boring. I tried to play "I Spy" with Cillian, but he didn't find it amusing. Then I thought he was going to make Finn pull over so he could grab his gun and shoot me between the eyes when I played the "Slug Bug" game with him.

"You need to loosen up, man," I tell him when we're about an hour out.

"Leave Cillian alone," Finn says from the driver's seat. "And fuck you for making me sound like Dad on a road trip."

That gets a smile from Cillian.

"How are things with Gemma?" Finn asks, trying to sound casual but failing miserably.

"Is that you asking, or your wife?" I reply.

Finn lets out a long-suffering sigh. "Listen, Alessia is concerned for her best friend. Considering I told you to stay away from her and you didn't listen, Alessia just wants to make sure you're not dicking her around."

"If anyone is in danger of being dicked around, it's me."

I see Finn arch a brow in the reflection of the rearview mirror. "Really?"

"Yeah. Really."

And that's where the discussion ends. My brother and I aren't ones to wax poetic about the women in our lives to each other—or anyone else, for that matter. It doesn't take a genius to see he's wholly and happily obsessed with his wife, just like he doesn't need me to elaborate on my feelings for Gemma. I never expected lightning to strike with the blue-eyed, blonde she-devil I met at a wedding, but here we are. I was perfectly happy screwing my way through Boston, not giving anything beyond one night and a good time more than a passing thought. Hell, probably not even that much of a thought. But Gemma Dalton changed all of that for me. Sure, it was lust at first sight. You'd have to be blind not to see what a stunning knockout my woman is. But the obsession I chased her over has become an all-consuming need to keep her by my side, and that sure as shit has never been something I thought I'd say.

Cillian, Finn, and I hop into the white delivery van driven by Tommy before going through the gates at the harbor. Cillian printed off some bogus paperwork about picking up a shipment before we left, and that's all that was needed to get through the gate.

We find the freight easy enough because of Cillian's thorough plans. I have the lock picked and the door open less than a minute later. Finn and I never partook in stealing shipments from rival families. By the time he came into power, that part of our operation had long since been discarded. But our grandfather used to tell us stories of his father coming to the States and stealing shipments of liquor and various other things from rival families. Thieves and bootleggers, that's how the Monaghans made their fortune back in that time. It sort of feels like we're visiting our roots as we load the crates of guns into the van.

"Fuck, it's going to be a tight fit," I comment as we get the last crate inside.

"Just for a minute til we get back to the car, princess," Cillian says.

"Are you…making a joke?" I ask, fake shock on my face.

"Hey, let me see your paperwork." The five of us turn and see three security guards making their way toward us.

Fuck.

"Sure thing," Cillian says, pulling the fake papers from his jacket.

The one in front takes them as the other two eye us.

The guard looks at the paper and I see the second he realizes they're fakes. "This isn't—"

Before he finishes his sentence, Cillian throws a punch to the guy's jaw, and he immediately falls to the ground. The other two rush to Cillian but don't make it there before Finn and I are on top of them. I take a quick swing, but the guy ducks and strikes me in the side of the ribs. *Damn, I wonder if he's had training.* I send a fist to his face, but he doesn't go down easily. I almost feel bad for it, these guys are just doing their jobs, but like hell I'm going to be busted by port security.

He comes at me again, but his punch goes wide. I hit him in the jaw, and he falls to the ground, knocked out cold. I look over and the other two guards are lying unconscious on the pavement in front of the carrier. Tommy grabs their walkie-talkies, and Declan has the van running as the three of us jump in the back with Tommy in the front.

"Let's get the fuck out of here before they wake up," Finn says, slamming the back door behind us.

We make it out of the gate with a nod to the security

at the front, then drive two blocks to where our car is parked. We hop out of the back and Tommy dumps the walkie-talkies on the side of the road before heading back to the highway to get the hell back to Boston.

Easy fucking peasy.

CHAPTER FOURTEEN
GEMMA

"HOW DO YOU DO this?" I ask Alessia while we're sitting on the couch in my apartment, drinking a glass of wine after eating the dinner she and Enzo brought over.

Since the threat of the Russians emerged, Enzo has gone everywhere with her and is currently sitting in one of my chairs watching a televised MMA fight. It's just like old times when we lived together in college. Except we're older and have better taste in wine.

"Do what?" she asks, turning her attention from the TV screen to me.

"The waiting. You're cool as a fucking cucumber, and I'm over here sweating bullets."

Since Eoghan left this morning to firm up plans with Finn, I've been a nervous wreck. I attempted to do some work—that's always been my go-to in the past to get my mind off whatever's going on—but after going over the same spreadsheet three times and still not comprehending the numbers on the page, I finally gave up. I cleaned my apartment from top to bottom, hoping the mundane tasks would calm my racing mind. But apparently, I need to move into a bigger place if I keep seeing Eoghan because it didn't take long enough. I considered going to the gym but was afraid I'd miss a call or Eoghan coming back, even though he said he wouldn't be home until well past midnight. Finally, I called Alessia and she came over with takeout and alcohol.

"Trust me, sister, I'm anything but. I've just had more practice with the waiting. It doesn't get easier. Not by a long shot."

"I'm sorry. Does talking about the worry go against some rule in the mob wife handbook?"

Enzo grins and Alessia laughs outright.

"There's no handbook. And I sure as hell wouldn't have followed any of the rules if there were."

This is the first time I've been in the thick of the dangers that only pertained to my best friend's world in all the years we've known each other. When things went down with Cataldi, I had no idea it was happening. If I had known that Eoghan was calling me from the Black Roses clubhouse that night a couple weeks ago, I wouldn't have been so damn glib with him. Maybe. Okay, probably not. I was still firmly of the mind that we were never going to get together. But knowing he's out there doing something incredibly dangerous so he can weaken the threat against me and will most likely eventually kill the man who fathered me, well, it's scaring the absolute shit out of me.

"We'll be the new generation. You, me, and Giada."

Alessia eyes me with interest over the rim of her glass. "But you're not an actual mob wife."

"It won't be a requirement," I say, shrugging as I take a sip of the wine. I don't want to get drunk tonight. I mean, I do, but I'm not going to. This will be my only glass, just in case...well, just in case.

"It's kind of in the name, sweetie."

"Oh, come on, Alessia. We're breaking rules and bucking traditions here."

"I just find it interesting that you're including yourself in anything pertaining to any sort of wife title, mob or not."

Alessia and I haven't talked a lot about what's going on between me and Eoghan. Honestly, we haven't had time. Or opportunity.

"We can talk later," she says, her eyes traveling to Enzo.

I wave off her concerns. "Please, the man knew my menstrual schedule when we were roommates."

"I did not," Enzo says without taking his eyes from the fight.

"We sent you to the store the same time every month for ice cream."

"I just thought you liked ice cream." He shrugs.

"Anyways," I say, turning back to Alessia. "Things with Eoghan are...different than what I expected."

I've never needed someone the way I need Eoghan. The feelings I had for my ex weren't even in the same ballpark as what I feel for the man currently risking his life for me. I never expected to feel this way about the cocky asshole I met at my best friend's wedding. Honestly, I never expected to feel this way about anyone. I'd only ever cared about two things—my career and not turning out as anything even remotely resembling my mother. Now, Eoghan has firmly rooted himself in a part of me I didn't know existed, and I'm sitting here with my best friend, trying to distract myself from this feeling of impending doom.

"I'll say. I didn't even know you had any expectations."

"There wasn't for a while, but he finally wore me down, I guess."

"Ah, that's a great start to a lasting love story," Alessia says, and we both laugh.

I tell her the story of him "randomly" showing up at the gym and the club and how I kept denying my attraction. I tell her about the horrible date I had with the asshole photographer and that Eoghan, once again, showed up there.

"God, it sounds like he was stalking you or something. How the hell did he keep finding you?"

"I have no idea, but I don't think it was by any legal means or any sort of coincidence like he tried to play it off as."

"Jesus, he's lucky you didn't file a restraining order. Or tell his brother that he was bothering you."

"I don't think Eoghan would have cared if his brother told him to stop. He was like a dog with a fucking bone."

"And now he takes you to pound town every night."

I choke on my wine, nearly spitting it all over my sofa. "That was so bad, Alessia. *Jesus.*"

Even Enzo is shaking his head at her ridiculous joke.

I'm still laughing when I hear my phone ring from the table next to me. *Unknown Caller.* There's only one person this could be. I consider not answering, but fuck that. I have a few things to say.

"Hello, Angela."

Alessia's expression turns cold when she hears the name I say out loud. If there's one person who hates my mother as much as I do, it's her. Not because she's brought trouble to her doorstep, though that's a big part of it, but because of all the shit she put me through and is still putting me through. When I told Alessia that Nikolai was sending someone to keep an eye on her in Virginia, she didn't understand why I would bother, saying she deserves what comes to her. I don't know; what I said to Eoghan still holds true. I don't wish her dead, even though she deserves it. But that doesn't mean I want to have anything to do with her.

"Hey, baby," she says, and I can tell right away she's been drinking or getting high. Probably both now that she has some money from Viktor. "Listen, I'm sorry about the last time we talked. It's been stressful here. And I think Reggie has been running around on me. I need money so I can get the hell out of here."

"What you got from Viktor isn't enough?"

My mom is silent on the other end.

"Yeah, Angela, Daddy Dearest and I had a nice little

chat after you sold my whereabouts to him."

She's quiet for so long I actually check to see if the call disconnected. Since she's still on the line, I know she's thinking hard about how she's going to spin this to her advantage.

"I know how these guys think, Jenny. He would have a nice, rich husband picked out for you in no time. You would be set for life. A powerful husband with a home of your own. Isn't that the goal?"

"Are you fucking kidding me? You ran from the man when you were pregnant because he has a reputation for killing pregnant mistresses. In what world do you see him picking out a nice, rich husband for me? The only thing he wants from me is to marry me off so he can get more power. Do you really think anyone he chose for me would be able to give me a happy life?"

"Happiness is overrated. You always had some notion that being happy was what's important in life. The best we can hope for is a man who takes care of us."

"Wrong. That's the best *you* can hope for. I have no intention of settling for a man who's rich and will probably beat the hell out of me anytime he pleases, just for fun. You put everyone I love in danger when you made that call. Including yourself. And for what? Because you needed to feed your habit and I refused to be your personal bank account?"

"I told you. I needed money to leave Reggie and—"

"I don't fucking believe you!"

Alessia is staring at me with her mouth gaping wide,

but this conversation is a long time coming. When I was in college, we would get into some pretty good fights over the phone, but instead of ever telling her exactly how I felt, I changed my number and cut contact with her. I never told her what a horrible parent she was.

"All you ever cared about is where your next fix was going to come from and what man you could scam to get it. Turns out, once I grew up and got some money of my own, I was the person you were hell-bent on bleeding dry. Let me be one-hundred-percent clear on this. I will not give you money. You played the only hand you had left with Viktor. Now that it's blown up in your face, I'm the last person who will give you a fucking dime."

"I did it so you can have a secure future. He wants you to have a husband," she tries to justify in that obnoxious pleading tone of hers that used to work like a fucking charm. "I just hope when you have children, they aren't as ungrateful as you turned out to be."

I have to take a moment to absorb what she said. It doesn't surprise me at all. This isn't the first time she's spouted the same rhetoric toward me. But it is the first time I've had a man and a family of my own making who I know would have my back and handle any sort of dangerous person in my life. And my mom has proven herself to be the most dangerous one of all.

"I really need you to hear me on this, Angela," I say in a low, collected voice that holds all the menace I feel for the woman on the other end. "If you think Viktor is scary, you have no idea who you're speaking to right now. There are people in my life who won't sit idly by while you put me in danger. Do you understand what I'm saying? If you ever call me again, or Viktor for that matter, I'll be sure to send a lovely bouquet to your funeral that will be taking place a hell of a lot sooner than you think."

"Are you threatening me?" she seethes.

"No. Threats are empty. What I'm doing is making a promise to you. Daughter to mother. If you try to interfere with my life ever again, I'll make damn sure it's the last thing you do."

I disconnect the call and wish like hell I had one of those old phones that you can slam down. It would have been so much more satisfying. I stare at the dark screen, then a giggle erupts from my throat at that thought. Alessia looks at me as though I've lost my damn mind.

"You think she got the hint?" she asks, still unsure that I'm not completely cracking under pressure.

"I sure as hell hope so."

"You know, the Monaghans have a rule about women and children, but after what your mom did, I have a strong feeling Eoghan would make an exception for your mother." She sips her wine and turns back to the television. "And if he didn't, I would."

I smile at my best friend and squeeze her arm in thanks. Nothing like a little threat of matricide to bring two best friends even closer together.

Enzo and Alessia head home an hour after both of us received a text that Eoghan and Finn were on their way back from New York. It calmed the nervous anxiety I had thrumming through my body all day to know that everything went smoothly and they were safe.

When I feel a hand brush my cheek and smell the woodsy, citrus scent that is distinctly Eoghan, a smile stretches across my face before I open my eyes. When I do, his soft blue gaze is directed at me. He sits on the edge of my bed as I turn my entire body to him.

"You're back," I whisper into the dimly lit room.

"Of course I am. Did you think you were getting rid of me?"

"If I could only be so lucky," I reply with a wink.

"Sorry, blondie. I'm superglue, remember?"

My eyes roll toward the ceiling, and Eoghan's low chuckle sends shivers down my spine. "What time is it?"

"About two. I'm going to take a shower before I come to bed. Go back to sleep." He leans down and kisses me sweetly on the forehead.

When I hear the shower turn on in the bathroom, images of him naked in the shower with all that water running over the hard planes of his chest and back, down his muscular thighs that look damn fine in a pair of workout shorts...yeah, I'm not going back to sleep.

Slipping the covers off my body, I walk into the bathroom and hear the sounds of Eoghan washing his body on the other side of the curtain. I slip out of the T-shirt I stole from him that I was sleeping in when he got home. I'm almost embarrassed to admit I needed something so damn sappy to comfort me, but as soon as I pull back the curtain and see Eoghan's tight muscles rippling while he scrubs at his face, all thoughts of anything other than feeling his body under my touch drift away.

Then I notice the dark bruise forming on his left side.

"Jesus, Eoghan. What the hell happened?"

He spins in the shower and faces me, seeing where my eyes have landed. "One of the security guards got a punch in. No biggie."

My finger grazes the discolored flesh. "Does it hurt?"

He winces when I press. "Only when you do that." He takes my hand in his and brings it to his lips, kissing my knuckles. "It's fine, sweetheart."

Then I notice his swollen knuckles. I turn my hand and hold his between us. "What about this?"

"Same guard. They got the jump on us when we were just about to leave."

"You didn't..." I don't want to ask if they killed anyone tonight, but I need to know. I need to know if this shit with my father spilled onto innocent men just trying to do their jobs.

Eoghan shakes his head, his gaze softening as he looks into my eyes. "No, Gemma. No," he assures me as his palms slide to my cheeks, holding me in place. "We knocked them out and left. They were employees of the port. A few guys there to do their job. We don't kill people over that."

Relief washes through me. Innocent people didn't get caught up in this shit. At least not tonight.

"Sorry, I'm still getting used to this. I don't know what I can ask or what women normally ask or know in general."

Eoghan shrugs. "You can ask me anything. Tell me anything. If you want the full story, I'll give it to you." And it really is as simple as that for him.

"I talked to my mother tonight. She called while Alessia was here."

Eoghan's jaw tics, as it has every time my mother has been brought up in conversation this past week. "What the hell did she have to say for herself?"

"She was calling for money again. I told her I knew Viktor paid her for the information on me."

"God, I hate that woman. I know she's your mother, but fuck her."

"I certainly don't hold any warm and fuzzy feelings for her. She tried the whole *she did me a favor, that I was going to be set up to marry a rich and powerful man and never want for anything.* Then it turned into *I'm an ungrateful daughter and she hopes I never know the pain of having a child like me.* Same shit, different day." I look at him through my dampening lashes. "Then I told her if she calls me or contacts Viktor again, I'd kill her."

Eoghan isn't surprised by my statement. Or if he is, he doesn't let it show. "Do you want to call Nikolai's man off her? Let fate decide if she lives or dies?"

I shake my head before he can finish his sentence. "No. Once all this is over then she can make her decisions. I told her the consequences if she chooses poorly. Call it my last favor to her for getting us out of New York. But this is it. She tries to fuck with me or puts the people I love in danger, she's finished."

"I'd do it, you know. If you decided that she was too much of a liability in your life, I'd end hers for you."

Most girls would be completely freaked out by such a statement, but I've been learning more and more throughout my relationship with Eoghan that I'm not most girls. And some people are evil and don't deserve to breathe the same air as those around them. My mother is one of them.

"Is it weird I find that incredibly sweet?" I ask, wrapping my arms around his middle. "God, I must be fucked in the head."

"If this is you fucked in the head, then I like it," Eoghan says with a sly smile. "But I'd rather you get fucked somewhere else."

"Oh yeah?" I purr as he backs me up into the wall of the shower.

When he kneels in front of me and slides my leg over his shoulder, all thoughts of my mother and this mess with Viktor evaporate from my mind. Some girls may want to be held and have reassurances whispered in their ears. Me? I'll take the Irish mobster worshiping me on his knees any day of the week.

Chapter Fifteen

Eoghan

"That was an...interesting touch," Nikolai says when he calls to let me know how our little mission went the other night. "The families were certainly in for a shock when they opened the crates with my father standing there. I don't know that I've seen the man so angry. It was everything I could do not to laugh." His chuckle is strange to hear through the phone. I honestly don't think I've ever heard Nikolai Petrov laugh. I guess planning his father's demise brings out his humor. "A little heads-up would have been nice."

"It was a last-minute decision." A smile stretches across my face, imagining that fuck Viktor looking like an incompetent asshole in front of the Italians he's been trying to form alliances with.

"Tell your brother to wait on moving the guns. My father will be keeping an eye on the major players to see if he can suss out who stole the crates."

"Finn's in no hurry. Let us know if we can be of service again."

"Of course. The sooner we get my father out of the way, the better we'll all sleep at night."

That's the damn truth. Though Gemma says she's doing okay with everything that's been happening, I see the dark circles under her eyes and hear when she wakes suddenly from a nightmare. It doesn't matter how thoroughly I tire her out before her head hits the pillow. Since Viktor showed up at her place, she isn't sleeping. Every night, she leaves her bedside light on. It's something I know she did before I started spending the night, but with me here, she shuts it off because she feels safe. Even though I've told her we're handling the Petrov situation, there's a part of her that needs it for an extra layer of perceived protection. If she feels better having it on, she can keep the entire apartment lit up all night like Fenway Park, as far as I'm concerned.

"Amen to that."

Nikolai says goodbye and the call disconnects. For the last two days, Gemma has been doting on me, even taking Monday off from work. Hell, if I knew all I had to do was come home with busted knuckles and bruised ribs, I would've had one of my guys rough me up weeks ago. I insisted she go to work today, though. As much as she doesn't want to feel like a burden, I don't want her fussing over me when she's been so busy at work. If Gemma considers us long term, then she needs to know I don't expect her to drop everything anytime I have a night like the other one. Chances are, there's going to be more like it, maybe even worse. Her career is far too important to her—and, by extension, to me—for her to put it on the back burner for my sake. I've never carried the expectation that a woman needs to take care of me, and I sure as hell would never expect it of the blonde vixen who has gotten so far under my damn skin I can't imagine what it would be like to not have her there.

I'm in love with the woman.

Have I told her that?

Of course not. Gemma gets as skittish as a damn alley cat if things move any faster than a snail's pace. Until she comes to the realization for herself, we'll move at her speed. Call me optimistic or overconfident—hell, even a cocky son of a bitch—but I know damn well she feels the same.

I've been working from her apartment today, making phone calls and placing orders for our four bars. But that only lasted a couple hours. Now, I'm sitting on her chenille couch, remembering the night we had when I made her come twice on it.

Fuck, I must be turning into one hell of a needy asshole because I miss her. A thought starts forming in my head. We pretty much went from combative flirting, as I like to call it, to sleeping together secretly, to being thrown into this shit with her father and brother. But so far, I haven't had a chance to really wine and dine her. Jesus, I'm a right prick for not thinking of it sooner. She's used to going on actual dates, not just watching some underground fights in a bar and getting fucked til she passes out.

Tonight that needs to change.

Me: *What are you wearing?*

I figure it's as good as hello.

Gemma: *You saw me leave this morning. Do you think I change when I get here or something?*

Me: *Maybe I forgot. Why don't you spell it out for me. I'm most interested in what you*

have on underneath that tight as hell skirt you left the apartment in.

God, she looked good this morning in that silky blush button-down shirt and a black high-waisted, knee-length skirt. I don't know how she walks around in those heels of hers, but I was having some very naughty fantasies of her with that skirt lifted to her hips and those heels digging into my back...

Gemma: *You're an idiot.*

Me: *That's not an answer.*

Gemma: *Is that why you're texting me?*

Me: *I mean no...but I wouldn't be opposed to a picture.*

Gemma: *What do you want??*

When I picture her mouth pinching in that adorable, irritated scowl she's been known to wear around me so often, a smile spreads across my lips.

Me: *A picture of your tits.*

What can I say? Fucking with her is the highlight of my day, as I'm sure it is for her as well.

Gemma: *I swear to fucking Christ, Eoghan.*

Me: *Okay, okay. I was wondering if you had plans tonight?*

Gemma: *No...*

Eoghan: *Good. I'm taking you out.*

Gemma: *I thought we talked about the proper way to ask me out on a date.*

Eoghan: *You're right. Gemma, will you do me the honor of allowing me to escort you to dinner, ply you with wine, then give you several orgasms before the end of the evening?*

Gemma: *You don't have to get me drunk to give me orgasms, but I'll be happy to take you up on dinner and drinks.*

Eoghan: *I know, but I was hoping if I get you relaxed enough, you'd let me fuck your ass tonight.*

Gemma: *For God's sake, Eoghan!!!*

I laugh outright at her response, picturing her sitting behind a desk and getting more and more annoyed with my texts.

Me: *That's not a no...*

Gemma: *It's pretty fucking far from a yes.*

Me: So I have a shot?

Gemma: *I need to get back to work if you're taking me out tonight.*

Still not a no. Interesting.

Eoghan: *Okay. I'll see you tonight. Prepare to be wined and dined, Ms. Dalton.*

Gemma: *I'll be home by six.*

Eoghan: *See you then, blondie.*

Looking at the clock on my phone, I realize I only have a couple hours to run out and get a few things for our date tonight. As I'm grabbing my keys and am about to walk out the door, my phone dings with an incoming text. It's a photo from Gemma, and when I open it, my mouth instantly waters. She undid several buttons of her shirt, and her tits stare back at me, encased in one of her sexy-as-hell pale-pink bras. Her finger grazes the edge of the material as though she's going to pull the lace away and let me see her perfect rosy nipple underneath.

Damn blonde temptress. Now I'm going to have to get in my car with a raging hard-on.

When Gemma walks in the door, I greet her with a chilled glass of her favorite sauvignon blanc.

"I could get used to this," she says, taking the glass from my hand.

I grab her briefcase and bag as she removes her shoes and walks over to the couch, eying the vase of flowers I picked up from a neighborhood florist my dad visits regularly.

"Wine and flowers? You must really be gunning for anal tonight."

I laugh and grab my beer from the kitchen, then have a seat next to her. Gemma is leaning back into the cushions, practically melting into the plush sofa. I lift her feet and set them on my lap, massaging her arches.

"Fuck, keep doing that and you can have whatever you want." She lets out a loud groan as my fingers dig in, hitting a spot that sends shivers through her entire body.

"If you're too tired, we can stay in. I'll order takeout."

Her eyes meet mine and she gives me her soft smile. "No, I want to see what you have up your sleeve."

"I thought I'd take you out for that steak I promised you. Afterward, I'm going to take you to one of our bars. There's a band playing that I think you'll like."

Something I discovered about Gemma is her love of Irish folk music mixed with a little rock. She plays it when she's working from home or cooking dinner. Her TV is rarely on when I'm here, but there's always music.

Her eyes light up when I tell her my plan. "Sounds perfect."

When she finally emerges from the bedroom, I'm so damn hungry I could eat an entire cow by myself. I take a long look at her and can say without a shadow of a doubt, the wait was worth it. Her hair is in long, messy waves down her back, and she's changed into a loose low-cut tank top and a pair of jeans that make her ass look absolutely edible. She traded the heels that I love for a pair of black motorcycle boots, and she did that smoky thing with her eye makeup that makes the light blue of her irises even more shocking.

I let out a low whistle and she smiles. "Damn, blondie. I'm about to say screw going out." I walk up to her and help her into a light leather jacket before nuzzling into her neck.

"Not on your life. I'm fucking starving."

When I pull away, my wide grin matches hers. "Then let's get you fed."

We drive a bit out of Boston. There's a dive bar on the outskirts that serves the best damn steaks I've ever had. A hell of a lot better than any of the fancy restaurants I've been to in the city limits. Not that I go to many.

I open the door for her, like the gentleman my mom tried to raise me to be, and we're met with some old rock playing from an ancient jukebox as we make our way to a table in the low-lit bar. Gemma slides into the circular red vinyl booth first, and I follow, throwing my arm around the back. When the waitress comes over, I order my usual beer and Gemma orders a glass of red wine. When the waitress drops off the drinks, she takes our order and Gemma settles into the cushioned back of the booth.

She sips her wine and smiles at me. "Mmm, this is delicious. Not what I'd expect in a dive bar." She eyes me with a knowing gaze.

"I may have dropped off a bottle that I know you like."

"I usually drink white."

"Oh, I brought that too. I wasn't sure which one you would have picked, but this is the same red my mom served at Alessia's birthday party that you liked."

Gemma blinks at me a few times with a blank face. I'm not sure how to read her reaction, and to be honest, it's making me a bit nervous.

"So let me get this straight. You went out today and bought me flowers, picked up my favorite bottle of white wine, then picked up two extra bottles so they would have it where we were going to dinner?"

"Yes?" Shit. Should I not have?

"Goddamn, Eoghan Monaghan. You surprise me at every turn." She leans over and gives me a completely inappropriate kiss not meant for public consumption. Not that I'm complaining.

"So, I did good?"

"You've set the bar so damn high; I don't think anyone else will ever come close."

"That's the point. I want you so enamored with me that you'll never feel the need to look anywhere else."

"I don't." She looks into my eyes as though she wants me to understand exactly what she's saying without actually putting words to what she's feeling. "I won't look anywhere else, Eoghan."

It's not an enthusiastic I *love you*, but it's as close as she's ready for, and that's fine with me.

"How did you get so good at this, anyways?"

I chuckle and take a sip of my beer. "Watching my dad with my mom. He always made sure to show her how much he cared in the little things he did. He'd show up on random Tuesdays with a bouquet of flowers for her just because. Then, of course, there's my brother. When he met Alessia, he was smitten from the gate. It took him a minute, but he's come up with some pretty good dates himself."

"They hated each other at first," she says with a laugh.

"Hmm, sounds familiar."

Gemma rolls her eyes. "Tell me about your day."

I go into the boring details about the calls I made, then mention the conversation with her brother before the waitress drops off our steaks.

"So everything is going according to plan?" she asks, cutting the perfectly cooked meat in front of her.

"So far, so good. Though I wish I would've been there to see the asshole's face."

"I'm sure opening that shipping container to find it empty threw him for a loop."

"Oh, it wasn't empty," I say with a grin on my face as I chew my food.

"I thought you went there to steal the shipment."

"We did. But we left something in its place."

Her brow quirks in question, waiting for me to elaborate

"You kind of inspired me."

"Oh, Jesus. What did you leave?" she asks, bringing the glass of red to her lips.

"Crates filled with sex toys."

Gemma chokes midsip, and it takes a moment to compose herself. "What the hell?"

A laugh bubbles from my chest at her reaction. "Nikolai called me the day after I saw you using one, which I would love to catch you doing again in the very near future, and I don't know, rather than open the shipping container to find it empty, I thought this would be more fitting. You know, like a big go fuck yourself."

"You're really something else, Eoghan."

"Thank you," I reply with a shit-eating grin spread across my face.

"I'm not sure it was a compliment."

I shrug. "I can live with that."

We finish our steaks and enjoy another drink before it's time to head to The Celtic Cross, one of the other pubs my family owns. This isn't one we have fight nights at, but we bring in a pretty penny with live music. And being that it's a cash-only establishment, it's a prime business for us to clean some of the money we make by less than legal means.

When we walk in, I greet a few of the regulars and introduce them to Gemma. Of course, a couple of the old-timers take it as an opportunity to flirt with my girl, which she takes in stride, even tossing them a playful wink when they tell her if I'm not treating her right to come find them, and they'll straighten me out right away.

Fucking tossers.

The place is starting to fill up as the band sets up on the stage against the far wall. Gemma and I grab two chairs at the bar since I don't really have a table here, unlike at Clovers, where I spend most of my time. We order a couple drinks from Lilah, my bar manager, and I notice one of the bartenders that was scheduled isn't here yet.

"Where's Brenda?" I ask Lilah.

"Kid's sick again. I told her not to worry about it."

Brenda's son has terrible asthma. I covered one of

her shifts last week when her son was having a bad day. This time of year, when everything is blooming and the weather is starting to get humid, is tough on him. I'll have to remember to put a little something in her paycheck to help her with medical stuff since she's a proud-as-hell woman and wouldn't take a handout from anyone.

I nod in thanks when she hands us our drinks and Gemma is staring at me.

"What?" I ask, handing her the glass of wine she ordered.

"It's so different seeing you here. It's almost like here you aren't Eoghan Monaghan, Irish mobster. Here, you're just Eoghan, who runs a bar and laughs with the regulars."

"I am that man. And the other. Just like you're Gemma Dalton, the badass creative director who fought tooth and nail for everything she has, and Gemma, who gives me a hard time but is really a softy underneath all that prickly." I shoot her a wink.

"Not many people see the soft."

"I see everything, blondie. And I really fucking like it all."

"Me too."

We're startled out of the moment by the lead singer of the band, who begins his guitar intro, and the crowd starts cheering. Gemma leans in for a kiss before turning her attention to the stage and begins cheering along with the crowd. Fuck, this woman is stunning.

And so far out of my league, I have half a mind to pinch myself every time she turns that breathtaking smile toward me. For the first time in my life, I can imagine lazy Saturdays spent in bed and Sundays spent with my family. I imagine the day when she lets me slide a ring on her finger and her belly swollen with our child. Instead of breaking out in proverbial hives, like I would if anyone mentioned those things before Gemma, I allow my mind to wander to the future that's becoming more and more clear, and fuck me if it doesn't feel perfectly right.

Chapter Sixteen
Gemma

THE CROWD'S ENERGY IS rubbing off on me. This is exactly what I needed tonight, and leave it to Eoghan to give it to me. The way this man takes care of me and can tell what I need without me saying a word has me convinced he's some sort of mind reader. Never in my life have I felt so completely seen. Not even with Richard, who I dated for years. Though it might have something to do with the fact he was getting his dick sucked between legal briefings. I'd always held something back with Richard, maybe knowing somewhere in the back of my mind he was never going to be "the one"—whatever that means. But with Eoghan, it's been different. I told him things about my past I'd never told anyone. And when said past came back with threats against me and the people I care about, he stepped in the line of fire for me, the girl whose own mother sold her out, who no one ever really gave a shit about other than her best friend from college. The girl who told him over and over that she would never give him a shot.

The same girl sitting here tonight realizing that

love can come in unexpected ways, from unexpected people.

Never in a million years would I have thought Eoghan Monaghan would be the man I'd fall in love with, but damn it to hell, it's true.

The band is amazing and the place is starting to get packed. Eoghan glances from the two bartenders behind the bar to the sea of waiting customers, then back to me.

"I'm going to jump back there and help out for a minute, yeah?" he yells over the music and the cheering crowd.

"Okay."

I turn in my seat and watch him walk behind the bar. The bartenders' relief shows on their faces. Eoghan smiles at the customers who have been waiting and begins pouring drinks, handing them off and collecting cash. He works the crowd like a pro and moves around the other bartenders with effortless ease. A couple of women send him flirtatious smiles and stand just a tad taller when he talks to them. With the music so loud, it's impossible to hear what they're saying, but Eoghan smiles graciously back at them, that adorable dimple on display. I honestly don't think the man can help his naturally flirtatious personality, nor would I expect him to suddenly stop talking to half the world's population. I'm not the jealous type by any stretch, and when he looks at me after the girls have gone off to meet up with the rest of their friends, the smile and wink he gives me is the reason I know I'll never have a reason to be suspicious of Eoghan. He can turn his flirtatious smile toward anyone, but the one that holds sinful promises—and something else that I'm hoping I'm not imagining—is all for me.

The thought that he could feel the same about me is exhilarating. It doesn't scare me or make me wonder if this is too much too soon. Eoghan has always let me lead this little dance we've been doing with each other, and I know this is going to be no different. Though I have to admit, this is one instance where I wouldn't mind him taking the lead. Maybe it's my insecurities rearing their ugly heads, but the only thing that scares me is me saying the words I want to hear from him first and him not reciprocating.

Get out of your damn head and enjoy the music, that little voice in the back of my mind tells me. So, I do.

An hour passes, and once the crowd has thinned to a manageable pace, Eoghan comes back over to me. The band is taking a break with one more set before they call it a night, but I'm ready to go now.

"There's something about seeing you back there that I really liked," I tell the man smiling down at me.

"Really?" Eoghan places his hands on the bar on either side of me, caging me between his strong arms against the bar.

"I never had a thing for bartenders, but you may have just changed my mind."

"Well, good for you that I've always had a thing for

feisty blondes with an attitude and a fantastic ass."

"So, I'm your usual type."

"Blondie, I can say with utmost certainty there's nothing usual about you."

He leans in and kisses me breathless in front of everyone, and when he pulls away, I can almost hear the breaking hearts of every single woman in the room.

"What do you say we get out of here and go home?" I ask.

"I say that's music to my ears. You know what else I want to hear from you?"

"What's that?"

He leans in close, his lips brushing my ear as his warm breath tickles the column of my neck. "I want to hear you screaming my name while I eat your pussy. Then I want to hear you begging me to fuck you, to fill you with my hard cock. I want to hear how hard I make you come, how no one else will ever be inside your cunt again because you're mine."

Never in my life have I considered myself someone who likes to be referred to as *mine* by any man in that possessive tone. Never. I thought it was antiquated and stifling to my autonomy as my own person. But hearing those words from Eoghan's mouth has me throwing those thoughts straight out the fucking window.

I lean back and finish the glass of wine sitting on the bar top. "Well, we should probably go then. Sounds like you have your work cut out for you."

Eoghan backs up a step to allow me space to get off

the stool. He waves at his bartenders then grabs my hand, hauling me out the door to his waiting car, then speeds off toward my apartment. Once we're inside my building, he presses the elevator call button, and thankfully, the door slides open right away. Eoghan wastes no time pushing me against the wall of the elevator as the doors close and takes my mouth in a brutal kiss.

"Fuck, blondie. I've wanted to ruin your lipstick since you walked out of the bedroom."

"Funny. I've been waiting all night to see how it looks around your cock," I say, rubbing his hard length through his denim.

"Fuuuck," he breathes out, pressing his forehead to mine a moment before diving back in for another kiss.

The doors open on our floor and Eoghan picks me up, rushing to my front door. It takes a minute for me to navigate getting the door unlocked while being wrapped around him as he trails his tongue and teeth over my neck. When I finally manage, Eoghan opens the door with such force it bounces off the doorstop and nearly slams back into us before we make it across the threshold. He slams it closed with his foot then shoots off like a heat-seeking missile to the bedroom. I love this wild side of his. The one that can't seem to go another second without touching me or being inside of me. I've never felt that kind of basic, nearly feral need from myself or any other man for that matter, just with Eoghan.

"You're wearing too many clothes," he growls, setting me on my feet before ripping the jacket from my arms and throwing it across the room. Laughter bubbles from me at his desperate need to get me naked and sink into me, that any little hindrance causes him the utmost frustration.

"I don't know why you're laughing instead of stripping," he says when I take a step back.

"Didn't anyone ever tell you that patience is a virtue?" I ask as I play with the hem of my shirt.

"Fuck patience." Eoghan grabs the hem and whips the shirt over my head before removing his. The harsh bruise still mars his otherwise smooth skin, but if he's in any pain from the injury, it doesn't show. The only thing I see on his face is molten desire mixed with irritation that I'm still clothed.

His mouth attaches to my nipple over my bra, and a bark of surprise followed by a moan from deep inside my chest falls from my lips. My fingers tunnel through his thick hair, gripping the soft strands. Eoghan reaches for the clasp of my black lace bra with one hand and manages to snap it open, yanking the straps down my arms before he throws the material over his shoulder.

"Nifty trick," I moan as his mouth finds my bare nipple and he sucks it into his hot mouth. God, I love the way he uses his mouth on me as though he needs to devour every inch of me.

He releases my nipple with a pop and kisses his way up my chest before claiming my mouth, his tongue delving in. Eoghan's hands grip me around my waist as I clutch at his shoulders, both of us still standing at the foot of my bed half-clothed.

"If you like that one, you'll love what else I have in store."

He lifts me and tosses me onto the mattress before kneeling on the bed, taking one boot off, then the other.

"Brute," I say when he crawls over me to take my mouth in another kiss.

Looping my legs with his, I flip us over so I'm positioned on top. The surprised look on his face makes me chuckle as I sit on top of him, my center rubbing deliciously against the hard bulge behind his zipper.

"You have some of your own tricks, I see." He cups both of my breasts and rubs his thumbs over my stiff nipples, sending tingles straight to my core.

"I did a little jiujitsu training with Alessia and Enzo. Comes in handy sometimes."

I lean down and graze my lips across Eoghan's before running them down his neck and over his firm chest, dipping my tongue into every groove of muscle as I go. When I get to the zipper of his pants, my hand pulls at the waistband, not enough to take his pants off, but enough that the head of his hard cock is exposed. I lean down and lick the saltiness from the tip, and Eoghan hisses, his hand lifting my hair back into a ponytail so he can have a front-row view. I swipe my tongue a few more times, rubbing the rest of his hard length through the jeans.

"Fuck, blondie. Stop teasing me," he says with a groan, tightening his grip on my hair.

"Why? You tease me all the time."

"I swear to God, I'll never do it again. Just please take my cock out and put it in your mouth," he begs, but I'm not done. Instead of doing as he asks, I wrap my lips around what's peeking out the top of his pants and moan, causing the vibrations to travel down his length. Eoghan jerks his hips and curses under his breath, and I can't help the smile that forms. God, I love taking him to the point where he's about to break. And I love it even more when he does.

When I lift my gaze to his and shoot him a wicked grin, Eoghan shakes his head. "You're an evil, wretched woman."

"I mean, I could stop if it's that bad." I shrug as though it doesn't matter one way or the other to me.

"Don't you fucking dare."

I give him a wink and slowly undo his zipper before pulling his jeans down his legs and sliding them from his body.

"Your turn," he says, pointing to the fabric still covering me. I stand from the bed and slide out of my jeans and panties before crawling between his thighs and lowering my mouth over his length in one motion.

"Fuck," he moans into the otherwise silent room as I bring my mouth to the tip and suck the head before moving my mouth back down.

When my eyes move up, he's lying back on my

mattress, and our eyes meet. His arm is slung behind his head, with his other hand holding my hair away from my face. The toned muscles of his torso are tight with anticipation, probably also holding himself back from pumping into my mouth as I continue to bob my head up and down. He loses the battle with himself and pumps his hips up, causing his cock to hit the back of my throat. Instead of gagging, I open my throat and swallow around him. When his eyes roll to the back of his head, I know he's close, even though he's desperately trying to stave off his impending orgasm.

"Fuck, baby. I want to come inside you."

I pop my head up and before I can blink, Eoghan sits up from the bed, taking my mouth in another brutal kiss. "Your mouth is too fucking good, blondie."

He reaches over to grab a condom from my bedside drawer, but I put a hand on his arm and shake my head.

"I don't want…I don't want anything between us."

Eoghan stills and stares into my eyes, not saying anything.

"I have an IUD and tested negative on everything at my last visit."

He still isn't saying anything, which is freaking me the hell out and making me second-guess every clue he gave me that this thing between us is more than two people dating and only living together for appearance's sake. What was I thinking? Eoghan is charming, but that doesn't mean he's serious about anything between us—

His lips crash to mine, cutting off my train of doubtful

thoughts.

"Same here. Not the IUD but the testing negative. I haven't been with anyone since, except for you."

Eoghan kisses me again, his hand cupping both of my cheeks, relieving the doubt and second guesses that were plaguing me only moments ago. But hasn't that always been the case? I can be a mess of self-doubt and insecure about my emotions where Eoghan is concerned, but as soon as his lips meet mine, it's like my brain...just stops. It's a comforting silence I've only had with him.

Lifting my hips, I position myself over his cock, holding it in my hand as I slide onto his length, bare for the first time. I swear to Christ, the world around us narrows into this one singular sensation, this one moment of being closer to him than I've ever been with another person.

I break the kiss to look at Eoghan's face. Our lips are parted as we tumble headfirst into the incredible sensation of him being inside me bare for the first time. Our breaths mingle, sharing the same air as I slide up and down his length. There's so much in the depths of his blue eyes, things I've never seen before. A connection so strong it's as though it would be impossible for either of us to look away.

Eoghan takes my mouth in another kiss and leans back, pulling me with him. Our chests are pressed together when his hands find my hips, and he guides me up then slams me down, thrusting forcefully into me from underneath.

"God, it feels so good. You were fucking made for me, Gemma."

My walls clench around him as he continues controlling my hips, pumping in and out of me. It's almost too much but not quite enough at the same time.

"I'm so close," I pant into his open mouth.

Eoghan moves one hand between us and his thumb begins strumming my clit with expert precision. That's all I need before I explode around him, my pussy tightening, making each stroke of his cock inside me that much more intense.

"Goddamn baby, strangle my cock just like that. Fuck," he hollers as I feel him jerk inside me and his release washes through him.

I collapse onto his chest, the damp heat between our bodies feeling so euphoric, I can't even think about moving, let alone actually do it. Eoghan traces the tips of his fingers up and down my damp back for several long moments. I want to tell him I'm in love with him, that when all of this is over, I don't want him to move out. I don't want to spend another day coming home to an empty apartment or sleep in my bed alone. But I don't. I keep all those thoughts locked tightly in my heart. I'm not ready to voice them. I will. Just not tonight.

"I hear your brain going into overdrive, blondie."

I chuckle and kiss his slick chest. "Let's get cleaned up. Some of us have to go to work in the morning."

"And some of us want to push you up against the shower wall and eat your pussy. Me. I'm the *us*."

I laugh and lift myself from his chest, my muscles still feeling like jelly from the orgasm I just had. "Well, let's not keep *us* waiting."

I am tired as hell at work today, but it's so worth it. The live music, the sex, the shower, all of it has had me smiling like a giddy schoolgirl throughout the day.

I'm about to shut down my computer and leave for the evening when there's a knock at my door, and Natalie peeks her head in.

"Hi. I'm glad I caught you before you left." She steps into my office and shuts the door behind her before walking in front of my desk and taking a seat.

"It's seven o'clock; I thought you would be gone by now."

"It's been a hell of a day, or I would have been in here sooner."

"What's up?" Jean and Natalie have been having some closed-door meetings the last week. I haven't pried since if it's something I need to know, they'll tell me. Besides, the new campaign has been keeping me plenty busy, but that doesn't mean my curiosity hasn't been killing me.

"You know how much Jean hates the Massachusetts

winters."

Of course I do. Come February, the man threatens to pack it in and move to the Caribbean every damn year.

"Well, he's decided that he wants to open another office and studio where he can get away for the winters. We've been looking at properties in Southern California."

"Wow, that's a big step." I had no idea they were even considering an expansion.

Natalie nods. "It is. His haute couture studio will still be based in Boston. But he wants to move operations for the ready-to-wear line to California. And we think you should head the office there as VP of marketing."

I'm stunned speechless as I stare at Natalie. VP of marketing? That's been my dream. What I've worked my ass off for since coming to Aubine.

I blow out a long breath, trying to find my words. "That's an amazing offer."

"We've seen how tirelessly you work, Gemma. The ready-to-wear launch went amazing, thanks to you and your team. We want you to re-create the magic in California."

Her smile is bright, like she just handed me the opportunity of a lifetime, which she has. Except...no, this needs to be a decision that I make for myself. This has been my goal since before coming to Boston. If I start making decisions based on a man, I'm no better than my mother, who would gladly give up her independence and worth time and time again for the opposite sex.

"When are you thinking of going out there?" How much time do I have?

"We have an appointment with a commercial realtor to look at properties next week. Jean wants something by the beach." Natalie rolls her eyes. "I have a feeling he's going to be a bit of a prima donna about the entire thing."

I laugh with her, but the sound rings hollow in my ear.

Her smile is still wide as she stands from the chair. "I should have more information for you in a few days."

Nodding, I keep the fake smile on my face as she walks out the door. God, I hope she's taking my lack of words as being so excited I can't talk. And I am excited. This is *huge*. But there's an uncomfortable tightness in my chest and a little voice in my head that says the last place you belong is in California.

I pack up my things on autopilot and walk out of the office. The ride down the elevator into the parking garage doesn't even register. When the doors open to my level, I grab the phone from my bag to call Alessia, but she doesn't answer. She's probably at the casino being the badass host that she is.

When her voice mail picks up, I leave her a message before getting into my car: "Hey, so I just got the offer of a lifetime. Jean is opening an office in California and wants me to relocate out there as VP of marketing. I...I don't know what to do. Call me when you get a chance. I really need to talk this out."

I grab my keys from the bag, holding my phone and briefcase in one hand as I press the fob to unlock my car. From the corner of my eye, I see a man approach, and as I turn, I recognize him immediately.

Andrei.

"What do you want?" I ask.

"Your father would like a word."

"He can call me, then. I'm not at his beck and—" Before I finish the sentence, a hand covered in a sweet-smelling cloth clamps around my mouth. The last thing I see is Andrei's smirking face before my eyes close and I lose consciousness.

CHAPTER SEVENTEEN
EOGHAN

TONIGHT, I'M GOING TO tell Gemma that I love her. I should have said it last night, but I chickened the fuck out. It felt goddamn amazing being inside her body without a barrier, and I was afraid if I said it then, she would have thought it was some sort of sex-haze confession and I didn't mean it. I don't know, maybe she would have seen the truth in my eyes like I swear I saw in hers when I was moving inside her. But my woman tends to be skittish, and I didn't want her to doubt for even a second that my words weren't one-hundred-percent true.

I try calling her again. It's nearing eight o'clock. Even though she told me she was working late tonight, I expected her home by now. I even made her dinner—a rack of lamb that I called my mother to help me with. She thought it was absolutely adorable that I called her to have her walk me through the steps. Finn has never called her for cooking tips, so I'm pretty sure my position as favorite son still holds.

Gemma's favorite bottle of red is open, with two glasses sitting at the table ready to be poured. Now the woman just needs to get her fine ass home.

I'm going through the playlist I've made on my phone of songs I think Gemma will enjoy listening to with dinner when Nikolai's name pops on the screen.

"Petrov," I say in greeting.

"Where's Gemma?"

"On her way home from work. Why?"

"One of the guards I had on her mother was found shot behind her house. No sign of the husband or Gemma's mom."

Icy dread like I've never felt in my entire life works its way down my spine. I stand from the couch and stare at the front door as though I'm willing her to walk through the damn thing right fucking now.

"I expected her home already. I tried calling her about twenty minutes ago, but it went to voice mail."

"Shit." He doesn't speak for a few moments while I continue to stare at the door. "I'm about five minutes from her apartment. Is that where you are?"

"Yeah."

"I'll swing by and pick you up. We'll meet her at her building."

I hear his unspoken thoughts. *If she's there.*

"Okay."

Nikolai disconnects the call, and I immediately dial my brother's number.

"Hey, brother. I'm just about to head out to the casino floor. What's up?"

"I think Gemma is missing." Grabbing my keys, I walk

into the bedroom where I keep a gun locked in a small safe I brought to Gemma's when I started staying here. I open the safe and grab my 9mm and an extra magazine. I don't know what we're going to find when we go to her work, but I sure as hell am going in prepared.

"What do you mean 'think'?"

"Nikolai called and said the guard he had on her mother was found dead, and her mom and stepdad were nowhere to be found. Gemma should have been home by now, but she isn't, and I can't reach her. Nikolai is on his way here, and we're going to go check out her work."

"I'll meet you there."

He disconnects the call, and I head out the door dialing Gemma's number again.

No answer. I pull up the tracking app I installed on her phone. I didn't give a shit if it was an invasion of privacy when I put it there, and sure as shit don't now. The app shows she's at her office building, at least her phone is.

As I'm standing in front of the apartment building with thoughts of where Gemma is and why she isn't picking up her phone swirling through my head, Nikolai pulls up in a blacked-out luxury sedan. He rolls down the window, and I take a quick look inside. I'm not saying I don't trust the man, but I'm not saying I do. At least not enough to jump in a car with him without checking to make sure no one else is in there.

"Have you tried calling her again?" he asks as he pulls away from the curb.

"Yeah. She still isn't picking up."

His hands tighten around the wheel as his eyes stay fixed on the road ahead of him.

"How'd you find out about the guard?"

"I've had two men in Virginia rotating shifts. When the other guard came to relieve the one at her mom's house, he wasn't in his car. My guy looked around and found him shot between the eyes and placed behind some shrubbery at the back of the house. He went inside and saw signs of a struggle, but no one was home. It was obvious someone broke in, so he called me."

"Her mom seemed to be married to some shady son of a bitch. Could have been anyone." I'm desperate to believe it was anyone other than Viktor.

"Maybe. But who would have thought to kill my guard then hide his body? This has my father's stench all over it."

I can't fault his theory, no matter how much I pray it isn't true.

We pull into the parking garage Gemma uses, and I see her car still sitting in a spot.

"That's a good sign. She's probably working later than she thought she'd be."

Nikolai doesn't say anything as he parks and gets out of the car.

We get in the elevator and head to the lobby of her building. When we step off, we see someone locking the glass doors that lead into the offices of Aubine. The young woman looks startled when she turns and finds us standing there. I don't fucking blame her. Two men who probably look like they're ready to commit murder have just walked up behind her.

"Can I help you?" she asks, her gaze darting between us.

"My girlfriend works here. I was just coming to surprise her and take her for dinner with her brother from out of town," I say, laying on the charm, dimpled smile and all on full display.

"Uh, no one is here. Who's your girlfriend?"

"Gemma Dalton."

"Oh, Gemma left about an hour ago." She shrugs and hikes her purse over her shoulder.

I force the smile to stay on my face so as not to alarm the poor girl more than we already have.

"Darn. I was hoping to catch her," I say with a fake pout. "Okay, thanks." Nikolai and I head back to the elevator to make our way back to the underground parking.

When the doors close, my hands fist my hair. "Fuck!" I yell into the small space.

The door opens, and I march over to her car. Before I have a chance to look around, my brother's SUV pulls into the parking garage, and he steps out from the driver's side. Then the passenger door and back door open, and there's Alessia with Enzo right behind her.

"Tell me she's in her office, Eoghan, and we're all overreacting here," Alessia commands as she stalks to where Gemma's brother and I are standing next to her car.

I shake my head, staring my woman's best friend in the eye. "I can't."

"What do we know?" Finn asks Nikolai as Alessia and I continue to stare at each other. I'm sure the devastation in her eyes matches mine.

"The receptionist was locking the door to the offices when we went upstairs. Said Gemma left an hour ago," Nikolai replies.

"Have you heard from her today?" I ask Alessia.

"She called a little after seven and left a voice mail. When I tried to call her back ten minutes later, she didn't answer."

"What did the message say?" Maybe there's a clue in there.

Something flashes in Alessia's eyes, but before I can consider it, it's gone. "She was just calling to check in and say hi."

I grab my phone from my pocket and pull up the tracking app again. It still shows that she's here. When I dial her number, I hear it ring in my ear, but there's another noise coming from somewhere close. I look around the ground then get on my knees and look under her car. Her phone is lit up underneath, with my name flashing on the screen. I pick it up and stand, holding it in front of me.

"Fuck," Finn mutters and looks around the garage. "There're cameras here. Let's head to the security office and look at the footage."

We get in our respective vehicles and drive to the street level before parking in a guest spot and finding the security office. When we knock on the door, a portly man in his mid to late fifties opens the door. He takes one look at us, and his hand goes to the baton at his waist. If I wasn't so scared for my woman, I probably would have laughed.

"I'm Finnegan Monaghan. That name mean anything to you?"

The man nods and looks at the three of us, along with Alessia and Enzo standing behind us. "What can I do for you, Mr. Monaghan?"

"We need to look at some camera footage."

The guard dips his chin and allows the five of us to crowd inside his small office.

"What times do you need to see?" the guard asks, sitting in his chair.

"Let's start with six thirty until now," Finn answers.

The guard presses a couple buttons on his keyboard, and I see the time on the screen set to six thirty. He presses another button and the footage moves faster across the screen.

When I turn to my brother. "Did you see what I saw?"

"Yeah. A whole lot of nothing. Not even us pulling in or out of the garage. Like someone has the footage on a loop."

I nod and turn to the guard. "How often do you leave the office?"

"I do rounds once an hour at the public parking lot

across the street."

"How long does it take you to do a round across the street?" Finn asks.

"About fifteen minutes."

My brother meets my gaze. "That's more than enough time to come in and fuck with the footage," I say.

"Reset your cameras," he says to the guard. "You didn't see us here."

My brother pulls a money clip from his pocket, peels off a few hundred-dollar bills and hands them to the man.

"Let's go back to our house. Cillian is meeting us there with a few things from the penthouse," Finn says then walks out the door with sure steps back to his car.

Alessia stares at me as I stand in the security office. Once I step foot out of this door, blood will fucking spill.

Alessia sees the murderous expression on my face and gives me a slow smile. "Let's go get her, Eoghan."

Nikolai is on the phone the entire way back to Finn's. Sometimes he's barking orders in Russian, other times in English.

"My men checked all of my father's usual safe houses. Nothing."

"Where would he keep her?" I ask.

"He has two others that he doesn't know I know

about. One is on the border of New York and Massachusetts."

"I thought you were his right-hand man. Why wouldn't he tell you about them?"

"Our families aren't the same. There is no absolute trust between me and my father, nor was there between him and his."

"That's fucking sad, Nikolai."

He shrugs. "Obviously it was smart on his end," he says with a slight tilt to the corner of his lips.

When we pull up to Finn's, Cillian's car is in the drive. We all make our way up the stone stairs, and when Finn opens the door, the four of us trail him down the stairs to his basement, where he keeps an arsenal of weapons. Cillian is already there, packing a few things. When he sees Nikolai, he stops and faces the man with coldness settling in his gaze.

"Are you sure you want him in on this?" he asks Finn without taking his eyes from Gemma's brother.

"I do," I reply for my brother. "Plus, he's the only one who knows where his dad's supersecret safe house is."

Cillian looks to me, then to Finn, then back to Nikolai. "Are you sure that's where he would have taken her?"

"No, but my men have checked all the other safe houses that my father uses. The one closest to us is one of two that he thinks I don't know about."

"Not a lot of trust between you and your father?" Cillian asks.

"As much as I would expect. He's always been one

to make sure he keeps something in his back pocket. My guess is he suspects I've been working against him. Whether he knows it's with you is yet to be determined."

"Let me make myself very clear to you, Petrov," Cillian begins. "If I think you're going to hurt my brothers, I don't give a shit who you're connected with; I'll put a bullet between your eyes."

Nikolai doesn't blink at the threat. "Understood."

"Great, you guys have measured your dicks. Can we please go get my best friend back from her sadistic father now?" Alessia chimes in from the doorway.

"Who's *we*?" Finn asks.

"Enzo and I should go with you. You have no idea what you're walking into and are going to need all the manpower you can get."

"There is no way in hell you're coming, Alessia."

"She's my best friend, *Finn*. Plus, I'm probably a better shot than any of you."

"Sweetheart," he starts in that cooing tone that says whatever he's about to tell her could possibly get him castrated if he isn't careful. "There is no way I'm going to be able to concentrate if you're with me. It's too dangerous for us if I'm distracted worrying about you." She opens her mouth to argue, but Finn cuts her off. "I know what you're going to say."

"No, you don't," she replies, crossing her arms over her chest and narrowing her eyes on him.

"You're going to tell me that you'll stay in the car. And I know you would, but that's still too close. We have no idea what we're walking into, and there're too many unknown variables in play. I need to know you're here and safe inside this room until we get back."

"You want me in the safe room all night?"

Finn nods. "I do. Viktor already threatened you. I need to be certain there's no way in hell he could get to you while I'm gone. I'll make sure the guards are on high alert, and if anything seems off, to shoot first and let God sort it out. But I want you and Enzo in here."

Enzo nods in agreement, understanding why Finn is so overprotective. Last time we went to kill a motherfucker, Alessia was in a fortified clubhouse full of bikers. But the time before that? Yeah, Finn isn't going to take even the slightest chance.

Alessia blows out a breath. "Please get her back. I can't…" Her tough exterior is starting to crack, and I know my sister-in-law well enough to know that's the last thing she wants anyone other than her husband to see. The only other person on this planet she's ever let see her vulnerable is Gemma, and I'll be damned if she's ripped from her life or mine.

Finn walks over to his wife and kisses her on the top of her head. "I promise, wife."

"Have you been to the property?" Cillian asks Nikolai. "Or do you happen to have an address, boss?"

"There's no address you can pull, but I know the coordinates."

"It'll have to do. Let's go upstairs and see about pulling up satellite footage."

"Damn, Cill. You know how to do that?" I ask.

"I like to dabble in a few things."

I don't think I'll ever know the full scope of Cillian's talents, but there's a reason he's Finn's lieutenant, and it isn't for his charming personality.

We collect all the weapons that will fit in the bags and head back upstairs so Cillian can pull up a visual on the safe house. Finn heads in the direction of his office and returns with several bulletproof vests and a medical bag. We don't know the state we're going to find Gemma in, and unless Nikolai knows of a doctor close to where we're going, we may have to make do until we can get back here to our family doctor fifteen minutes from Finn's house.

Alessia disappeared when we came up from the basement and now returns with a small bag, handing it to me.

"A change of clothes if she needs it."

I take the bag and look into her fearful gaze. Her eyes are rimmed red, but there're no tears on her face. She needed a minute to collect herself away from prying eyes. I offer her a small smile, but she doesn't return it.

"I'll get her back," I reassure. *Or I'll fucking die trying.* The unspoken words hang between us, but Alessia knows I won't be walking out of there without her.

I walk over to where Cillian and Nikolai are sitting at Finn's dining room table with the computer in front of them. They're going over some images of the house. Two SUVs are parked out front, so we know there's someone there.

The phone in my pocket rings, and when I pull it out, I see Jude's name lighting up the screen.

"Hey, now's not a good time."

"Fuck off, arsehole. My brother and I are in Boston drinking at your bar. Tear yourself away from your woman and come have a pint."

"Liam's with you?" I ask, hoping like hell his brother is willing to do me a giant fucking favor.

"That's what I said."

Jude's brother is an ex-Royal Marine who came to the states to start a security firm. The man has been in the middle of some incredibly dangerous missions, some very similar to this one.

"Listen, I need your help tonight." Fuck, I hope they're sober enough. "How much have you had to drink?"

"Working on our first. Hold on." A few moments later, the loud bar noise disappears. "What's going on?"

"My girl is in the hands of Viktor Petrov. We've been working with her brother, Nikolai, to take the Russians down."

"Wait, if Nikolai is her brother, then that means Viktor Petrov is Gemma's father?"

"Yup."

"Do you know where he has her?"

"Yeah."

"Hey, you fucking wanker, give me my phone back," Jude yells at someone.

"Eoghan, it's Liam. Did you say Petrov, as in the head

of the New York Bratva?"

"I see you're familiar."

"Where are you?"

"At my brother's, about thirty minutes outside of the city."

"Text Jude the address. We'll be there in twenty."

Liam hangs up without giving the phone back to Jude, and I promptly text him my brother's address.

I turn to the other three men, locking my gaze with Finn's.

"Grab a couple more vests. The fucking British are coming."

Chapter Eighteen
Gemma

THE FIRST THING I notice when consciousness slowly creeps back in is the disgusting taste in my mouth. God, I hope Eoghan is still asleep so I can brush my teeth really quick. No way in hell am I giving him a good-morning kiss with this breath. When my heavy eyelids peel open, the tightness in the rest of my body screams at me. What the hell?

I blink a few times and stare up at a stained white ceiling, the sheets beneath me feeling scratchy as hell and certainly not the ones I have on my bed. I jolt upright, and my head swims for a moment before I can focus on where I am. Taking a look around the old dingy room, I realize I have no fucking clue where that is. Then the memories come crashing back. Walking to my car, leaving Alessia a message, and Andrei showing up as I was about to get in my car. He said my father wanted to meet with me, and when I started to tell him off and move to get in my car and the hell away from him, a hand clasped around my mouth, and I inhaled something. Those motherfuckers used chloroform to knock me out and kidnap me.

I'm going to kill all of them.

I swing my legs off the bed and stand, still a bit woozy from the drug. Shit, good thing they didn't overdose me if I feel this bad after however long it's been since they took me. On shaky legs, I make my way to the door and twist the handle. Locked. *Of course it is.* I walk over to the one window with heavy drapes over it, stepping lightly so as not to alert anyone to the fact that their captive is awake and moving around.

When I part the heavy curtains, I'm met with bars on the window and the dark sky. I'm effectively caged in this room.

Double shit.

Next, I scan the room for anything that can be used as a weapon. There are a few boxes in the corner, but when I open them, they're filled with women's clothes and nothing else. Not even a pair of heels I could use to shove into someone's eye socket. Why the hell are there a bunch of women's clothes? A memory blinks in my mind; Nikolai saying something about shutting down his father's trafficking operations. Is this where they take the women before they're sold to whatever sadistic piece of shit who thinks buying human slaves is just fine and dandy?

Footsteps sound in the hall, and before the door opens, I scurry back to the bed and pretend to be asleep, not wanting to give anyone the impression that I'm awake and already trying to find a way out of this hellhole. My eyes close, and I attempt to relax my tense body to make it look like I haven't woken yet.

Whoever opens the door shuts it before their heavy footsteps take them to the side of the bed.

A hand slaps my cheek a few times. "Wake up."

I open my eyes and see Andrei staring down at me with a harsh coldness in his gaze.

"Where are we?" I croak out, pretending that I just woke in confusion.

"Safe house. One not even your traitor of a brother knows about. Here." He throws a paper plate with a sandwich and an apple on the bed, then a bottle of water. My stomach roils at the sight of the peanut butter and jelly sandwich. So many dinners consisted of just that when I was growing up with my mom. I haven't touched the stuff since leaving Virginia. But I do grab the water and unscrew the cap, grateful for the cool liquid running down my burning throat. Chloroform fucking sucks.

"Do you feed all your captives before killing them?"

A disgusting smile spreads across his face as dark as the night sky outside the barred window. "This isn't where we bring girls to kill them. This is where we prepare them for their new owners."

So I was right. And that knowledge brings me absolutely no relief.

"I thought Viktor just wanted to talk to me," I say before taking another sip of the cool water.

"He does. He wants to tell you what happens when you disobey his orders. He gave you a chance, girl, and you fucked it up. Now it's time to pay the consequences."

God, are Giada and Alessia here too? He made it clear if I screwed him over, they would pay, same as me.

"Am I the only one here?" I doubt he'll tell me anything, but I need to know if I got my friends killed. Or worse.

"Nope. There's someone who's dying to say hello downstairs waiting for you."

It can't be Giada. She's in Italy with Luca. She just sent me a picture of her and her husband in Naples eating from a bowl of pasta, *Lady and the Tramp* style. There's no way they could have gotten her here that fast, right? But that means if it's not Giada, it's Alessia. Maybe that's why she didn't answer her phone when I called. Maybe they got to her the same time they grabbed me. And that means they had to get through Enzo to get to her.

Fuck, fuck, fuck.

Calm down, Gemma. Freaking the hell out isn't going to save you.

"Get up. Time to talk to your father."

Andrei turns from me, and I take the opportunity with his back facing me to make my move. I jump from the bed and race toward the door, knocking him over as I pass. My hand grabs the handle, and I twist. It's fucking locked. Goddamnit, I didn't hear him lock it again when he came in.

I whirl around and Andrei is standing upright with a set of keys in his hand. He shakes them at me with a caustic laugh.

"This isn't my first rodeo," he informs me.

I jump at him, attempting to grab the keys, but he lowers that arm and raises the other one, grabbing me around the throat before I can make contact with the keys. My fingers claw at his arm, my legs kick out, trying to find purchase on any part of his body, but his grip never loosens.

"I knew you were going to be a pain in the ass," he says with a sneer. The last thing I see is his fist flying toward my face, and it's lights out again.

The next time I wake, my head is pounding a hell of a lot harder than it was the first time I woke. I'm also no longer in the room with cheap-ass sheets but handcuffed to a folding metal chair in a damp basement. I shake my head a few times, but the only thing that does is make it pound even harder. There's one light about ten feet from where they have me restrained. It doesn't do much to illuminate the space we're in, as though the darkness of this house is absorbing any light.

"Jenny," I hear a familiar voice say next to me.

There's only one person who still calls me that.

"Mom?" I squint my eyes, but it's still dark as hell, or it could be he hit me so damn hard my vision is fucked to hell now.

I make out her silhouette a few feet from where I am. The harder I focus, the more I see. She looks like shit, even in the poorly lit space. Her hair is a mess of shaggy blonde strings, and there's black makeup running down her cheeks. I can't make out much more than her too-skinny body slumped over in the chair she's restrained in.

"Yeah, it's me," she answers. "Those bastards grabbed me yesterday and knocked me out good. I tried to tell them I hadn't done anything. That I gave Viktor what he wanted and I wasn't asking him for anything else. But they wouldn't listen."

Trying to save her skin, as usual.

"They figured out we were working against him. That's why he took you. He told me if I double-crossed him, he would come after you."

"But you did it anyways?" she screeches before a raspy cough shakes her body.

"Still smoking like a chimney, I see."

"Don't change the subject. God, what were you thinking? How could you do this to me? I can't believe you were so stupid to think you could get away with this."

A humorless chuckle falls from my mouth. "That's right, Angela. Blame me for this shitstorm we're in. It couldn't possibly be because you opened your fucking mouth and brought a dangerous criminal into our lives for a quick payout."

"This is your fault as much as mine, Jenny. Or should

I call you Gemma? That's who you are now, right? Some fancy stuck-up bitch who doesn't give a shit about the position she put her mother in."

"Again," I grit out. "This was you."

"I gave you everything. It was only fair that your father paid me back for all the money I spent on you throughout the years. I considered it back child support. But oh, no. You couldn't just trust your parents to do what was right for you."

"You are fucking delusional. The drugs have rotted your goddamn brain. You never did shit for me when I was growing up. The only thing you ever did right was get out of New York and keep your slimy pedo boyfriends from taking it too far with me. That's the only reason I had Nikolai send a guy to protect you. Otherwise, I would have handed you to Viktor myself."

"You ungrateful—"

"Family reunions are so much fun," a disembodied voice calls from the other side of the darkened basement. When the man steps from the shadows, I see a face so similar to mine staring between my mother and me.

"Viktor, I gave you what you wanted. Why did you bring me here? Jenny is the one who fucked up, not me."

"Gemma didn't live up to her end of the bargain. I was very clear what the consequences would be, was I not?" he asks, turning his attention to me.

I remain silent. There's nothing I can say that will get me out of whatever he has planned for me, and I refuse to give him the satisfaction of witnessing my terror. Men like this thrive on it, get off on it. He's the same as all the men my mom had parading through our small apartment when I was growing up, just in a better suit.

"Viktor, if you let me go, I'll disappear. I won't tell anyone where she is. I swear. Or maybe we could work something out. I was your favorite once. You told me that. I could be your favorite again."

The man looks at my mother with disgust smeared across his face. "You're about thirty years too late, Angela." He pulls his gun from the holster at his hip and shoots her between the eyes before she can utter another useless, pleading word. I barely hold in the scream that threatens to erupt from me. He just killed the woman who gave birth to me like it meant nothing to him, which I suppose it doesn't. In his mind, her death was probably a long time coming.

"God, now I remember why I was ready to cut her loose in the first place. The woman is annoying as hell. Well, *was*, I suppose." He looks at her body slumped in the chair, a pool of blood and brain matter on the floor around her dead body. "She knew how to use her mouth in other, more creative ways, though. Pity."

Disgust churns around my stomach. Viktor turns his gun toward me, and I'm convinced these are my last moments on earth and definitely the last place I ever pictured myself spending them. Just yesterday, I'd pictured myself growing old with Eoghan and being surrounded by the people I loved. Maybe even having a couple kids with the infuriating man. The man I love more than the life that's about to end, and I never told him. I have no regrets about anything except that. I'm going to die, and he'll never know about the future I wanted with him more than anything else in the world.

"I would have given you a husband. A life where you wouldn't have to worry about anything. You would have been set up. Now I have to punish you, then your brother, for betraying me. Stupid Nikolai. That boy always trusted too easily. He didn't even see the discontent some of his men had when he started working with the Irish. Even the most loyal can be pushed too far, and working with Irish scum like your boyfriend was too far for a few. "

I'm still silent, staring at him with blazing hatred rolling off me.

"You don't have anything to say for yourself?" He sounds like a father chastising his daughter for sneaking out past curfew or getting a bad grade on a test. It's fucking creepy.

"What would you like me to say, Viktor? Sorry for not rolling over and doing your bidding? Sorry for not wanting a husband who would probably be as evil as you? Sorry for being loyal to the family that I chose, that I love? Take your pick."

"You could have been showered in riches beyond your wildest imagination. You could have bore sons and daughters that would have made your husband proud. Now you'll die a drugged-up junkie like your mother.

Well, after the men who intend to buy you are finished. At least they like their girls compliant, so you won't have to sell yourself on the corner for the shit they'll gladly push in your veins."

He nods his head, and Andrei steps out of the shadows. "Take Gemma to where the rest of the girls are, then have someone clean up this mess. The buyers are going to be here first thing in the morning."

Viktor turns back toward the shadows and disappears from sight before Andrei steps closer to me. He kneels in front of me, pulling out a key, presumably for the cuffs around my ankles.

"Don't get any ideas. Not only will it piss me off, but Viktor will have no problem handing you over to his men until the buyers get here. Actually"—he looks at me with a sinister grin—"maybe you should fight me. At least a little."

I keep my mouth shut and let him unlock the cuffs. It takes everything in me to not kick this disgusting piece of shit in the face.

He grabs me roughly by the arm and hauls me from the chair, his grip digging into the muscles of my arms. After leading me to the other side of the basement, he takes out his keys and unlocks a door, flipping on a light switch. What I see in the bright room has my heart dropping into my stomach. Cages. Four of them, two on each side of the wide room, with two scared-looking women in each. They don't say anything; most of them try to hide their faces, but a couple look at Andrei with hatred brimming in their gazes.

Unlocking one of the cages, he unceremoniously throws me in, pulling the door closed and locking it again. Then, without a word, he walks out the metal door and slams it shut, locking us in here.

I look around the room at the girls, all of whom are staring at me. Some of them don't look to be more than fourteen, some maybe in their twenties.

"Does anyone know where we are?" I ask the group, searching their faces.

"I'm not sure, but I think somewhere between New York and Massachusetts. They took me from New York City and we only drove a couple of hours. Three at the most."

"Do you know which direction they drove in?" I ask.

"North, maybe? They shot me up with something, but it wasn't enough to knock me out. I have a higher tolerance than that."

The girl can't be more than eighteen. When I look at her too-thin arms, I see track marks. I also notice a thin sheen of sweat covering her entire body. She must not have had a fix for some time. The other girls start chiming in from where they were picked up. Three of the other girls were from the city. Two from Albany, and they both said they don't think they were in the van for very long, but can't be sure, then two from Baltimore. They were in the car the longest. There was a third with them, but she had a reaction to whatever they gave her and died before they made it here. The two girls watched as Andrei hauled her over his shoulder and threw her on the ground a few feet from the house like a pile of trash. Neither of the girls saw what they did with her after that.

Fucking animals.

Andrei said we were somewhere Nikolai doesn't know about, but we're still on the East Coast and most likely still in New York, though I suppose Viktor could have set something up anywhere. I'm not sure how far out of Boston we are since it was starting to get dark when they took me, and then it was pitch black when I woke up in the room before being carted to the basement. Viktor also told Andrei the buyers would be here in the morning, so that means it's possible it's before midnight, which also means we're only a few hours from Boston. Not that it will make much difference if no one knows where to look. The more I think about it, the more the dread creeps in. Eoghan has to know I'm missing by now, but what can he do if he's searching for a needle in a two-hundred-mile-radius haystack?

If we're going to get out of here, I need to think of something and fucking fast. In a few hours, my life and the lives of the other eight girls in this place are going to be sold to the kinds of people nightmares are made of.

I can't let that happen.

I won't.

But I have no clue how to stop it.

CHAPTER NINETEEN
EOGHAN

"WE HAVE ABOUT A three-hour drive," Finn says as we load into the large SUV. He pulls out his phone and fires off a text.

"Who are you texting?" I ask from the back seat where I'm sitting next to Jude.

"Enzo. Just letting him know if Alessia tries to open the safe room door, he has permission to tie her to a damn chair."

When we left her in the room, Finn wasn't entirely convinced she wouldn't try something and somehow stow away in the SUV or something. I can't exactly blame her, but I need Finn focused on Gemma, not worrying about his wife.

When Liam and Jude made it to Finn's house, Liam let us in on one of his mission objectives. He told us that he's been looking into Petrov for several years but hasn't found a way into his organization yet. From whispers and clues on the dark web, Liam knew Viktor was a major player in the sale of women.

"I thought you only worked with high-paying clients?" I asked him while he was going over some aerial images with Nikolai.

"It pays the bills and funds my other endeavors quite nicely," he informed me.

I'd say so. Liam is the man the rich and powerful call to help them with various jobs when the police or legal channels are of no use. And he charges accordingly. It's even been rumored he's involved himself with a coup or two over the last few years.

Before we left, Liam made a call to a doctor he knows in New York and to a few members of his team, who were given the coordinates to the safe house. They may not make it in time to go in and get my woman, but from What Nikolai says, the house they're at has been used as a meeting spot where some of his father's customers go to buy girls. It's entirely possible that Gemma isn't the only one there. His guys will make sure if there are other girls there, they'll be taken care of.

Nikolai and Liam are taking another one of my brother's SUVs since we don't know if or how many other girls are there. He let Nikolai know that as payment for helping him, he wanted all the information Nikolai has about his father's operations and the locations of safe houses he uses as a landing spot for the women he kidnaps and sells. Nikolai was all too happy to give him the information, seeing as one of the things he was adamant about was stopping the operations his father so gleefully raked in millions of dollars from.

Silence fills the SUV as I stare out the window, repeating the same thing over and over in my mind.

She's alive, she's alive, she's alive.

Her father wouldn't kill her. Not when he stands to make money from her or to still form an alliance with another family. It just doesn't make good business sense. But the things he could and probably is doing to her in the meantime have my blood boiling with rage. Even Jude isn't making his normal jokes or ribbing everyone in the silent car.

"A while back, I was in a similar situation with my woman," Jude says quietly beside me.

"I remember." He didn't call me for help, which I would have gladly given.

"There was never a point where failure was an option. Didn't matter what we were walking into, I didn't allow myself to imagine a scenario where we didn't get her back. And there's no chance we won't get your woman back, either."

I don't reply. Instead, I just keep my eyes on the passing scenery for the next two hours.

We will get her back, and before the dawn breaks, every motherfucker in that house will die.

We stop about a mile from the house and silently get out of the vehicles. Cillian opens the trunk of our SUV and reveals the secret compartment we have outfitted in several of our cars to hide the cache of weapons stored. Each of us grabs a vest and begin loading ourselves with various guns with suppressors attached, knives, and extra ammo. We're to kill these motherfuckers as silently as possible since

Liam informed us when we were back at Finn's that if these men are tipped off, they're likely to dispose of the women so as not to be identified if the women are rescued.

"I couldn't get a layout of the house, so we're going in completely blind," Liam tells us.

"There wouldn't be any plans for this house or records. It's completely off the grid," Nikolai says.

"I've gone in on less," Liam says. "The one thing we have on our side is the element of surprise. As far as Viktor's concerned, no one knows about this place. Typically, places like this will have some sort of basement or possibly an outbuilding where they keep the girls. No other buildings were detected on any of the satellite images, but there are a shit ton of trees that could be obstructing our view. Keep an eye out for any smaller structures as we approach."

We all nod as he continues, the five of us listening intently, considering it seems Liam has quite a bit of knowledge of what we're potentially walking into.

"There will likely be at least two exits from wherever they are keeping Gemma and any other girls that may be in there with them. One accessible from the house, and one accessible from the outside. I'd imagine there to be at least one man guarding the exit that leads directly outside, maybe two. Most of the men will be inside the house and a couple with the girls themselves. We have no idea how many men are on the property, but there were two cars, so we can count on at least four, probably more. These guys travel in pairs."

Liam meets the eyes of every man in front of him, and when they finally land on me, his lips tip up in a small grin.

"Let's go get your woman back."

We quietly make our way through the dense thicket of trees before Viktor's safe house is in view. We don't meet any of his guards on our way, but there are two standing on the front porch, enjoying a smoke. Liam signals for Finn and Cillian to go around back and check on things there. When they return, Finn informs us of another set of guards standing outside the back door. They aren't sure if the door leads to the basement or the house. We really don't know much, but that's fine with me. I'm ready to go in and start killing these assholes.

Liam nods at Jude and raises his gun, indicating for Jude to do the same.

"Just like South America," Jude whispers.

I'm not sure what that means, but the two men fire off a silent shot and each guard crumbles to the ground with a bullet between the eyes. We're all still for a beat, but when no one comes outside and no alarms seem to have been triggered by the dead guards, we proceed.

Low and fast, we rush the house, Nikolai and I taking the lead with the other four men at our back. We creep up the porch on soft but hurried feet. Pressing my ear to the door, I hear the soft murmur of the television but nothing else. I twist the handle and as soon as the door opens, I clock the man in the black leather recliner facing the television before his eyes swing to me. He doesn't have more than a chance to widen his eyes before I put a bullet between them.

Nikolai is right behind me when a man comes from the kitchen at the far end of the room and throws a knife, hitting the man in the throat. No sound is heard, though his mouth is open in a silent scream as he drops to the floor, and I put a bullet in his head, too.

I look to the right, where Nikolai's standing beside me.

"Fucking show-off," I mutter, and we make our way to the back of the house while Finn and Cillian have disappeared down the hallway to the left. When they come out, Finn raises one finger then slices it across his throat, signaling that one more dead guard is in the house.

I tilt my head toward the kitchen, and the six of us file past the dead man with Nikolai's knife protruding from his throat. There are two doors. When I stop at the first, the five men circle my back. I lift my gun and open the door. And come face to face with shelves of canned food, beans and rice.

"We found the pantry," Jude comments quietly.

That leaves only one option. I press my ear to that door but don't hear anything. If this is another pantry, I'm going to lose my shit.

We take the same formation, and I open the door. A set of stairs that lead to a black abyss at the bottom greets us.

It's fucking go time.

Taking the lead down the stairs, all of us step with light feet so as not to alert anyone of our presence. When we get to the bottom, the basement looks empty, but I spot two doors at the far end with a staircase in the middle. That must be the door that the other two guards, who at this moment are still alive, are guarding from the outside.

We're tucked within the shadows when one of the doors opens, and I see that fuck Andrei walk out of a room. Before he closes the door, my eye catches on something in the room. A corner of what looks like a chain-link cage. He opens the door of the room on the other side of the staircase and it's a poorly lit, dingy office. He doesn't notice our presence when he walks into the room and shuts the door behind him.

"We need to move this along, gentlemen. There's no telling when the other two guards are going to do a perimeter sweep and find their dead friends," Liam whispers in the silent basement. I nod and start walking toward the office. Placing my ear against the door, I listen for any sign of how many people could be in the office with Andrei.

"Yeah." I hear him say, then he's silent. "I'll let them know that something came up." Silence again. "It's fine. Viktor has to deal with the Italians, so I'm here to facilitate the transfer. We expect the buyers in the next hour." Silence again. "Okay. Bye." When I don't hear him talking to anyone else, I can only assume he's the only one in the office.

Turning around to the five men at my back, I raise one finger then tilt my head to the door. My hand goes to the knob, and I throw the door open, immediately raising my gun and pointing it at the asshole behind the desk. He looks up in surprise and tries to grab for the phone he was just talking on, but I rush forward and press the muzzle of my gun to his forehead.

"Not so fast, Andrei."

He leans back with his arms raised and spots the other men in the room. "You're all going to die for this. You think Petrov isn't going to come after every last one of you and take everything you love before killing you? Fucking fools." His eyes meet Nikolai's. "Your father knows you've betrayed him and his organization. There's nowhere you can hide where he won't find you."

"Let him come after me. I look forward to putting a bullet in him," Nikolai responds with a slight tilt to his lips.

The sound of a door opening and slamming shut breaks our attention from the man at the desk, and Jude and Liam whirl around.

"Andrei!" someone shouts from outside the room.

"Kill the girls!" Andrei shouts back before I fire my weapon and Andrei slumps in his seat with a bullet hole in his head.

Liam and Nikolai rush out of the office to stop the guard from carrying out Andrei's order. A loud bang echoes through the basement then several softer pops.

I charge out of the office to find a dead guard on the ground in front of the other door and Nikolai slumped against the wall, holding tightly to his left side.

"Fuck." I hurry over to Gemma's brother.

"I'm fine," he tells me, though I can tell he's anything but by the way blood is oozing from between his fingers.

The door at the top of the stairs between the two rooms opens again and another man comes flying down. Finn immediately opens fire on the man, peppering him with at least five bullet holes before he falls the rest of the way down the stairs and lands dead at our feet.

As far as we could tell before we walked in the house, that should be everyone, but whoever Andrei was talking to said that more men were going to be showing up in a matter of minutes. We need to be long gone before they get here.

I raise my gun and open the last door in the basement, having no clue if there's another guard in there. What I find chills me to my fucking bones. Cages. Four of them, two on each side of the room. And inside are women. Some of them scream when they see a man in the room with a gun, and some sit silently, staring at me with fear and resignation in their eyes. As though they've accepted their fate. They don't know who I am, just that they've been taken to be sold. In the last cage with two other women stands a blonde, relief warring with anger in her crystalline-blue eyes.

"I hope you shot that asshole Andrei," Gemma says as I lower my weapon and walk straight to her.

"Between the eyes, blondie."

"I would have aimed for the dick," she replies.

I look at the padlock holding the door together and grab the small lock pick set I brought with me before kneeling down and making quick work of the lock.

"I have a key," Jude calls as he rushes to the other three cages.

When I open the door, the other two girls rush out toward the door where Liam is waiting. He takes them out of the room, then Gemma throws herself in my arms.

She buries her head in my neck and lets out a gut-wrenching sob.

"Shh, I've got you. But we need to go."

Her tear-soaked face lifts to mine.

"Where else are you hurt?" I ask, examining the bruise on her face.

"This is it. Andrei fucking knocked me out when I tried to escape. Viktor"—she swallows hard—"he had my mom here. She's dead. He shot her right in front of me."

My arms tighten around her. "He wasn't here when we showed up. But Andrei was on the phone and said the buyers are on their way."

"Let's get the fuck out of here then."

We make our way past the two dead guards and up the stairs where Liam and Cillian are getting the girls into the two SUVs we saw.

"We can't take these. They could have trackers," I say to Liam.

"Relax. We're just going to take them to where we parked. These girls don't need to be traipsing through the forest and Nikolai needs to get to the doctor ASAP."

"Nikolai?" Gemma asks, looking at me.

"That's how we found you. His father didn't know he knew about this place. He was shot by one of the guards."

"Oh God, where is he?"

Liam points to one of the cars, and she rushes over. Just as she opens the back car door, a black SUV and a gunmetal-gray truck approach at breakneck speed. Finn, Cillian and I raise our guns, ready to shoot out the windows, when Liam calls over the loud rumble of engines.

"Relax, boys. Those are my guys."

The SUV and the truck slam into park and two men from each open the doors and exit their vehicles.

"You missed all the fun," Liam says to one of the men holding a medic bag. "He's over there." Liam points to the SUV Gemma ran to, where her brother is.

Without saying a word, the man jogs over and opens the door.

"What do we got?" one of the other men asks, approaching Liam and me.

"A shit ton of dead bodies and eight girls that were going to be sold. We're taking them and Petrov to the doc about an hour from here."

"Oh shit, what did you have to promise her to get her to help you after last time?"

"Fuck off, Hendrix, she loves me." Liam waves his hand at the tall man with long hair who's covered in tattoos.

"What about the buyers that are coming?" Hendrix asks.

A look passes between them, but I can't decipher it.

"Kingston can take Petrov to her. She likes him better anyways."

Liam stares at Hendrix for a beat then nods. "Okay. Let's get the girls and Nikolai to the other vehicles then we'll come back here. By my account, we don't have much time."

"I'll tell the guys to set it up like Mexico City?"

A chilling grin spreads across Liam's face. "Perfect."

My eyes swivel back and forth between the two men, still having no idea what the hell's going on.

"Mexico City?" I ask Liam when Hendrix walks away to relay the message to the other two guys.

"We're going to wait for the buyers. See if we can get some information then dispose of them accordingly," he tells me as Cillian makes his way over to us.

"Need some help?" Cillian asks.

Liam stares at Cillian for a beat then nods. "Go talk to Hendrix. He's the tall wanker with all the tattoos."

Cillian jogs over to the three men and grabs supplies from the back of the truck. I don't know what's in the duffel bags they're opening as Cillian nods at whatever directions they're giving him. Wait, are those bars of

C-4?

Finn walks over and looks at Cillian then back to Liam.

"Your man offered," Liam says, holding his hands in the air.

"Just see to it he makes it out alive," Finn says.

"We'll be an hour behind you." It doesn't go unnoticed to me that Liam doesn't make that promise to my brother.

Finn dips his chin then turns to me. "Let's go."

Chapter Twenty

Gemma

WHEN I OPEN THE door to the SUV I was probably brought here in, Nikolai's pale face greets me, with Jude on the other side of him, holding a bloody rag to his side.

"Jesus, you look like shit," I say and climb in.

A gun is sitting on his lap, which I take and place in mine.

"Are you okay?" he asks, his breathing labored.

"Better than you, by the looks of it." My eyes meet Jude, and his jaw tenses when he notices the bruise on my face.

"I'm sorry," Nikolai says. "I didn't realize our father was suspicious."

I shake my head. "Shh. It's not your fault. We're going to get you to a doctor and they'll patch you right up." I look to Jude again, but his face doesn't give anything away.

"He'll be fine. He's a tough-as-fuck Russian badass. Right, Petrov?"

Nikolai wheezes out a shallow laugh that doesn't exactly inspire confidence in me.

The door next to me is thrown open, and I don't recognize the man. Before he can get a word out, I grab the gun in my lap and point it directly at him.

"Whoa, whoa," Jude rushes out. "That's Kingston. He's part of my brother's outfit."

I don't lower the gun for a few moments as Kingston holds my stare. My nerves are fucking shot. I just watched my mother die in front of me and thought I was going to be sold as a sex slave and never see anyone I cared about again. My father is still out there, and my brother is sitting next to me, bleeding all over the fucking place. I don't know which way is up.

"Gemma, you can put the gun down. He's one of the good guys, I promise," Jude coaxes.

Are there good guys in this life? Is anyone actually safe?

I lower the weapon and stare at Kingston. He's not angry that I just had a gun trained on him. It's almost as though he could hear the thoughts that were racing through my head and was letting me work it out. Brave fucking man. *Or stupid fucking idiot.*

"Come over on this side," Jude says, and Kingston gently closes the door he was holding without speaking.

"Man of few words," I mumble, and Jude chuckles.

When he opens Jude's door, the biker slides out and Kingston takes a look at the wound. He pours something over it and Nikolai hisses.

"Slows the bleeding," Kingston comments, then places a bandage over the wound. "We need to go."

He gets out of the vehicle, and through the window, I see him walk over to speak to Liam as Finn and Eoghan make their way to us.

Finn jumps in the driver's seat and grabs the keys from the visor. "Hate the Russians, but appreciate the predictability," he says as he starts the SUV. Eoghan opens the door to the back seat, but Kingston walks up behind him and tells him he needs to sit in the front.

"Fuck that," Eoghan mutters.

He walks around the hood to my side and opens the door. "Slide over for a second."

I do as he asks, not that I can go far with my bleeding brother next to me. When he sits in the car, his arm goes around my waist and he hauls me onto his lap.

"There. Get in, Kingston."

The other man doesn't say anything as he hoists himself into his seat and Finn takes off, leaving Jude to drive the other SUV filled with the girls that were in the basement with me. We're only in the car for a few minutes before we arrive where they parked the vehicles they took here. Nikolai is looking worse than before, and I look at Kingston, who doesn't seem particularly bothered by his state. The bleeding seems to have stopped, but if I had to guess, I'd say he's going into shock.

The other girls pile out of one SUV and into the other with Jude again at the wheel. From wherever we're going, Kingston assures me he'll find places for the girls to go, either home or to a house they have set up for the girls who were working the streets before being picked up by Viktor's men. No one looks for missing prostitutes, he said, but he assured me if they want a way off the street, Liam has places set up for them so they can get a fresh start.

"We're a little less than an hour from the doc," Kingston tells Finn once we have Nikolai situated in the back. Then Kingston gives my brother a shot of something, and he seems to finally rest on our way to the doc.

Forty-five minutes later, we pull up to a nondescript farmhouse off a dirt road and I'm worried we're making another stop that we really don't have time for. A woman who looks to be a couple years older than me, wearing a pair of dark-blue scrubs, meets us on the front porch of the two-story white home.

"Was Liam too chickenshit to face me?" she asks Kingston when he opens the door.

"He's busy tying up some loose ends, Doc. We expect him in the next hour or so."

Kingston steps out of the way and the doctor takes a look at my brother and shakes her head. "Jesus. Get him inside. Courtney's in there and we have the OR prepped." Then she catches sight of the other eight women spilling out of the SUV Jude was driving. "Who are they?"

"Hitchhikers," Kingston says.

"Right," the doctor replies. "Liam is damn lucky Talia's with my mom for the night." She looks at the girls and sighs. "Alright, ladies, come on in. Mi casa es su casa, I guess."

Kingston meets my questioning gaze as I stare at the woman who has the bedside manner of a fucking rattlesnake.

"She's good at what she does, and we can trust her. That's all you need to worry about," he says before he and Jude haul my unconscious brother from the back seat and up the porch stairs.

When we get inside the house, the doctor walks us through what looks like your typical family home with flowery wallpaper and pictures of a little girl and the doctor, smiling and happy. Huh, so the scowl isn't permanent. Then we head to a set of stairs that leads to a basement. I stop at the top and stare down. There's a light at the bottom, and I hear two women talking with soft music playing. Even the steps are illuminated along the bottom, but I can't move. The last basement I was in, I thought life as I knew it was over. And in a way, I suppose it is.

"Blondie?" Eoghan asks behind me.

I'm safe. With Eoghan here, nothing bad is going to happen to me. I know all this in my head, but my damn feet still won't move.

"Do you want to wait in the living room with the other girls while I find out what's going on with your brother?"

I stand motionless at the top of the stairs for a few more moments, staring down them to the light I see at the bottom. *It's not the same stairs or the same house,*

Gemma.

I shake my head and exhale a long breath. "No."

"Okay. How about I go first?"

I offer Eoghan a weak smile and nod. When he grabs my hand and begins walking down to the basement, his grip keeps my mind rooted in the present instead of flying off to the last twelve hours. God, has it only been twelve hours since Viktor took me? The sun was just peeking over the horizon when we pulled up to the farmhouse, and the sun was setting yesterday when I left my office. One night. That's all it took for my life to change irrevocably.

There's a young girl at the bottom landing wearing a pair of cheery yellow scrubs that look wholly out of place after the night we just endured. She smiles at me with a clipboard in her hand.

"I'm Felicity, one of Dr. Lasher's nurses. Do you know your brother's blood type?"

I shake my head. Hell, I don't know anything much about the man. "No."

"That's okay. We have a lot of O-neg on hand," she says and notes something on her paper.

"I'm O-neg," Eoghan says. "Can I donate while I'm here?"

"Sure," Felicity says with a little bounce to her step as she walks away.

I take a moment and let my eyes wander around the basement of the house. It's the complete opposite of the one I was in earlier. The walls are stark white with a row of uncomfortable-looking plastic chairs against one side, just like the ones you would find in a regular hospital waiting room, and a metal desk sits on the other side of the room with several large filing cabinets behind it. Next to those are giant glass cabinets with all manner of vials and medical equipment inside. Jude and Kingston walk out of the door at the opposite end of the basement, which leads to where I assume the OR is that Dr. Lasher was talking about.

"How is he?" I ask Kingston when he and Jude step over to the metal sink in the corner and begin washing the blood from their hands.

"He'll be fine. Doc is prepping him for surgery now," Jude answers.

"Does she have everything she needs?" I find it hard to believe in a space so small, but I suppose looks can be deceiving.

"We aren't the only clients of the doc's. Or the only ones who donate to her cause. Trust me, there's nothing any other hospital would have that she doesn't. Hell, her stuff is probably top-of-the-line and more advanced compared to anywhere else." Kingston's comment inspires the barest of confidence in me.

Felicity comes back through the door to the OR with empty blood bags and a couple of those blue sterile packages in her arms.

"Ready?" she asks Eoghan in an upbeat voice.

He nods and squeezes my hand before letting go to walk to the large chair like you would see in a phlebotomist lab.

"Nikolai is going to have a little Irish in him, just like his sister," he jokes then shoots me a wink.

Jude coughs a laugh, and I send Eoghan a narrow-eyed look. "You're ridiculous."

"You love it, blondie."

Felicity gets to work getting Eoghan prepped, and Kingston makes his way up the stairs.

"Want to come and see what we can do for the girls?" Jude asks as the blood begins pouring into the bag. I can't take my eyes off it.

"No. I'm going to stay here with Eoghan," I reply.

"We'll be done in just a minute, then I'll come up and see what they need. Would you mind grabbing a few sets of scrubs in case any of the girls need them right away?" Felicity asks Jude.

It strikes me as funny as he takes a couple piles from the shelves next to the stairs that Little Miss Sunshine has no qualms about bossing around bikers or mobsters, in her own sweet way, of course. Makes me wonder what kind of people come through these doors.

When Eoghan's bag is full, she hands him a cookie and a little bottle of juice from the small fridge behind the desk. I laugh outright, watching him eat it and down the juice while she cleans up and takes the blood to the OR.

"What?" he asks with his mouth full, dusting the crumbs from his shirt.

The laughter immediately turns into sobs. God, I'm a fucking mess. My boyfriend is donating blood for the brother I still hardly know because he was shot rescuing me from our father's human trafficking operation. I've barely had a chance to get used to the idea of having a brother and he could very well be dying on a metal slab in an illegal OR run by a woman who I know nothing about.

"Come here." Eoghan opens his arms and I walk over to him, positioning myself on his lap before burying my face in the crook of his neck. I hear the door close and Felicity softly tells Eoghan to meet her upstairs when we're ready.

Once I have my emotions back under control, I raise my tearstained face to his and offer him a smile. "I'm sorry. I can't seem to get it together."

"You don't have to." His warm hands cup my cheeks as he stares into my eyes, imploring me to hear his words. "Not with me. It's only been a couple hours, Gemma. No one expects you to be some emotionless robot. Least of all me."

But I do. I shouldn't be freaking the hell out like I am. The bad guys are dead, except for Viktor. Everyone I care about is safe. My mother...I don't know how to process that one yet.

"Come on," I say, standing from his lap. "Let's go see what we can help with."

Liam and Cillian arrive at the house shortly after we've all sat down to eat. Thankfully, Dr. Lasher had a case of burgers in her freezer. Jude manned the grill outside, and the girls sat on the doctor's wooden deck under the breaking dawn. Some just picked at their plate and others gobbled the burgers down, even asking for seconds. I have no idea how long some of them were in the basement, and none of us have any clue what the next step is.

When Liam opened the back door and popped his head out to tell us he was here, the relief was evident on Jude's face. Finn looked at Liam with a question in his eyes.

"Cillian's in the living room. Everything was taken care of."

Jude and Finn head inside, probably to get a debriefing of what went down with the buyers when they showed up, but Eoghan stays on the back patio with me.

"You can go in if you want," I say, trying to not sound like that's the last thing I want and probably failing miserably.

"Nah, I'm good where I am," he replies, leaning back in the chair next to me.

We stare at the light-blue sky together in silence for

a few minutes, and the memories of yesterday before being taken swirl through my mind. The East Coast is all I've ever known. I can't imagine being away from Eoghan, but yesterday, my life took a turn I didn't see coming. The danger we're all living in has never been more apparent than it is now, sitting here with eight other women who were kidnapped from wherever they were. Liam and Cillian just got back from killing a group of people who buy women, for God's sake. My brother is still in surgery from a gunshot wound he got while rescuing me from our deranged father, who killed my mother in front of me. How is this my life? Do I even *want* this to be my life?

"Yesterday before I...was taken...Natalie came to see me in my office."

Eoghan's hand is still holding mine. Still keeping me tethered as his thumb gently runs back and forth across my hand as I stare at the sky.

"She had an offer for me, a really fucking good one." My gaze turns to Eoghan. "Her and Jean want to promote me to VP of marketing."

"That's amazing, blondie. Fuck, you deserve that," Eoghan says, leaning over and giving me a kiss. "I'm so damn proud of you."

"Thank you. There's a catch, though." I inhale a shaky breath before I continue. "It's in California. Not exactly sure where. Natalie and Jean are going out next week to look at properties. He wants something by the beach."

My eyes stay locked with Eoghan's while he processes

what I just told him. He isn't angry or sad. He still has a smile on his face, but I can tell it's somewhat forced. It breaks my heart that I'm even considering moving across the country, but after everything that happened in the last several hours, not to mention the fact that this is a huge opportunity that I worked tirelessly for, I can't *not* consider it.

The back door opens again before Eoghan has a chance to respond.

"Doc's out here with an update," Finn says, looking between me and his brother.

I get up first, and Eoghan follows me into the house. The doctor is waiting for us in the living room, where she seems to be having some sort of silent standoff with Liam. She looks pissed as hell, and he's smiling like the cat that ate the canary.

Liam turns his attention to us. "Oh good—just in time for the beautiful and ever-talented Dr. Lasher to give us an update on your brother."

"Don't think flattery is going to get you out of the enormous bill I plan on sending you, Liam."

"I'll gladly pay it, Doc. As I have many times before. I'll even throw in a bottle of your favorite wine. Do you still like that little winery in Italy?"

Her face turns beet red. "Do. Not. Bring up. Italy," she grits out.

I'm seriously concerned for Liam's safety while she stares at him with a violent promise behind her green eyes. He should probably watch what he says, considering she seems to be handy with a scalpel.

Dr. Lasher turns to me then, her face wiped of any emotion whatsoever. "Nikolai had a bullet in his spleen. I removed it and he'll be fine. I'll allow him to stay here for a day or two to make sure infection doesn't set in and keep him on IV antibiotics and pain medication, but after that, he needs to find a place to recover, preferably with someone who can help take care of him for the next week or two."

"He'll be staying with me," I say and she nods.

When she leaves, I fall into Eoghan before he wraps his arms around me.

"Everything will be fine, blondie. We'll get it all sorted."

I don't think he's only talking about my brother.

CHAPTER TWENTY-ONE
EOGHAN

"**B**RO, THAT'S FUCKING CHEATING, and you damn well know it," I holler at Nikolai, who's currently kicking my ass at the video game on Gemma's TV screen.

"Jesus, you're a sore loser," Nikolai comments from his spot on the couch opposite where I'm sitting in one of Gemma's chairs.

"Am I going to have to turn the TV off again?" Gemma says, walking up to me with her arms crossed over her chest.

"Sorry, *Mom*." I grab her around her waist and pull her onto my lap, nuzzling my face in her neck.

"That's just fucking weird, Eoghan," she chastises, and Nikolai laughs.

We've been home for a little over a week from the doctor, and we're staying at Gemma's. Everyone is still on edge because Viktor hasn't been caught, but Gemma refused to hide away when I told her it would be safer at my brother's or my penthouse until we found him. She refused to listen, saying there was no way in hell he was going to dictate where she lived or what she did. She did concede to keeping a guard in front of her apartment building. Not that I would have given her any sort of choice on the matter.

Gemma needs to feel in control of her life again after she felt like she had none when she was in that basement with those other girls. Finn is less than thrilled with us not being more protected here, but I reinstalled the app I had on my phone that's connected to a camera, so I have a full view of anyone who comes to her door.

We've been trying to act like life is normal, and for the most part, it is, but there's a low-lying tension that won't go away until we catch Viktor. Nikolai has been in contact with everyone who's loyal to him in their organization, which, at this point, isn't many. He's going to have a hell of a bloody time when he emerges from this apartment as the new head of the New York Bratva, but that's not going to happen until Viktor is put to ground. Too many people are still loyal to his father, including some of Nikolai's own men apparently, and without a clear new boss, they aren't switching alliances. Nikolai was prepared for that, which is why the endgame was to always kill Viktor. There's no other path to power for him.

Gemma hasn't gone to work since Nikolai has been here, either. She told her boss her mother passed, which was true, but she didn't go into details. Not that she could have or should have. The first few days were a little awkward between Gemma and Nikolai, neither of them knowing how to act. She was playing nursemaid, which doesn't come naturally to her, and he felt like he was imposing. The two of them still need to find their groove as brother and sister, but it's getting better. There have been a few mornings in the last week that I've come out from the bedroom and the both of them were sitting on the couch with cups of coffee in their hands, talking and getting to know each other. What breaks my heart is that they've been bonding over having fucked-up parents. Gemma has told him a few things about her childhood that had my blood pressure spiking, and Nikolai would look at her with sadness and understanding in his eyes. Fucking guts me.

"Has your mom tried to contact you?" Gemma asks Nikolai.

The first night he was here, she tried to call, worried that she hadn't heard from her husband or her son, asking where he was. He declined to answer. Later, he told us he figured out a long time ago that his mother would often get information from him and go back to his father with it, resulting in a punishment from Viktor.

"No. She's probably been in contact with him already. If she calls again, it will only be to find out where I am to tip him off, which she isn't likely to do. I have a feeling my mother knows her tricks no longer work on me."

"Do you think your father will do something to her?" Gemma doesn't seem particularly concerned, just curious.

"Doubtful. I know for a fact she's put safeguards in

place. If he takes her out, he goes down with her. My father hasn't always been completely honest with his business partners, and my mother knew where to look. Trust me, if anything happens to her, we won't be the only ones looking for Viktor."

"Maybe it would be easier to have a little birdie whisper in his business partners' ears than deal with it ourselves," I say.

Nikolai shakes his head. "I thought about that. If we do that, it gives them a chance to destabilize our organization, then gives them the opportunity to come in and take over. I'd rather handle it myself. My father's men will only respond to strength and brute force. If they think I can't handle it, they'll never fall in line."

He makes a good point.

One of the reasons I agreed to stay at Gemma's was to give Viktor the impression we weren't as protected as we would be in my brother's fortified penthouse like I originally wanted. He's more likely to try to pull something here where he thinks he has a shot at getting away with it. But the waiting and anticipation is fucking killing me.

We haven't left the apartment since picking up Nikolai from Dr. Lasher's house—or should I say meeting a decked-the-fuck-out ambulance there, courtesy of Liam. Nikolai was still in rough shape, so it helped Gemma's nerves when Kingston and Liam showed up at the doc's in that elaborate ride. The point of staying here is so Viktor has to come to us. I'm not sure if he knows Nikolai is here with us, but Gemma is a big enough target to draw him out. Do I love the idea of using my woman as bait? *Fuck no*. But that's why I also have three of my guys staying in the empty apartment next door.

"It's about time for me to go to bed," Gemma says, lifting herself from my lap. When she walks into the bedroom, Nikolai is spearing me with the hardened gaze he's known for in some of the less-than-savory circles we both traverse. It's uncanny how much it resembles Gemma's, given they didn't grow up together. Obviously, when she does it, it makes my heart beat faster. All Nikolai's does is make me laugh.

"Don't give me that shit, Petrov. My brother is Finn Monaghan, and I share a bed with your sister. I'm immune to the intimidating powers of that particular look."

"What are your intentions with my sister since you brought her up?"

I never realized before this moment how happy I was when I thought Gemma was an only child.

"Your sister is the one steering this ship. Why don't you ask her?"

"She told me about her promotion."

Yeah, that's not something we've talked about much. Or at all. Having Nikolai here hasn't given us much opportunity, and honestly, I'm being a fucking chickenshit. The offer is amazing, and I would be an asshole to ask her to pass it up and stay here with me. I can't exactly run our bars and money laundering or the fight nights from California. We've been living in limbo, busying ourselves with working from the confines of her apartment so Viktor has less of a chance of catching us alone then falling into bed with each other every night.

"If she takes it, would you let her go?" Nikolai prods.

A huff of laughter escapes me. "What gives you the impression I *let* Gemma do anything? It's like you haven't met her."

I would support her decision. It would fucking kill me if she left, but I would never stand in her way. At least, that's what I'm telling myself.

"If I had what you two have, I wouldn't so easily let something like that go."

"Okay, Nikolai, I've had about all the relationship advice from you I can take. It would break my heart if she chose California. Of course it would. But there's nothing I can do to stop her if that's what she decides."

"If you can't think of something that would keep her here, maybe you don't deserve her."

Anger boils to the surface, and knocking him the fuck out like I wanted to do the first time he was in her apartment is starting to sound like a damn fine idea. "Oh, fuck off with that bullshit. What do you suggest I do, chain her to me so she can't get on a plane? I don't have control over her, nor would I want it. One of the things I love most about that woman is her fiercely independent spirit. I'm not going to try to take that away."

"It's not about taking her independence. It's about giving her what she truly wants. What she's been searching for her entire life. It's about giving her a reason to stay."

"Since you seem to know her so fucking well after knowing her for two goddamn weeks, why don't you tell me what that is?" I'm trying to keep my voice down since the woman we're speaking about is in the other room.

He gives me a knowing look that absolutely does nothing but serve to piss me the hell off even more. "Well, like you said, I haven't known her that long. Sounds like it's something you'd have a better chance at figuring out."

He rises from the couch and dips his chin. "I'll see you in the morning." Nikolai goes to his room and shuts the door, leaving me to face all the thoughts I'd been too scared to think about. I love that woman more than the air in my lungs, but what can I promise her more than a life of living with a criminal and potentially being caught in the crosshairs once again?

When I make it into our bedroom, Gemma is lying on her side, facing me with her eyes closed. Her face is illuminated by the soft glow of the lamp on her nightstand. In the last few weeks, the only time I see her relaxed is when she's either asleep or I've just made her scream my name. Otherwise, tension, no matter how hard she tries to hide it, creases the lines on her face.

Once this is over, she'll finally be free. Maybe starting over is what's best for her. Maybe getting away from Boston and this life will finally give her the peace she deserves after everything she's had to deal with in the thirty years she's been on this planet. No one could fault her for wanting a fresh start on the West Coast. Beats the shit she's had to put up with on this one.

Her eyes flutter open, and a soft, sleepy smile stretches across her lips.

She raises a hand to me, and I take it in my palm, kissing the top.

"Come to bed," she whispers in a tired voice.

I let go of her hand, reach for the collar of my shirt and pull it over my head before dropping it to the ground. My jeans are next, followed by my black boxer briefs. I'm already half-hard from the hungry look on Gemma's face and the way her makeup-free cheeks blush a bit while she appreciates my naked form. She lifts the satiny sheet from her body, and her pajamas are nothing more than a loose tank top so thin I can easily make out her hard nipples through the white fabric. Who needs sexy lingerie when I have a woman that looks this fucking tempting in an old tank?

I lean in and kiss Gemma, letting my tongue slide into her mouth as I push her onto her back with the weight of my body. When her thighs wrap around my middle, I grind my hard cock into her center, not sliding inside of her but putting pressure on her clit as our tongues play. Her nails score up my back, and a deep groan vibrates within my chest while my fingers tangle in her blonde strands.

I break the kiss but keep my mouth mere millimeters from hers so we're sharing the same air, breathing each other in and out.

"Fuck, you're so wet for me already," I whisper as I continue to glide myself over her drenched pussy, hitting her clit with the head of my cock over and over. "Could I make you come like this? With nothing but my cock on your little clit?"

Her whimper is the only answer she gives.

"Or do you want me to fill your pussy? Feel me sliding so deep inside you with every stroke. Would you like that? Make you come around my cock so hard that you soak these fucking sheets?"

"God, yes. Please," she groans.

"Shh. You have to be quiet." My lips find hers again and she opens. God, her mouth tastes like the sweetest heaven. I can't imagine ever craving someone's taste the way I constantly crave hers.

I lift my hips and thrust inside her, sheathing myself in her tight heat. Her moan vibrates into my mouth, and I swallow that one down and all the others that follow as I slowly move in and out, going deeper and deeper with each thrust. It doesn't take long before I'm teetering on the edge of release. She feels too damn good with nothing between us. It's taking every ounce of control I possess to not spill inside her right fucking now. When her walls begin to ripple with her impending orgasm, I rip my mouth away and press my sweat-slicked forehead against hers.

"Fucking strangle me, baby. I need to get there. Fuck, blondie, I can't hold back."

My cock jerks inside of her as pulse after pulse of pure pleasure has my vision going hazy around the edges. Gemma cries out, her pussy tightening like a silken fucking vise grip as I seat myself deep inside her, her rippling walls pulling every last drop from me.

I'm lying on top of her, probably crushing her into the mattress, but I can't find it in myself to care, needing to be as close to her as I can possibly get. Always needing her. The words *I love you* and *don't leave me and go to California* are on the tip of my tongue, but I don't allow them to fall from my lips. We need to have a rational conversation about it, and after what has to be one of the most intense orgasms of my life, now isn't that time. I don't want her to think I'd ever manipulate her with orgasms and hollow *I love yous* just to keep her here. I was serious when I told her brother she was steering this ship. No matter how much I want to beg on my hands and knees that she chooses me, it has to be a choice she makes on her own. I want to make sure if she chooses me, there're no regrets. I never want her looking back, thinking she was backed into a corner or any such nonsense.

"I hear the wheels turning," she whispers as her fingers glide up and down my back, causing goose bumps to erupt in their wake.

Kissing her lips softly once more, I pull out of her and groan at the loss of contact. "Blondie, I think you fucked my wheels right off." She giggles at my half joke, half lie and doesn't press it further. Even if I tried to talk to her about it right now, everything is too jumbled in my head to make sense.

I roll onto my back and pull Gemma so she's lying over my chest. "Light on or off?"

"On, please."

It breaks my heart a little that she still needs that light on, even with me and Nikolai here, but I stay silent and wonder if there will come a day when she feels safe in Boston again.

We've been asleep for a few hours when the chirping of my phone rouses me from my light slumber, and it takes another second for me to realize it's the sound I have set to the app for the camera pointed at Gemma's front door.

Someone's outside.

I grab my phone and sit up, pulling up the app. I see a man wearing a baseball cap dressed in what looks to be some sort of maintenance uniform. Grabbing my jeans from the floor, I slide them on and shove my feet into the boots next to the bed before opening the nightstand drawer to retrieve my 9mm.

"Gemma, wake up." She turns over and sits up, immediately standing to lean around me as I watch the video feed of the person ducked in front of her door trying to pick her lock. We have a chain, but that'll be easily taken care of by the pair of bolt cutters I see sitting next to the man.

Gemma flips herself to the other side of the bed and opens the drawer on her nightstand, grabbing the revolver she's had stashed in there since Viktor showed up.

"Get dressed and stay in the bedroom."

I dart from her room and run across the hall, throwing Nikolai's door open. He jerks upright with a gun already in hand.

"We've got company."

I walk out to the living room, Nikolai right behind me, and watch the person on the other side of the door open it a crack before the bolt cutters come into view. Nikolai and I aim toward the door and hear the snap of the chain before it opens farther. My eyes meet Viktor's for a split second before he charges at me, knife in hand and rage on his pale face. My training in the gym means I'm quick on my feet, and I sidestep him at the last second, sending him tumbling over the coffee table. The knife is still in his hand as he flips onto his back with his arms at his sides. Before he can make a move, my foot stomps on his wrist, causing the knife to fall from his grasp as I feel the satisfactory pop of his bones beneath my foot. Nikolai walks up behind me, both of us with our guns trained on Viktor. His father's glare darts between us. He knows there's no way in hell he's getting out of this one.

"Who's with you?" Nikolai asks.

Viktor stays silent.

Nikolai shakes his head and pulls a suppressor from his pocket, attaching it to the barrel of his gun. Once he's finished, he points it at Viktor's thigh and shoots.

One quick howl of pain is all Viktor allows himself before he clamps his mouth shut.

"I'll let him fill you with lead all fucking night, Viktor," I say. "Answer the man's question."

His eyes are ablaze with hatred when he stares at me. "No one," he grits out from his clenched jaw. "They're my children. My mess to clean up."

I turn to Nikolai. "Do you think he's lying?" My booted foot digs into his wrist that much harder.

"No. He's thought himself untouchable for years. There's no doubt in my mind he thought this was going to be a quick in and out."

"You ungrateful little shit. You had everything handed to you, and this is how you repay me? I gave you *everything!*"

Nikolai points his gun at Viktor's other leg and fires. This time, his bleeding father cries out in pain over and over.

"Wrong. You took everything. Now I'm going to return the favor."

Just then, Gemma comes out of the bedroom with her

gun pointed at her father on the floor. She takes in the scene and walks right over to Viktor, kicking him in the side of the head like it's a fucking soccer ball, knocking him out cold.

"Get this piece of shit out of my apartment," she commands, staring at his unconscious, bleeding body with disgust curling her kiss-swollen lips.

"I know just the place." I grab my phone from my pocket to dial my brother.

"Yeah?" he answers on the second ring.

"I'm going to be making use of your kill room. Thought you might want in on the fun."

"I'll be right there."

Chapter Twenty-Two
Gemma

WE PULL INTO THE underground parking of Finn's penthouse. I was a little worried about Viktor waking on the way over here, but Nikolai assured me the little night-night shot he gave him would keep him under with plenty of time to spare. When the car stops underneath the building, our headlights point toward Finn and Alessia, standing arm in arm in front of the elevator door. Eoghan wasn't totally on board with me coming here with him, but there was no chance in hell I was going to miss this, and since I'm here, Alessia has insisted on being here with me.

Eoghan pops the trunk before exiting the vehicle, and I follow. Alessia walks up to my door and wraps me in a hug.

"It's almost over," she says quietly, and I nod, returning her embrace.

We walk around to the trunk and the five of us stare inside at the unconscious man who's responsible for so much fear and weeks of sleepless nights. At least for me, and in turn, probably Eoghan as well.

"How many bullets does he have in him?" Finn asks.

"Only two," Eoghan replies. "Plus, he's definitely concussed from Gemma kicking him in the head."

"You were out there when he broke in?" Alessia asks, turning her worried gaze to me.

"No, I was in the bedroom just like Eoghan asked. I was a good girl and followed directions." Eoghan scoffs next to me, and I shoot him a withering look. "I came out after Nik had already shot him, and they had him on the ground."

"Let's get this piece of shit inside," Finn says, nodding at two of the guards who are always here. There's a bunch of shit around here that even I don't know about, so this place is never left unattended.

They reach into the trunk and haul Viktor out, one grabbing him under the arms and the other grabbing his ankles.

"He looks so...weak. Like he's someone's drunk uncle they're carrying to bed," I say as I watch them take him through a door to the right of where we parked.

Alessia looks at me with raised brows. "Are you in shock?"

Am I? I shrug because it's entirely possible I'm losing my ever-loving mind at this point. I'm about to watch my father be murdered, probably tortured a bit beforehand, and I can't find it in myself to care one bit.

"We can go upstairs and wait for them to finish," Alessia offers, but I shake my head.

"No. I'm not sitting around waiting for them to tell me it's done. I need to see him take his last breath."

A look of understanding passes between the two of us. Alessia knows better than to argue with me, so she simply takes my hand and leads me into the room on the other side of the door.

One thing I never imagined in my entire life is what a kill room looks like. It kind of reminds me of those cop shows where there's a dark room with a two-way mirror facing a brightly lit white room with a chair in the middle. There're a couple folding chairs on this side and a tray of various instruments used for all sorts of gruesome things, I'm sure, on the other. The guards set Viktor on the chair and cuff his hands behind his back and his ankles to the metal.

Eoghan stands next to me and Finn is next to Alessia, but Nikolai is on the other side of the open doorway in the room with Viktor, staring at the man. Though I can't see his face, the hatred he feels is almost a tangible thing, with his body tense as though he's ready to attack at any moment. I have a feeling the torture part of this little show is going to go quickly. Nikolai doesn't look like he can handle his father taking many more breaths.

Eoghan turns to me, and I face him, our eyes locking. His hand cups my cheek before he rests his forehead against mine. "Are you sure you don't want to go upstairs?"

"No." My voice is firm. "I want to see the monster die."

Eoghan nods and kisses my forehead, holding his lips there for a few still moments. Then he releases me and steps through the door. Finn kisses Alessia briefly and follows his brother.

The door closes, but we can still hear everything they're saying, thanks to the speaker above the glass.

"Here," Finn says, holding a syringe to Eoghan. "Shoot this into his neck."

Eoghan takes the needle and does as instructed. The second he pulls the empty syringe from Viktor's body, the man wakes with wide eyes, immediately struggling against the restraints.

"Don't waste your energy, Viktor. You aren't leaving this room." Finn's voice is hard as he stares at my father.

Viktor takes in the scene around him. Eoghan is standing in front of him, with Finn next to the table filled with various items meant to inflict pain, and Nikolai is still standing next to the closed door, staring at our father.

Viktor's face contorts into an evil sneer when his eyes lock on Eoghan. "You think you're scaring me, boy? I was torturing our enemies for sport before you were a gleam in your whore mother's eyes."

Eoghan rears his fist back and plows it into Viktor's mouth.

The asshole chuckles. "Fucking mama's boy. You're weak," he says before spitting bloody saliva from his bleeding mouth.

"My mother is as close to a saint as I'll ever meet, but you insulting her doesn't piss me off. I just felt like hitting you." Eoghan is cool as can be, seemingly unbothered by anything that comes out of Viktor's mouth.

"What a disappointment you turned out to be," Viktor says, turning his attention to Nikolai, who, up until now, hasn't moved from his spot. "You going to let this Irish scum steal your glory? Come on, pull out that gun in your waistband and shoot me already. Get it over with. Or are you too much of a pussy to follow through?"

Only the side of Nik's face is visible from where I'm standing at the glass, but what I see chills me to the bone. A smile that holds murderous intent spreads across his face as he walks to the table Finn is standing next to.

"You used those words often when I was growing up. I'm a *pussy*, I'm *worthless*. Always telling me what a disappointment I am." He picks up a mean-as-hell-looking knife from the table and turns toward Viktor, examining the blade. "Yet I'm standing here, and you're tied to a chair, Viktor, trying to get me to end your life." Nik shakes his head. "Give me a hand?" he asks Eoghan before handing him a pair of clamps. Eoghan takes them and follows Nik to stand in front of our father. Nik grabs Viktor's face, roughly squeezing his thumb and pointer into Viktor's cheeks to separate his jaw. When his mouth opens, Eoghan shoves the clamp into his mouth and pulls his tongue out, dropping the clamp so it rests on Viktor's chin.

Nik grabs the rubberized handle and pulls his tongue taut. "I'm tired of your words, Viktor." He takes the knife and, with quick efficiency, detaches it from Viktor's body as blood pours from Viktor's mouth over his chin, drenching the front of his maintenance uniform.

I should feel sick to my stomach watching them torture a man in front of me. I should be running out of this room screaming. I've never been a part of this world, never wanted to. But I don't do anything except watch my brother exact retribution for the years of abuse thrust upon him by the man sitting in that chair. There's a sweet sort of justice to this whole thing, and it doesn't frighten me.

Viktor groans loudly as he fights to stay conscious, or maybe he wants to pass out. Maybe he's willing his body to give out on him. It's not like he hasn't already lost a lot of blood. The human body can only take so much, after all. But Nikolai isn't done.

He walks back over to the table and smiles when he sees something. He lifts the cattle prod from the metal table and smiles at Viktor, who's barely holding on at this point.

"You used to tell me stories of the old country. How your father would torture men for days with electrocution. Killing them and bringing them back to life over and over." Nik walks over to our father and stares down at him. "I don't think you have more than a few minutes, but let's see how this works." He turns the prod on and shoves it between Viktor's legs. I look at Eoghan, who winces and moves his hand in front of his crotch. Hell, I have the urge to do the same.

When he pulls it away, it takes Viktor a few

moments to stop twitching. He's passed out. Probably on the brink of death when Nikolai grabs him by his sweat-soaked gray hair and yanks his head up. Viktor's eyes blink open and Nik presses the barrel of his gun to his father's forehead. "I'll see you in hell," he spits at the man with years of hatred coating every word.

Then he pulls the trigger.

Nikolai lowers the gun to his side and turns for the doorway, opening the door and walking into the room where Alessia and I just watched as he finally got the revenge he so desperately needed for the murder of his girlfriend and unborn child. He doesn't say anything, doesn't look at me as he walks out the other door that leads to the garage.

Eoghan walks out of the room and right up to me, taking me in his strong arms, breathing deeply as he nuzzles his face into the crown of my head.

"Go check on your brother, blondie."

I nod and kiss him before turning and following Nik out to the empty garage, save for the two guards who are standing on the other side of the gate, keeping an eye on the street in front of Finn's building.

"You okay?" *God, that's a stupid fucking question, Gemma.* "Of course you're not," I mutter, wanting to smack my palm over my face.

"You know," Nikolai starts, staring at the cement block wall on the other side of the garage. "Our child would have been twelve yesterday."

"Oh, Nik." I place my hand on his arm and squeeze.

"I'm so sorry. I had no idea."

"I'm afraid that one day I'm going to forget their birthday. That the day will pass without anyone acknowledging the life that never was."

"It won't. Now that I know, I won't forget."

Nik offers me a sad smile and places his hand over mine.

"Did it help?" I ask, nodding toward the door.

Nik shrugs but doesn't answer. "Did it help you?"

He's talking about getting revenge for my mother's murder. For all the horrible things that man put me and so many people through.

"I'm not sure. But I'm not sad he's gone. I don't regret what happened in there," I reply.

"Sylvie was the love of my life. She may not have liked what I did in there, but she would have understood it. She accepted who I was and the things I did. She loved me in spite of it." He turns and faces me, his eyes boring into mine. "Eoghan looks at you the way I looked at Sylvie. You don't find that twice in a lifetime."

He's right. You don't. I can't believe I found it at all in the first place. Especially with the brash and cocky Irish mobster who I tried to shake for months. I should have known there was a reason I was trying so hard to convince myself he couldn't be anything more than a fun lay. Somewhere in the back of my mind, I knew that if I opened my heart to Eoghan Monaghan, he'd come in like a fucking wrecking ball and turn my world on its axis. What I didn't realize was how happy I'd be to let him.

"I think it's time for me to head back to New York," Nik says, startling me out of my thoughts.

"Right now?"

He smiles, and it's lighter than the tense one he was wearing just a few moments ago. "You think Eoghan will mind me borrowing his car?"

A laugh bubbles from my throat. "I'll smooth it over."

Nikolai nods and we walk over to the driver's side of the car we took here.

"Tell Eoghan and Finn thank you for me."

I dip my chin and he gets behind the wheel, the keys already inside. When he drives toward the gate, the guard nods as Nik drives through and turns right toward the highway.

The door opens behind me, and I turn my head, seeing Eoghan, Finn and Alessia walk out.

"Did your brother just steal my car?" Eoghan asks, looking toward the street.

"Yup." I turn toward him and wrap my arms around his middle. His arms immediately go around my shoulders, and I rest my forehead against his chest. "I'm fucking exhausted," I say, but my voice is muffled.

"Come on. We'll borrow one of Finn's cars and head to my penthouse."

Eoghan steps away, and Alessia takes his place. "You okay?"

"I'm...I don't know what I am," I reply honestly.

Alessia pulls me into a hug before Eoghan starts his

brother's car. "I'll call you tomorrow," she says, then steps back into her husband's waiting arms.

It takes us less than a minute to get to Eoghan's penthouse which is only a block over from his brother's. I feel like a walking zombie as he leads me to the elevator that opens into a spacious loft with exposed brick along the walls and plush, dark furniture dotted throughout.

"Did you and your brother have the same decorator?" I ask, taking in the similarities between the two penthouses.

"Yeah. Our mother."

I laugh as he takes my hand, leading me up the staircase to a loft bedroom. The bed is huge and framed in dark metal with black sheets. You know, typical bachelor shit.

"I need a shower," Eoghan says and walks into the large bathroom to the left. When he turns on the light, the white marble is almost blinding, paired with the stainless steel faucets and towel rack. He leans into the massive walk-in shower and turns it on. It only takes a few moments for steam to build in the bathroom, making me feel like we're in our own private little cocoon.

Eoghan strips me out of the oversized T-shirt and yoga pants I put on before we left my apartment, then rids himself of his own clothes. I walk in the shower first and let the hot water rinse the tension from my body before stepping out of the way to share the water with him.

The shampoo and conditioner I use at my apartment, along with the same body wash, sits on the seat in his shower. When I turn to Eoghan, he shrugs.

"I knew I'd get you to come home with me at some point. Figured I should have the shit you like here." He grabs me by the waist and turns us so I'm the one under the spray before picking up the shampoo and pouring a generous amount in his hand. "Come here." Eoghan rubs the shampoo into my hair, massaging my scalp and running his hands through my long strands before instructing me to tilt my head back to rinse the suds from my hair. He repeats the process with the conditioner, gliding his fingers through my slick locks. A groan of pleasure escapes me, and Eoghan pinches my ass. My eyes pop open, shooting him an annoyed glare.

"Careful, blondie. You know what those noises and that look do to me." He gives me one of his cocky little grins then steps back under the spray, washing himself with my body wash.

Leaning against the shower wall, I'm overcome by that smirk I've seen a hundred times. I used to hate it, at least I thought I did, but now I know what it means. That I'm the center of his world. It's not a look he shares with anyone else, and neither is the heart he holds in his chest.

"I love you," I say and Eoghan turns to face me, his breathtaking smile turned up brighter than any damn sun. "I'm not taking the job in California." I wasn't planning on saying that, but now that I have, it feels so right. Like a weight has been lifted from me. That weight was the idea of leaving Eoghan. "I might be out of a job soon, so there's every chance I'm about to become a kept woman, but I don't care. I can't imagine life without sleeping next to you every night or waking up without you. Or not going to your bars to see a band play and getting lost in the music for a few hours. Or watching your mom and brother give you shit at Sunday brunch. I can't imagine missing any of it." Eoghan stares at me, and all of a sudden I'm feeling a tad self-conscious that I just bared my heart to him, and he's simply standing there staring at me. "Are you going to fucking say something?"

Eoghan laughs, then presses me into the wall with his large body, his hands going to my cheeks to cup my face and tilt it toward his. "I sure as fuck am." He leans in and places a soft kiss to my lips. "I love you, too. And I'm glad as hell you aren't moving across the country. Saves me the trouble of having to track you down and steal you back to my penthouse until you promise to never leave me again."

I bark out a laugh. "Jesus. Stalker much?"

Eoghan smiles and leans down, speaking against my lips. "You have no idea," he says before pressing his lips to mine.

I immediately open for him, and it doesn't take more than a few seconds before the kiss becomes a passionate dance of tongues, teeth, and loud moans. He trails his mouth from my neck, sucking the water that flows over my breasts until he's on his knees in front of me.

"I want to hear you scream that you love me while I make you come with my mouth. Then I'm going to take you to bed and sink so deep inside of you that you won't be able to walk tomorrow. Then I'm going to do it all over again."

"How about instead of telling me what you're going to do, you show me?"

Eoghan shakes his head, the corner of his lips tilted up. "That fucking mouth."

"You love it."

"Damn right," he says, taking a long lick through my center and groaning at the taste of me on his tongue. "Now, let's get started."

Epilogue

Gemma

Three Months Later

"Thank you all so much for being here with us to celebrate. Aubine wouldn't be where it is today without each and every one of you, and I know damn well we're going to absolutely crush it in California. And added bonus, no one will have to listen to Jean lament about the Boston winters for the entire month of February." The crowd laughs and Natalie raises her glass. "Cheers."

I take a sip of champagne with Eoghan standing next to me and Alessia and Finn on my other side.

"Jesus Christ, lady, you're going to poke my eye out with that rock if you're not careful," Alessia says as she sets her glass down on one of the tall cocktail tables Natalie had brought into the conference room at Aubine.

It's Friday night, and on Monday, Natalie and Jean are headed to Beverly Hills to set up the new offices for Aubine Couture. When I told her I couldn't leave Boston, and I understood if she and Jean needed to find someone else who was willing to relocate, she laughed in my face and told me there was no one who would ever bring to the table what I'm capable of bringing. Instead, they decided to move the couture side of the business to California, and I'd stay here and head the ready-to-wear side from Boston. She also mentioned this little thing called air travel and said if Jean's needed here for appointments, he can always fly back, but the couture clients were damn well rich enough to fly themselves to the West Coast for fittings.

I look down at the diamond on my left hand and thank my lucky fucking stars again that Natalie is the amazing boss that she is. I didn't want to choose between love and my career, not that it wasn't decided the night Viktor took his last breath.

Two months after that night, Eoghan got down on one knee in the middle of The Celtic Cross while the band was on break and proposed. Alessia and Finn were there with us, and my best friend broke down in the happiest tears I've ever seen. Underneath that tough exterior, the woman is a romantic softy. Or it could have been the hormones.

"Wait, you better not be drinking champagne with my little niece or nephew in there," I scold, pointing to her flat stomach.

"Relax. Finn brought a very fine vintage of sparkling grape juice."

"Only the best for my wife," he says from the other side of her.

"Peanut is safe and sound tucked in there," Alessia says, rubbing her stomach.

She was scared as hell when she told me she was pregnant. It's been a sore subject for years. But that was a different time with a completely different man, one who had no chance in hell of ever hurting her again. Finn saw to that. Then she started crying, saying she was going to be as big as a whale when Eoghan and I walked down the aisle. I assured her we were in no rush, and since I didn't know anyone with kids, I'd wait for hers to be the flower girl or ring bearer. Eoghan grumbled about not wanting to wait years to make me a Monaghan, but I shot him a look, and he shut right the hell up. I love that man to hell and back, but I'll be damned if anyone makes my best friend cry.

I turn to Eoghan, and he's wearing a smile on his face as he looks between Alessia and me. It's one I've seen a few times since she told us that she was pregnant.

"Wipe the grin off your face, Eoghan. You aren't knocking me up anytime soon."

"Who said anything about getting you pregnant?" he asks innocently.

"Your mother would have an absolute conniption if we weren't married before I got pregnant, and since that's still a ways off, you can get those thoughts right out of your head." Marriage is one thing. Kids are a whole other ballgame that I am far from ready for.

"So, you're saying if I knock you up, you'll have to marry me sooner?"

"Are you saying you'd trap me into marriage?" I arch my brow, throwing him a look that says he had better be real fucking careful how he answers.

"I would never take away your choice or consent in the matter. I'm simply considering our options if it were to happen."

"You're fucking ridiculous."

"And you love me."

"Yeah, got me there." I smile and lean in to give him a soft kiss on the mouth.

When I pull away, I see Finn look down at his phone. "It's Cillian. I'll be right back."

He walks away, and I turn to Alessia. "Cillian hasn't been around much."

"He's been doing some work with Liam. I think he's in New Orleans right now."

I shrug, not wanting to ask any questions. Eoghan tells me what he thinks I need to know, but I don't need the ins and outs of anything. My life isn't wrapped up in their business. I have my hands full as the new VP of marketing for Aubine ready-to-wear.

Finn returns and kisses Alessia on the cheek.

"Everything okay?"

He nods and looks at Eoghan. "Seems he's on his way home with a stowaway."

Eoghan's brows draw down in question. "Who?"

"Didn't say. Just that she needed a ride to Shine. Apparently there's some connection with her and the Black Roses, and he did not sound happy about it."

Sounds like someone finally got under the man's tough as hell armor.

Eoghan shrugs, then turns to me before grabbing me by the waist and lowering his mouth to my ear. "How long do we have to stay? I haven't been inside of you since last night."

I laugh and try to push him away, but he doesn't budge. "You're a brute."

"Why? Because I want to spread your legs and lick you until you come on my face?"

"Shh. *Jesus.*" I look around but no one is paying us any mind. Well, except for my best friend, who's standing next to me with a smirk on her face.

"Come on, blondie. We christened my office. It's only fair we christen yours."

"You think that's going to work on me?" I ask when he gives me that damn smirk. Goddamnit, he's right, and it is.

I turn to Alessia. "We'll be right back."

She laughs and shakes her head. "Just make sure your blouse is on right side out this time."

"I'll never live that down, will I?"

"Nope."

I shrug, and Eoghan starts to pull me in the direction of my office.

Yeah, I can live with that.

The End

Thank you so much for reading Eoghan and Gemma's story! If you enjoyed their book, I would be incredibly appreciative if you took the time and left a little review on the retailer's site. Reviews are an amazing way to help out indie authors like me spread the word about their stories!

Want to get to know the guys from the Black Roses MC? They have a series too! And I wrote a little novella about what it was like growing up in Shine for a few of my guys. You can get a copy by signing up for my newsletter with the QR code or by going to my website katerandallauthor.com. Don't worry, I'm not an email spammer!

<u>Stalk me on my socials!</u>
TikTok
Facebook
Instagram
Goodreads
BookBub

Scan the QR code to follow me on my socials and to sign up for my newsletter!

Acknowledgements

I want to start by thanking YOU! You took the time to read my words and that means the absolute world to me!

My editor, Victoria. You have been with me since the first in this series and take such good care of my babies every step of the way. I'm so glad I reached out to you and get the honor of working with you.

Kiki, Megan and Anna at the Next Step PR. If it wasn't for you ladies, I'd still be wondering what the heck to do in this indie author world. You always keep me on track and have been there for me since I started this entire thing!

Molli, my sister from another mister. You're my sounding board, my therapist, my best friend all rolled into one mighty package. I love you sister!

Of course, my husband and partner in life, Matt. Thank you for always being there and believing in me. If it wasn't for you saying *go for it, babe* I don't know that I would have had the courage to actually do it. You are amazing and I love you.

Also By Kate

The Ones Series
The Good One
The Fragile One
The Other One

The Black Roses MC
Linc
Jude
Ozzy
And more coming...

The Boston Syndicate
Finn
Luca
Eoghan
Cillian

About Kate

Kate is a lover of all things books. It doesn't matter what sub-genre, as long as there's a HEA, she's in. She started reading romance in high school and would hide novels in textbooks to read during class. Becoming an author was always a dream she had and finally decided to put pen to paper (or finger to keyboard) and write what she loves. She grew up in the beautiful upper peninsula of Michigan then became a West Coast girl where she lives with her amazing husband and hilarious son. She would love to hear from readers so check out all her socials and sign up for her newsletter so she can keep you up to date on her books and whatever other ramblings come to mind.